"Wait, don't walk off. I don't even know your name."

Dusty grasped her hand.

Her mouth curved into an impish smile. "Why, I thought you knew who I was," she said.

"A princess?" he guessed.

"Only until midnight." Her smile grew more mischievous, and she lifted the hem of her satin gown, revealing shapely feet encased in clear high heels.

"Ah . . . you're Cinderella, glass slippers and all."

"And you are?"

Dusty yielded to impulse. "Prince Charming, at your service."

At that, his warm lips ...... her wrist, and ...... "You don't loo ...... ased. "You look like ......

He chuckled, and ...... resonant sound, feelings that had be ...... pressed for so long began to stir within her.

"Prince Charming is merely a state of mind," Dusty murmured.

Dear Reader,

Welcome to the Silhouette **Special Edition** experience! With your search for consistently satisfying reading in mind, every month the authors and editors of Silhouette **Special Edition** aim to offer you a stimulating blend of deep emotions and high romance.

The name Silhouette **Special Edition** and the distinctive arch on the cover represent a commitment—a commitment to bring you six sensitive, substantial novels each month. In the pages of a Silhouette **Special Edition**, compelling true-to-life characters face riveting emotional issues—and come out winners. All the authors in the series strive for depth, vividness and warmth in writing these stories of living and loving in today's world.

The result, we hope, is romance you can believe in. Deeply emotional, richly romantic, infinitely rewarding—that's the Silhouette **Special Edition** experience. Come share it with us—six times a month!

From all the authors and editors of Silhouette **Special Edition**,

Best wishes,

Leslie Kazanjian,
Senior Editor

TRISHA ALEXANDER
Cinderella Girl

Silhouette Special Edition

Published by Silhouette Books New York

America's Publisher of Contemporary Romance

This book is dedicated to the memory of my parents, Ann and Pat Sfara, who always believed I could do anything, and to my sisters, Gerri, Margie and Norma, who still do.

Special thanks to Radha Mohini, whose teaching inspired me; to my critique group—Susan Brown, Betty Gyenes, Elaine Kimberley and Alaina Richardson—whose honesty drove me to do my best; and to Dick, Kim, Sandy and Shelley, whose support never wavered.

SILHOUETTE BOOKS
300 East 42nd St., New York, N.Y. 10017

ISBN: 0-373-09640-2

First Silhouette Books printing December 1990

Printed in the U.S.A.

TRISHA ALEXANDER

was encouraged from childhood to believe she could do whatever she set out to do, and this perennial injection of confidence became the mainstay of her life. Professionally, she has held many positions, from secretary to ad salesman. After years of considering the prospect, Trisha began writing seriously. She found that she liked everything about it: reading, research, talking about writing, the act of writing itself, writers' conferences, critiquing, revising, editing—you name it, she loves it. *Cinderella Girl* is her first published novel.

Chapter One

JUST DUSTY
by Dusty Mitchell

This reviewer always tries to present local singers and composers in the best possible light, but Dusty Mitchell's debut album is a disappointment. Mitchell, a local singer/composer, wrote all the songs on this first effort, and, although some of the tracks show promise, overall the album is a serving of commercial pabulum for the musically unsophisticated listener and typical of the junk pop music filling the airwaves.

Mitchell panders to the romantic daydreams of teenagers with offerings like *Sweet Baby* and *Last Night I Dreamed of You*, two songs with bland lyrics and predictable melodies. Two others, *Texas Lady* and *Dance With Me, Darlin'*, which lean more toward basic country music with its starker, honest appeal, are better but still lack that spark of magic we expect from top-notch composers and lyricists.

The one really bright spot on the album is a seductive, bluesy number, *Close Your Eyes*, that is reminiscent of Jocco Riley's early music. If Mitchell's other selections had been of this caliber, he might have had something more than this mediocre collection.

Production quality is tinny, with some unidentifiable background noises. Recommendation: Don't waste your money. (Gulf Coast Productions)

—V.M. Patterson

As Victoria Patterson Jones typed the last letter of her name, she sighed and leaned back in her swivel chair. To relieve the sharp pain between her shoulder blades, she rotated her head in slow circles, then stretched. She felt bone tired, she had a headache and she wished she could go home.

"I need a nap," she said aloud. Then she muttered under her breath, although no one could hear her from behind her partitioned cubicle. "What I don't need is a late night out. Not when I have all those papers to grade tomorrow."

Well, the nap would have to wait. Victoria had one more review to write before calling it an afternoon. Why had she allowed Grant Gyenes to talk her into filling in for him while he was on vacation? She smiled. Could it have something to do with the fact that Monty Brown, her boss, had added his persuasive voice to Grant's?

"Oh, Monty," she'd protested, "I hate pop music. You know that. It isn't fair of you to ask me to do it. I'm your classical music reviewer. Besides," she added slyly, "I'm only supposed to work twelve hours a week. This'll add extra hours." Monty was a notorious penny-pincher.

"Doesn't matter. There's no one else to do it, and you're a good reviewer, Jones. You can handle it." His pudgy face had taken on an adamant expression, and Victoria knew it would be useless to protest any longer. Not if she wanted to keep her part-time job at the *Houston Herald*.

"If only I didn't need the extra money," she muttered. Sighing once more, she squinted at the amber screen and read what she'd just written. A small twinge of remorse nagged at her. Had she been too hard on this guy, Mitchell? There were glimmers of real talent in his work. For a few seconds, her innate sense of fairness battled with her fatigue, but fatigue won out, and Victoria punched a few keys and sent the review to the proofreader's desk.

She reached for her notes to begin her next review when the telephone on her left buzzed. Frowning, Victoria snatched the receiver from its cradle. "Entertainment desk. Jones."

"Why are you still at work? It's five o'clock. You should be at home getting ready for my party."

Victoria smiled, her irritation instantly forgotten. The indignant voice at the other end of the phone belonged to Sissy Farraday, Victoria's best friend.

"I like the paycheck the *Herald* gives me twice a month. It keeps me in diamonds. Besides, I've got plenty of time. You know I can get ready for anything in thirty minutes flat."

"But I want you to be here early, Tory."

There went her nap. "I will. I promise."

"Good." Now that she'd accomplished her mission, Sissy sounded as complacent and contented as her two fat Persian cats. "Well, I've got a jillion things to do, so I'd best fly. See you at seven."

Victoria grinned as she replaced the receiver. She and Sissy had been best friends from the instant they'd set eyes on each other in kindergarten, attracted to one another as only complete opposites can be. Sissy—small, golden and effervescent—had grown up to marry and then divorce a wealthy oil baron, one of Houston's elite. Victoria—taller, darker, quieter—had been dazzled by Sissy's bright-eyed optimism. That optimism and Sissy's loyalty had helped Victoria survive her own disastrous marriage to Chris Jones—a charming, immature, would-be photographer who had left her a widow at twenty-two. A widow with no skills and a small baby to support. A familiar ache of sadness gripped her as the image of Chris's handsome face filled her mind. Such a terrible waste.

Shaking off her momentary depression, Victoria picked up her discarded notes and forced herself to concentrate on the next review. If she didn't hurry, there was no way she'd make it to Sissy's by seven. And even though she wasn't really looking forward to this party, she owed it to Sissy to keep her promise and show up on time.

Dusty Mitchell stretched his long legs out in front of him and contemplated the toe of his elephant-skin boots. "What do you think, Spence? Should I go to this party as a cowboy?"

Bob Spencer looked up from the notebook he was studying and blinked. "What?"

Dusty sighed heavily. "It's a sad state of affairs when the hired help doesn't even listen to the boss," he complained. "I asked if you thought I should go to this costume ball as a cowboy." Spence was more than hired help at *Mitchell's,* Dusty's club, and Dusty knew it, but he enjoyed teasing his best friend. For the past year Spence had assumed more and more of the daily responsibilities of running the popular Village hangout, leaving Dusty free to concentrate on his music.

There was a good-natured twinkle in Dusty's hazel eyes. Spence ignored the complaint and studied Dusty's outfit. "But if you go as a cowboy, you won't be in costume," he said reasonably. He wiped the already spotlessly clean bar top.

"True."

"On the other hand, maybe that's what those society types will expect."

"Also true."

"So why not compromise?"

Dusty raised his eyebrows.

"Why don't you wear that flashy outfit you bought a few years back?" Spence grinned as Dusty grimaced. "Yeah, that's it," he added mischievously. "That black satin job with the sequins. That'll get 'em. All you'll need is a black mask, and there's a costume store right over on Kirby. If you hurry you can get there before they close."

Dusty stood up. Spence's suggestion was the easiest solution to his problem. "I guess that's better than some silly costume like Count Dracula or the Devil," he muttered. "But I'd sure like to skip the whole thing. I always feel uncomfortable around people like Sissy Farraday."

"Why?" Spence stopped polishing. "What's different about her? She got two heads?"

Dusty squirmed under Spence's penetrating blue stare. "Who knows? I've never met her. We've only talked on the phone."

"Why'd you say that, then? You don't even know what she's like."

"Yeah, that's true, but I've got a good idea. I've read enough of Maxine's column in the *Chronicle*."

Spence laughed. "Oh, you mean this Farraday woman probably has lunch with the Baroness and lives in a *swankienda*."

Dusty chuckled at the absurdity of the popular gossip columnist's coined word, but under his amusement was an uneasiness he couldn't shake. Whether he liked it or not, Houston's jet set could put him on the map as a performer. If Sissy Farraday and her crowd liked him, they'd boost his career as no amount of paid publicity could. "Yeah," he said. "It's a whole different world in River Oaks."

"So what? You got nothing to be ashamed of."

"I know that, but I don't move in those circles. I don't talk their language. I won't have anything in common with the men, and the women...."

"Knowing you, you'll meet some gorgeous, rich chick who'll fall at your feet and kiss the ground you walk on and make a pest of herself coming in here looking for you."

Spence flashed Dusty an evil grin. "After all," he said slyly, "why should River Oaks women be any different than all the rest?"

Dusty's eyes narrowed. "You know, Spence, no one is irreplaceable—not even you."

Spence began polishing the first of a long row of glasses. "So replace me."

Dusty shook his head in mock exasperation. "Women aside, I guess I have to go, don't I?"

"Chances like this don't come along often," Spence said without looking up. "Do you want to concentrate on your composing and making it as a performer, or do you want to be a saloon keeper all your life? That's the question."

Dusty looked around the quiet club. There were a couple of people sitting at the other end of the bar, and a few more playing darts in the corner, but it was too early for most of the Saturday night crowd to have arrived. The club had been good to him since he'd opened it ten years ago, but he'd never meant it to be his life's work. It *was* time for him to concentrate on his goal to be a composer, to make a living at writing songs and performing them. And if he were ever going to make it big, he had to focus his energies in one direction only.

Thoughtful, Dusty looked at Spence. The other man's head was once more bent over the inventory list. Even in the dim light, Dusty could see the spot where Spence's hair had thinned. Good old Spence. He always cut to the heart of anything, and he was reliable and loyal. What would Dusty have done without Spence over the years?

Spence glanced up, blue eyes gleaming. "You'd better get a move on if you're gonna make that costume store."

Spence was right again. Dusty didn't want to be late. He wanted to make a good impression on these people who could be so important to his future with their contacts and their influence. Like it or not, most of the other guests were the kind of people whose interests were broadly publicized in the Houston press—people whose tastes were emulated.

They could really boost his career...save him a lot of time...whether he liked it or not. But someday, he vowed, someday he wouldn't need to worry about impressing anyone. His music would speak for itself.

He waved goodbye to Spence and strode out of the club.

Victoria shifted self-consciously in the low-cut satin ball gown, her feet burning in the clear plastic backless shoes. The heels were four inches high. But if she were going to be Cinderella, she had to wear glass slippers. At least that had been her rationale when she'd discovered the shoes, a holdover from when the silly things were stylish, lurking at the back of the spare room closet.

The River Oaks mansion shone from its polished parquet floors to its gleaming Baccarat crystal chandeliers. A quartet played softly in the next room, and tuxedoed waiters hovered near the laden buffet table.

Standing to one corner of the immense room, Victoria watched as Sissy greeted her guests. Sissy loved the pretentious parties favored by Houston's rich and famous, although she always justified her own extravagance by giving her parties to benefit one of her many charitable interests. Victoria enjoyed watching her friend in action, charming and dazzling her guests.

"Colonel Kimberley, how nice it is to see you again," Sissy gushed as she greeted a short, white-haired man dressed like Napoleon who was accompanied by a robust woman.

Victoria watched as her friend masterfully guided each guest past her and into the glittering room. Sissy had always reminded Victoria of a butterfly—gossamer and fluttery—alighting only long enough for a person to admire her beauty, then soaring away to new sights and sounds. Tonight she was dressed as Venus, and the softly draped folds of her white chiffon toga hugged her shapely curves, while the sparkling gold girdle she wore emphasized her tiny waist. Her bright hair was twisted into a topknot and studded with gold sequins that sparkled and flashed as she inclined her elegant head.

Sissy's tinkling laugh drew Victoria's attention to another guest who was standing—no, *towering* above her. A giant of a cowboy dressed all in glittery black bowed low over Sissy's hand. He swept off his large black hat, revealing golden-brown hair that curled in thick disarray. A black satin mask covered the upper half of his bronzed face, but Victoria's breath caught involuntarily as his mouth curved into a heart-stopping smile. Who was he? Some wealthy rancher's son, from the looks of him.

Her attention was distracted by movement beside her.

"Would you like a glass of champagne, ma'am?" asked a solicitous waiter.

"No, thank you." As the waiter moved on to another guest, Victoria turned her attention to Sissy. The tall cowboy was gone, and in his place was a reed-thin brunette who kissed Sissy on both cheeks.

Victoria looked around, but the cowboy had disappeared. Feeling oddly disappointed, she strolled to the buffet table and was gratified to find that Sissy had plenty of alcohol-free punch as well as champagne. She accepted a glass of punch from the attendant. She'd made a vow and hadn't drunk an alcoholic beverage since Chris's death. Sipping slowly, she let her eyes scan the room.

The quartet began to play dance music. Couples strolled toward the adjoining ballroom. Victoria's feet burned. The headache she'd had since afternoon was still throbbing. Wondering if she'd last the entire evening, she looked for an empty chair. Spying one in the far corner of the room, she turned to place her empty glass on the table behind her and was nearly knocked off her feet when she collided with a California redwood.

"That's what always happens when I approach a beautiful woman to ask her to dance," drawled a low, amused voice. "She throws herself into my arms."

Big hands grasped her shoulders.

Victoria looked up. And up.

He didn't remotely resemble a California redwood. And his smile was even more potent up close than it had been from a distance; its dazzle belonged in a toothpaste ad. Her heart pumping just a little faster than normal and arms tingling where his warm hands met her exposed skin, Victoria tried to regain her composure. Although his satin mask covered nearly half his face, she could see the sparkle of green-gold eyes and the strength of a square jaw and wide mouth. A slightly crooked nose kept him from being too handsome, giving him a roguish look that was almost irresistible. Broad shoulders. Narrow waist. Long legs. His entire bearing exuded an aura of strength and power.

"I'm sorry," she said. "I wasn't looking where I was going."

"And here I thought it was my good looks and charm that had bowled you over," he said, his grin growing wider.

Victoria felt herself blushing. For the first time that evening she was grateful for her mask. What on earth was wrong with her? She didn't normally react like a giddy teenager, someone more the age of her daughter, Julie, when a man flirted with her.

"So what do you say?" he said.

"About what?"

Releasing his grip, he moved back a step, swept off his hat and bowed low. "Ma'am . . ." he drawled. "Would you do me the honor of dancing with me?"

Victoria's heart tap-danced. She couldn't help it. He was outrageously charming and probably worked hard at it, but she nodded wordlessly anyway. Mesmerized, she drifted into his arms.

Dusty slowly and expertly guided her through the wide doorway and into the crush of swaying bodies. He was delighted that the classy beauty had agreed to dance with him. Arms tightening, he pulled her close. She stiffened, then relaxed against him. From his first glimpse of her, he'd known her skin would feel as silky as her dress, that she'd smell like spring flowers, that she'd be as enchanting as she looked.

Her shining dark head with its rhinestone tiara fit under his chin as if she'd been made with him in mind. Her tall, slender body felt exactly right in his arms—the fullness of her breasts pressed against his chest, the firmness of her back moving against his palm as their steps matched each other's.

As the last notes of the song died away, she stirred. Dusty felt an unfamiliar reluctance to let her go. His arms remained firmly around her, holding her close. "Dance the next one with me, too," he urged softly.

Forgotten were her tired feet. Forgotten was her headache. Victoria's normal reserve and coolness melted under his warm gaze, and for the first time in a very long time, she let herself live for the moment. Tilting her head up, she smiled.

Dusty could see enough of her eyes to know they were the most incredible shade of dark blue, almost violet. They reminded him of the periwinkles that grew in wild abandon during the hot Houston summers. Combined with her creamy skin and hair like brown sable, she looked like a princess in a fairy tale. The purple satin gown, with its off-the-shoulder neckline, revealed her rounded breasts and slender waist and emphasized her lush curves.

The musicians began their rendition of "Lady in Red," and Dusty pulled his princess close, giving himself up to the feel of her body and the enchantment of her warm, flowery scent. His earlier irritation over the necessity for attending the charity ball vanished; the evening had been transformed into something magical with the advent of the tall beauty in his arms.

All too soon, the song ended, and she drew away. Reaching out, he grasped her hand, enfolding it in both of his. "Wait. Don't walk off. I don't even know your name."

Her mouth curved into an impish smile, a tiny dimple appearing at the right corner of her mouth. "Why, I thought you knew who I was," she said, her voice lilting and musical.

"A princess?" he guessed.

"Only until midnight." Her smile grew more mischievous, and she lifted the hem of her satin gown, revealing shapely feet encased in clear plastic high heels.

Dusty raised his eyes to meet her sparkling gaze. Laughter danced in their brilliant depths.

"Then my coach turns into a pumpkin..." she prompted.

"Ah...you're Cinderella...glass slippers and all."

She nodded. "And you are..."

Caught up in the whimsy of the moment, Dusty yielded to impulse. He took her hand, raised it to his lips and lightly kissed its silky warmth. "Prince Charming at your service."

When his warm lips met the tender underside of her wrist, a queer breathlessness seized Victoria. "You don't look like Prince Charming," she teased. "Your clothes aren't right. Are you sure you're not Zorro?"

He chuckled, and at the warm, resonant sound, feelings that had been suppressed for so long began to stir within her again. Her eyes were drawn to the caressing twinkle in his, and for a long moment, their gazes held.

"Prince Charming is a state of mind," he said.

A liquid, silky sensation curled into Victoria's stomach. She knew they were playing a game, pretending to be people they weren't, but at the moment, it didn't matter. All that mattered was the warmth that filled her and the look of admiration in his eyes.

Dusty wanted to put his arms around her, wanted to kiss the corner of her mouth where the enchanting dimple peeked in and out, wanted to carry her off somewhere far away from all these other people. Instead, he said lightly, "My white horse is just outside. Would you like to see him?"

She shook her head. She didn't trust herself to speak. She especially didn't trust herself to go outside with him. The way she felt, she just might run off with him into the velvet night and never return to the real world. She certainly didn't feel like Victoria Patterson Jones, music teacher at the University of Houston, thirty-three-year-old widow and the mother of a thirteen-year-old daughter. Instead she felt like . . . Cinderella.

Victoria floated through the next few hours. Her prince never left her side. His admiring attention made her feel as if she really were a princess in a fairy-tale world. Even when someone else asked her to dance, the bronzed giant stood watching and waiting for her return.

And return to him she did. She was inexorably drawn to him; she felt as if she'd known him forever, this splendid male creature who was all hard muscle and solid strength— this gorgeous man who held her so tenderly and looked at her as if she were a precious piece of crystal, someone sparkling and special and wonderful—all the things Victoria knew she wasn't. At least not in her real life. She closed her eyes and gave herself up to the feelings his nearness evoked. So what if she woke up tomorrow as the same old person she'd been all of her life? Tonight she'd play let's pretend.

A rousing version of "Boogie Woogie Bugle Boy" dissolved the make-believe world into the rowdy sounds of jitterbugging.

"No, no," Victoria laughingly protested as her prince tried to lead her into the dance. "I don't do this kind of dancing."

"Oh, come on. It's easy. Try it."

"It might be easy for you, but it's not for me." Victoria tugged her hands free and escaped through the arched doorway into the brightly lit main room.

"Hey, Cindy, wait for me." His warm breath feathered her ear as he leaned over her. "Let's get something to eat, okay?"

"Are you following me?" she said with mock indignation. They were standing near a long table covered with tempting dishes.

"Damn right. I don't intend to let you out of my sight. Not ever," he vowed.

Victoria's heart skittered at the promise in his low drawl. Her reaction surprised her—in some ways it frightened her. She couldn't remember feeling this trembling tension ever before. Not even with Chris.

When he picked up two plates and handed her one, smiling down at her with his sexy smile, Victoria felt helpless to do anything other than follow his lead.

The enormous buffet table was arrayed from end to end with food that looked sinfully rich to Victoria: crystal bowls piled high with pink shrimp, tiny meatballs in a bubbly sauce, hot mini quiches, mini egg rolls, French bread and melted Brie, caviar and toast points, lobster Thermidor, oysters Rockefeller, sliced smoked ham and turkey, salads, fresh fruits and cheeses, and dozens of other dishes Victoria couldn't put a name to.

Victoria stood there watching as her prince piled his plate high. Finally he turned and looked at her practically empty plate. "What's wrong? Aren't you hungry?"

"Not really," she lied, knowing she wouldn't be able to eat while he was near.

"That's okay," he said. "I've got enough for both of us. Come on."

Holding his plate in one hand, he nudged her toward the open terrace doors. As they emerged into the navy night, he nodded toward a half-hidden bench at the far end of the terrace.

Colorful lanterns gently swayed in the tall oaks surrounding the terrace, and the March air smelled of freshly mown grass and the sharply sweet scent of the heavily blooming Indian hawthorne. Buckets of scarlet geraniums stood like sentries at the perimeter of the terrace, and rows of purple pansies grew from carefully tended beds on either side of the walkway weaving from the terrace through the grounds.

They sat next to each other on the bench, the long length of his leg against Victoria's thigh. He dug into his food with enthusiasm. Victoria couldn't eat; his nearness was too disconcerting, too distracting.

She nibbled on a piece of melon. What was wrong with her? She was acting ridiculous. Why was she so nervous? This man was a stranger. She would probably never see him after tonight. There was no sense in letting him unsettle her. So he was handsome and charming. So they were having a wonderful time flirting and playing a game, pretending to be Cinderella and Prince Charming. It was only a game— she had to remember that. She picked up a tiny quiche and tried to ignore his nearness.

But the warm contact of their touching thighs and his overpowering maleness were impossible to ignore. Victoria sneaked a peek at him. He smiled at her. "I'm hungry."

"I noticed."

"It takes a lot of food to keep me going."

"You don't have to make excuses. I didn't say a word."

"You didn't have to." His laughing eyes held hers. Suddenly his teasing mood disappeared, and he put his half-full plate down. Then he gently took her plate from her suddenly lifeless fingers and set it next to his. Swinging his arm around the back of the bench, his palm settled on her bare shoulder. His fingers softly stroked her skin, and she could feel the roughness of calluses on his fingertips. Her heart thudded up into her throat even as she wondered if he played the guitar.

He leaned close and murmured against her ear. "Do you know what I want to do more than I want to eat?"

Unable to speak, Victoria shook her head. His face was so close she could smell his after-shave, something sharp and tangy. From the depths of the distant darkness she heard the hoot of an owl, and a stillness settled over the terrace. Even the birds seemed to be holding their breath as if waiting for something. Victoria's pulse raced as, very slowly, her prince lifted her mask away from her face and dropped it into her lap. She trembled at the touch of his fingers against her skin, then held her breath as his warm lips nuzzled her ear in a whispery, soft kiss. Her insides felt like melted butter. She couldn't move. She couldn't breathe. His hand lifted her hair, and his moist mouth moved in a shivery trail to the hollow of her throat.

"Sweet princess," he whispered.

Victoria closed her eyes, powerless to stop him, powerless to stop the rising rush of emotion flooding her.

Dusty knew her mouth would taste like honey and, like a bee to a flower, he was drawn to it.

Victoria knew she shouldn't let him kiss her like this, but the starry night and the spell that had held her enraptured all evening refused to release her now.

Somewhere close by, a thrush sang sweetly, its trilling voice blending perfectly with the soft sounds of the music drifting from the house. Victoria's heart joined in the song as he pulled his mask off, then slowly encircled her in his arms.

Without thinking, Victoria moved her head until his questing mouth found its target. Turbulent emotions tumbled through her as his insistent lips claimed her. She clung to him, dizzy with intoxicating joy.

As they slowly drew apart, the magic of the moment seemed to grip them both, and Victoria knew her eyes shimmered with the same wordless wonder she saw reflected in his green-gold depths as a finger of silvery moonlight illuminated his face.

"Well, for heaven's sake! I've been lookin' all over for you two!"

Victoria jumped at the sound of Sissy's faintly accusing voice.

"We've been right here," drawled her cowboy prince, "getting to know each other."

"So I see..."

Victoria flushed and was glad of the darkness on the terrace. She hoped Sissy hadn't seen them kissing; she knew she'd never hear the end of it if she had.

Sissy laughed. "Well, I'm afraid the ball is nearly over, and it's time for the featured entertainer to do his thing."

Featured entertainer? Confused, Victoria looked from Sissy to the man who had transformed her into a blob of Silly Putty with one kiss.

Dusty grinned. He couldn't believe how fast the time had gone in the company of his delightful companion. He stood and reached a hand down to assist her. When she placed her slender hand in his, he felt a surge of tenderness at the look of confusion and vulnerability on her face. She seemed as bemused by the evening's events as he was.

"Come on," he said. "Come and watch me."

As they followed Sissy into the house, Victoria struggled to get her tumultuous feelings under control. It was silly to let one kiss affect her like this. She was so out of practice, so unused to men flirting with her, she'd allowed herself to fall to pieces just because a good-looking man had kissed her. One kiss wasn't a big deal. But her wayward heart refused to settle down, and she was acutely conscious of the feel of his warm hand enveloping hers.

Leaning down, he said, "This'll take about twenty minutes. It's eleven-thirty. Promise you'll stick around and wait for me to finish."

"Eleven-thirty! Oh, dear, I completely forgot. I have to make a phone call," Victoria said. When he didn't release her hand, she said, "I'll be back."

"Do you promise?"

"Yes. I promise."

His eyes gave her a silent kiss. "Good. We have to talk." Then he squeezed her hand, winked and walked away.

Victoria watched his loose, easy stride as he followed Sissy, who was threading her way through the crowd. And although Victoria would've liked to stand there watching him, she had to call Julie. She'd told her she'd call before eleven. What was she thinking of—forgetting her daughter like this?

Victoria rushed out of the large room and down the hall to Sissy's study. Opening the door, she moved quickly to the cherry-wood desk and the white and gold telephone sitting on top of it.

Kicking off her shoes, she picked up the phone and pressed the numbers of Julie's friend's house, then flexed her aching feet as she waited for someone to answer at the other end.

"Hello," said a young, female voice. Victoria recognized it as belonging to Kate Richardson, Julie's best friend.

"Hello, Kate? This is Mrs. Jones. I'm sorry I didn't call sooner. May I speak to Julie?"

Sounds of a quartet warming up filtered through the open study doorway, along with the chatter and laughter of the guests.

"No problem. We were watching television," Kate said. "Hold on."

As Victoria waited for her daughter to come on the line, she realized that a hush had fallen over the crowd outside. Then she heard a low male voice begin to sing. The tune sounded familiar, but she couldn't place it.

"Mom?"

"Oh, hi, honey. Sorry I didn't call earlier," Victoria said.

"I told you there wasn't any reason for you to call at all."

Victoria tried to ignore the resentment in Julie's voice, but a knot twisted in her stomach. She knew Julie hated it when she hovered; she knew she was overprotective, but she couldn't seem to help it. She sank into Sissy's leather swivel chair and propped her aching feet on the desk. Keeping her voice light, she said, "So what have you and Kate been doing all evening?"

Julie's sigh came over the phone clearly. "Mom, we rented a movie, and—"

"You don't want to talk. You want to get back to it. I know."

"Yeah. Listen, I'm fine. I'll be home about noon tomorrow. Quit worrying about me."

They said goodbye, and as Victoria slowly replaced the receiver, she heard a great burst of applause, then another hush as the musicians started another song. She winced as she slipped her feet back into her shoes.

As she neared the ballroom she realized the same male singer was singing—a slow, sultry love song—again tantalizingly familiar, which was strange, because Victoria seldom, if ever, listened to popular music.

She drifted into the ballroom. The insistent beat of the song reminded her of the beat of her heart when her handsome cowboy had kissed her. The singer's husky voice picked up in volume as Victoria worked her way to the front of the crowd so she could see better.

She smiled in delight. It was him. Her cowboy stood on stage—singing. So that's what Sissy had meant.

He sounded wonderful. He looked wonderful. His golden-brown hair gleamed under the spotlight, and the sequins on his black satin shirt shimmered as he moved. His husky, sexy voice slid over Victoria, and she stood entranced as she watched him captivate the crowd. The words of the song didn't matter; it was his caressing voice and the hypnotic beat that held his listeners.

The music was so different from Victoria's beloved classical music. It was immediate, demanding, light-years away from the remote romanticism and rarefied poignancy of the music she had always preferred.

His brilliant eyes swept the crowd, then lighted on Victoria. He smiled—that warm, lazy smile she already adored. As he finished his song, he bowed low, and as Victoria clapped along with the rest of the guests, his eyes held hers. Still watching her, he picked up a guitar and pulled the strap over his shoulder until he could hold the instrument comfortably. He strummed a few chords, then moved closer to the mike.

"The next song is dedicated to a very special person. Her name is Cinderella."

Victoria felt a warm glow surround her.

He inclined his head in her direction, smiled and began to sing. "Close your eyes and pretend we're together..." His rich, vibrant baritone rumbled through Victoria.

"...and we'll never be apart..." His eyes, golden in the spotlight, never left her face. "...I'll close mine, too...and picture you...and hold you in my heart."

Victoria's heart thumped in her ears. No one existed except this man. Each word of the sensual song beat away at her defenses until she felt stripped to her soul.

"...we can never be lonely...we can never be blue...just close your eyes...and I'll be there with you..."

Close your eyes. Why were the words so familiar? Why was the melody so familiar? *Close your eyes.*

...The one really bright spot on the album is a seductive bluesy number... The words of her review flooded her mind, and she reeled as the knowledge reverberated in her brain.

Oh, God, she thought. It can't be. He can't be Dusty Mitchell. *Mitchell panders to the romantic daydreams of teenagers...overall the album is a serving of commercial pabulum for the musically unsophisticated...typical of the junk pop music filling the airwaves...* Her own words mocked her. Oh, God. She wished she could crawl right through the floor.

What would he think of her? What could she say? How could she explain it to him?

As the last note died away, the crowd applauded wildly. Cries of, "More, more," came from every direction. A beautiful redhead dressed like Miss America said, "God, what a hunk! Too bad I'm married."

"You never let that stop you before!" exclaimed a dark-haired woman standing beside her.

Sissy moved to the microphone. "Thank you, Dusty. That was wonderful. I'm sure everyone here enjoyed it.

Where can we buy this album? That's *Just Dusty*, by Dusty Mitchell, in case you're takin' notes.''

Dusty named some stores, and then people surged forward to talk to him. Soon his attention was captured by the crowd. Seized by panic, Victoria used the opportunity to slip into the other room. She had to get away. She had to think. She simply couldn't face him right now. She knew her face would betray her. Oh, God. That awful review would appear in the morning paper, and he would hate her when he read it. She couldn't bear to see hate in his eyes—those beautiful eyes that made her feel so special, so desirable. Victoria's heart ached as she imagined how those eyes would look filled with dislike.

Grabbing her purse, she sped through the open terrace doors. In her frenzy to get away, she tripped on the riser, and one of her shoes flew off, skittering to the other end of the terrace.

Heart racing, Victoria stopped. Oh, this was too much! Where had that stupid shoe gone? Her eyes rapidly scanned the terrace. No shoe. Indecision gripped her, but the sounds of the chattering, laughing guests made up her mind for her. Bending down, she removed her other shoe. Then she ran, as fast as she could, intent on one thing and one thing only: escape.

Chapter Two

Dusty stared at the plastic shoe in his hand. Then he scanned the surrounding shrubbery and towering oaks. Searching for the gleam of a satin dress, he slowly stepped off the terrace and onto the brick-paved walk that wound through the carefully tended grounds.

Where had she gone? And why had she left so suddenly, without warning?

His boot heels clicked against the rough surface of the bricks, and as he moved farther from the house, the sounds of music and laughter receded, becoming only a faint backdrop to the more immediate night sounds around him. Crickets sang, and somewhere in the distance two dogs barked. The rich perfume of gardenias scented the air, and a faint breeze stirred the branches of a nearby mimosa tree. Dusty was oblivious to the beauty of the night. He turned to his right, drawn by the aquamarine glow of the Farraday pool. No one sat in any of the dozen chairs ringing the pool.

Ten more minutes of searching the tennis courts, the cabana and the gazebo at the back of the grounds yielded nothing. Turning, Dusty slowly walked back to the main house.

She was gone. She'd disappeared and, just like Cinderella, she'd left her slipper behind—tangible proof she'd existed, that his imagination hadn't conjured her.

As Dusty stepped through the open terrace doors and entered the crowded room, he spied Sissy Farraday talking to a small group of people at the other end of the room. With sudden determination he strode quickly to her side and impatiently waited for a break in the conversation. He touched Sissy's shoulder. "Sissy, could I speak to you for a minute?"

"Oh, hello, Dusty," she said, turning her vivid blue eyes in his direction and smiling warmly.

One of the women in the group who had a wildly punk hairdo and was dressed as if she belonged in a heavy metal band sidled up to him. "I'm Lonnie," she purred. "But you can call me darlin', or anythin' else your little heart desires."

All the women in the group laughed. Dusty smiled automatically but kept his eyes on Sissy Farraday. "It's important," he said.

"Lonnie, hush up," Sissy said. She beckoned to him. "Come on back to my study."

As he followed her trim figure up the hall and into the paneled study near the back of the house, he wondered if she would be willing to tell him what he wanted to know.

Once inside the room, she turned toward him and leaned against a large cherry-wood desk. "Now, what was it you wanted to talk to me about?"

"Your friend. The girl I spent the evening with who was dressed like Cinderella."

"Tory?" Her blue eyes gleamed with curiosity. "What about her?" A smile lurked at the corners of her mouth as she studied him.

Dusty stiffened. What was so damned amusing? "I can't find her," he said. "I've looked everywhere, and she's disappeared."

Now her bright eyes were abrim with amusement, and Dusty could see that she was consciously fighting the urge to laugh. Was she laughing at *him*? A hard ball of anger knotted in his stomach.

"I wouldn't worry about that," she said airily. "Knowing Tory, she just wanted to get away from the crowd. She's probably outside sitting on the grounds somewhere, hiding."

He fought to keep his anger down. "I looked. She's nowhere on the grounds. Or anywhere else. She left."

Her smile faded. "Hmm. That *is* odd. I can't imagine her leaving without saying goodbye."

Now that she seemed genuinely concerned, his anger slowly dissolved. "I think it's odd, too. Especially since she promised to wait until I was finished singing."

Sissy stared at him thoughtfully. Had Tory pulled her vanishing act because of something Mr. Charm had said or done? Or had she simply been frightened by the evening's events and her uncharacteristic, uninhibited behavior with this good-looking hunk? Sissy could have sworn she'd seen the two of them kissing when she'd interrupted them on the terrace. She'd been astounded, because Tory hadn't shown any interest in any of the men who'd tried to date her over the past ten years. "Well," she said. "I can't imagine why she just took off like that, but Tory's unpredictable when it comes to some things. I wouldn't be too alarmed."

"Tory what?" he asked. "What's her last name?"

"Her name is Victoria Jones. I call her Tory, but most people call her Victoria."

Victoria. Nice name, he thought. Classy. Just like the lady herself. "Do you know her well?"

"Well! She's my best friend and has been since we were in kindergarten together."

"Would you mind giving me her telephone number?"

She grinned. "Not at all." She leaned over the desk and rapidly wrote on a piece of notepaper, then tore it off the pad and handed it to him.

Dusty tucked the note carefully into his breast pocket. "Thanks." He tipped his hat in a slightly mocking salute. "And thanks for inviting me tonight."

"My pleasure."

"Maybe we'll see each other again sometime."

The corners of her mouth lifted in a teasing smile. "There's absolutely no doubt in my mind that we'll see each other again."

He laughed. He liked her. She was direct and honest, two qualities he valued. "You're probably right," he agreed, "especially if my plans work out."

"I'd bet money on your plans working out. You strike me as the kind of man who usually gets what he wants." She stuck out her hand, and Dusty took it. They shook solemnly, but as he turned to go, Sissy winked. Dusty chuckled all the way out the door.

After he left, Sissy sat there, wondering if she'd done the right thing. Then she shook off her doubts. Dusty Mitchell was just what Tory needed: a real man, strong, sure of himself, and nothing like Chris. Chris had been weak and indecisive, happy to let Tory shoulder the responsibility of their lives. Dusty Mitchell seemed like a man who knew precisely what he wanted and wasn't afraid to go after it. Sissy had a feeling he would succeed in chipping away at that wall of ice Tory had erected around herself after Chris died. Actually, she thought, Dusty Mitchell's effect on Tory might be more like a blowtorch than a ice pick.

Maybe by inviting him tonight I've changed Tory's life. The thought warmed Sissy. Underneath her flippant exterior, she was a romantic, a fact most of her acquaintances would be astounded to discover. Sighing, she suppressed a twinge of envy. Lucky Tory.

Slowly, she stood up. She couldn't sit here all night and daydream about Tory and Dusty. She had guests to attend to. But a seed of hope began to grow. If it could happen to Tory, it could happen to her. Maybe one day she'd meet someone like Dusty Mitchell, too.

The first thing Victoria saw when she walked outside Sunday morning was the *Houston Herald* in its plastic bag lying at the edge of her driveway. After she'd fled the party the night before, she'd tried to put the review out of her mind. She'd tried to put everything, Dusty Mitchell and the entire evening, out of her mind. But she hadn't been able to. She twisted and turned for hours before falling asleep, and even then, she slept poorly, waking several times through the night.

If only he had been arrogant and conceited instead of utterly charming. If only he hadn't sounded so wonderful when he sang to her. If only she could dislike him intensely.

Sighing dejectedly, she picked up the paper and retraced her steps to the house. The beauty of the spring morning didn't penetrate her heavy feeling of gloom.

Victoria tossed the paper onto the kitchen table and poured herself a cup of coffee, lacing it liberally with sweetener. She scanned the headlines and pretended to herself that she was interested in the news, purposely ignoring the entertainment section.

When her telephone jingled, she jumped, sloshing some of the coffee over the rim of her cup. "Oh, drat!" she said as she grabbed the receiver from the wall phone. "Hello?" Cradling the receiver on her shoulder, she stretched to reach the paper towel rack.

"Is this Cinderella speaking?" drawled the vibrant voice Victoria hadn't been able to banish from her mind. "The same Cinderella who lost a glass slipper on the steps of the castle last night?"

Heart thudding, Victoria said, "How...how did you get my number?"

A low chuckle came clearly over the wire. "It was easy, Cindy. I just asked your fairy godmother." Then his voice deepened. "You didn't think I would just forget about last night, did you?"

Victoria wet her lips. Her heart refused to calm down. "I . . . no, I didn't think anything."

"So why'd you run off like that?" The teasing, playful note was gone from his voice.

"I . . . I just remembered something I had to do."

"And you couldn't even wait to say goodbye?" Skepticism radiated over the wire.

"It . . . it was an emergency," Victoria said, improvising.

"An emergency? Well, that's different. I hope it was nothing serious."

Victoria was ashamed of herself when she heard the note of concern in his voice. "No, nothing serious. Just a false alarm. It's all been taken care of."

"I'm glad to hear that. I was afraid something might have happened to you."

"No, no, nothing like that. I'm fine."

"And I missed you," he said quietly.

Victoria stared at the entertainment section of the newspaper. Had he seen the review yet? Probably not. He wouldn't be this calm and easygoing if he had. Then the realization hit her that even if he had seen the review, he would never connect V.M. Patterson with her. She blessed her decision to write under her maiden name.

"I want to see you again," he was saying. "How about if I come on over to your place and the two of us take a drive out into the country. It's a beautiful day."

"Oh, no. I . . . I couldn't."

"Come on, darlin'. That's not the way the story is supposed to go."

"Story?"

"You know . . ." His voice slid over her like gentle raindrops. "Prince Charming meets Cinderella. She runs from the ball and leaves her glass slipper behind. He searches for her, finds her, and they live happily ever after. . . ."

Victoria swallowed. *Happily ever after.* A part of her that she thought had been buried forever struggled to emerge from the depths of her heart. But the disciplined, reserved, sensible, cautious Victoria pushed the secret yearning down. "Mr. Mitchell," she said. "I barely know you. Last night...well, last night was just a fantasy...just make-believe. It has no basis in reality."

"Basis in reality?"

Victoria heard the incredulity. "Yes." Gaining confidence, she took a deep breath and rushed on. "Last night was a masquerade, Mr. Mitchell. I was pretending to be someone I'm not."

"I can't believe you were pretending to enjoy dancing with me. And I also don't believe you were pretending when I kissed you. Your reaction couldn't have been an act. You were feeling exactly what I was feeling," he said softly. "Something special happened between us last night. Something that might only happen once in a lifetime. Do you believe in love at first sight?"

His voice was husky and caressing. It sent little shivers up Victoria's spine. The warm, silky feeling she'd experienced when he'd held her close returned, sliding up her legs and curling into her stomach.

"Victoria, I know you felt it, too. What are you afraid of?"

Years of rigid discipline, of denying herself pleasure in favor of duty, in favor of pursuing her goals, welled to the surface. It would be so easy to give in to him, to yield to his soft, insistent voice, to allow him into her life. But how could she? Even if she hadn't written that review, even if he wouldn't change his mind about her once he knew who she was, even if it were perfectly safe to see him again, she couldn't.

Because Dusty Mitchell, with his seductive smile and indolent charm, was totally wrong for her, and she knew it. She'd set her goals eleven years ago, on the day Chris died, taking two innocent people with him. Never again would she allow herself to be swayed by charm, by unrealistic emotions. The next time around—if there was a next time—she wanted stability. A good, solid, dependable man who would be home with her at night. Not a singer and composer who would be traipsing around the country, spending his nights in music halls and his days in bed.

So Victoria pushed the feelings down. She straightened her shoulders and said firmly, "Mr. Mitchell, I'm not afraid of anything. I simply have no desire to see you again. Last night was a game of let's pretend. Today is reality, and the reality is, you and I are from different worlds. Under normal circumstances, we'd never have met. We have absolutely nothing in common. Please don't call me again." And then she quietly placed the receiver into its cradle, and if she felt an ache of sadness at the finality of the soft click, she pushed the ache down, too.

Dusty stared at the phone, his forehead wrinkled in thought. What had happened between last night and this morning to cause her to sound so cold, so remote? Victoria Jones might have been a complete stranger.

He frowned, confused but not angry. Today, talking to her, he'd sensed some struggle behind her words. He'd have bet money she had wanted to say yes to his invitation, but she hadn't. What *was* she afraid of? The passion that had ignited between them when he kissed her? The way he made her feel? Was that it?

That couldn't be it. She hadn't acted afraid when they'd kissed. In fact, up until the time Sissy Farraday came to get him at eleven-thirty, things had seemed great between them. And she *had* promised to wait for him.

No. It had to be something else. But what? Then a sudden thought struck him, chilled him. Maybe the answer to her reluctance to see him again was simple, so simple that he'd refused to see it. Maybe he wasn't up to her standards.

Dusty walked out to his minuscule kitchen and filled the teakettle with water. While the water heated on the stove, he leaned against the kitchen counter.

He hated the thought that Victoria might have been playing games with him last night. She hadn't seemed like that kind of person at all. In fact, he could hardly believe it. He considered himself a pretty good judge of people, and she had seemed completely genuine to him.

But what else could he think? As much as he didn't want to believe it of her, she was probably regretting her impulsive behavior of last night . . . thinking of it as slumming, or something. After all, Sissy Farraday had referred to Victoria as her best friend, and Sissy was as rich as Midas's wife. The logical conclusion was that Sissy Farraday wasn't likely to have a normal, everyday woman as her best friend. Victoria Jones was probably spoiled and rich. Last night wouldn't have meant anything more to her than a little casual flirtation. She'd even said as much when she said they came from different worlds. She was a society girl, and society girls didn't date cowboys who owned small bars and wrote songs. That had to be it. No other explanation made any sense. He'd been kidding himself by thinking she was the kind of woman who'd have enjoyed driving out to the ranch.

As usual, thoughts of the ranch reminded him of his younger brother, which produced a mixture of sadness and guilt in Dusty. As he turned off the gas, spooned some instant coffee into a mug and poured the boiling water over it, he decided that he'd forget about Victoria Jones and her rich friends. He'd drink his coffee, pack up his guitar and the song he was working on and drive out to the ranch. He hadn't seen Maggie and David in three weeks, and he missed them. They were *his* reality.

At ten o'clock that night, as Dusty drove along Interstate 10 to Houston, his mind was full of thoughts of his family. As usual, he'd enjoyed spending the day with them, but he was worried about his brother. David had seemed unhappy today, and that bothered Dusty. Then, just before Dusty had been ready to leave, David had said, "Come on out onto the porch. There's something I want to talk to you about."

"Sure." Uneasy at David's tone, Dusty had followed his brother's wheelchair as David deftly maneuvered himself through the screen door and onto the porch. Dusty perched on the porch railing. Dusk had settled over the ranch, and the western sky was a brilliant study of rose and violet as the sun sank slowly behind the hills. Horses nickered softly from the direction of the stables, and the night air smelled strongly of honeysuckle.

David sighed, and Dusty frowned. What was wrong with his younger brother? For months now, David had seemed discontented, in a way he hadn't been for years. Dusty had thought David was resigned to his paralysis, but lately, he'd wondered. "Look, Dusty, I know you're not going to agree with what I'm going to say, but I've been thinking and thinking, and I'm going to say it anyway."

"Okay. Spit it out, then." Dusty strove to keep his voice light.

"I want you to find me a place to live in Houston."

"What? What are you talking about?"

"Just what I said. I want to move to Houston. I want to study with Borghini, and I want to try to find a gallery that'll show my paintings." David's green eyes, a mirror image of Dusty's, gleamed in the soft light.

"That's ridiculous, David. Houston is no place for you. This is where you belong. The ranch is safe, protected, perfect for you. Houston is...Houston is *dangerous*." What was wrong with David to even suggest such a thing? Why, it was nonsense.

"Safe! I'm sick of that word, Dusty." David's muscled arms corded as he pushed himself up in his chair. Just as abruptly, he lowered himself back down and dropped his head into his hands. "I'm sick of everyone treating me as if I can't take care of myself, as if I'm a child." He dropped his hands and raised imploring eyes. "I'm not a child, Dusty. I'm thirty-four years old. I've been paralyzed since I was eighteen. I've had a lot of years to learn to look after myself."

"Nobody's saying you're a child. All I'm saying is that Houston isn't for you."

"*You* moved to Houston. *You're* doing what you want to do. Why shouldn't I?"

"That's different. I can take care of—"

"I can take of myself, too!" David said. "And I don't need your permission, you know. I have some money of my own."

"Calm down. I know you don't need my permission. But let's talk about this. What would Maggie do without you? She'd be lonely. And it's not like you can't paint out here. You can. You do."

"Mom would be just fine without me here. Her life is all tied up with this ranch. Shoot, she might even marry Luke if she didn't have me around to worry about. He's sure asked her enough times. I'm just another burden."

"That's not true, and you know it." Alarm and guilt combined in Dusty's mind. Although the accident that had paralyzed David had been no one's fault, Dusty had always felt guilty, as if he should have been able to prevent the horse from throwing David, as if he should have stopped his brother from a midnight ride after he'd been drinking beer. "You're not a burden to anyone. Maggie and I . . . we *like* havin' you to look after."

For a long moment, David didn't answer. Then, with quiet resignation, he said, "But I don't like being looked after. That's my whole point. I want to take care of myself. Please try to understand, Dusty. I have to try to take care of myself. I have to prove to myself that I can do it."

David's words echoed in Dusty's mind as his exit sign loomed ahead. Nothing had been settled today, but Dusty had felt a sense of disquiet since leaving the ranch. David had dropped the discussion, but Dusty knew the idea hadn't been dropped. And Dusty also knew he simply could never go along with David leaving the ranch. If David didn't know what was good for him, Dusty did.

He was still thinking about his brother as he unlocked the door to his apartment twenty minutes later. He could hear his telephone ringing, but he didn't hurry. Whoever it was would call back if it was important.

Sure enough, five minutes later, the phone rang again.

"Hello."

"Dusty, where the blazes have you been all day?" Spence's voice greeted him.

"I went out to the ranch. Why? What's up?"

"You read the *Herald* today?"

"No. I never even unwrapped it." Dusty could see the newspaper where he'd tossed it this morning—in the corner of the sofa.

"Well, I think you should go read it."

There was a strange note in Spence's normally cheerful voice. Foreboding.

"What is it?" Images of tragedy teemed in Dusty's imagination.

"A hatchet job, that's what it is," Spence said.

"A hatchet job! My God! Who? What?"

"Go get the paper and find the entertainment section and turn to page five. You'll see what I mean."

"The entertainment section?" Dusty wondered if Spence had lost his mind. "Why would a murder be written up in the entertainment section?"

"Who said anything about a murder?"

"You did. You said a hatchet job—"

"Oh, shoot, I didn't mean it literally. I meant the music reviewer for the *Herald* did a wonderful hatchet job on *you*—on the album—that's all." Then in a softer tone, Spence said, "Go read it. Then call me back. We'll talk."

Dusty picked up the paper from the corner of his brown leather sofa. He found the entertainment section, turned to page five and immediately saw the header.

Reading rapidly, he could feel his face growing hot. Anger boiled up. He wadded up the paper and threw it against the wall.

Who the hell did this V.M. Patterson think he was, anyway? Taking the work of years and dismissing it like so much garbage! *Commercial pabulum...junk pop music...panders to romantic daydreams of teenagers...mediocre...don't waste your money.* The words of the review sliced through his vanity like steel knives.

V. M. Patterson had probably never attempted to write a note of music in his life. What was that old saying? *Those who can, do. Those who can't, teach. Or write reviews.* Dusty angrily stared out his living room window. The lights of the cars dashing along the Southwest Freeway created ribbons of red and white, and the towers of the buildings in Greenway Plaza were inky silhouettes against the purple night sky. So who cared what V. M. Patterson thought? The guy was a snob, and he had lousy taste.

The strident ring of the telephone cut into his furious thoughts. "Hello," he said through clenched teeth.

"You read it."

Spence's quiet tone was calming, and Dusty let his muscles relax and his breathing slow. "Yes."

"Listen, Dusty, I know it's a lousy review, but nobody pays attention to reviews anyway."

Dusty closed his eyes. Every penny of his savings had gone into the production of the album.

"The only person that really matters is Chester Lansky, and I don't think that old coot even reads the paper," Spence said.

Chester Lansky. He'd forgotten all about Chester Lansky. The eccentric old wildcatter had half promised that if sales on this album went well, he'd help finance the recording of another album, this time in one of the better studios where the production quality would be more professional.

"Well..." Spence's voice trailed off. "I guess we'll know if he saw the review soon enough, won't we?"

Chester Lansky and his sidekick, Toby Perkins, came into Mitchell's every Monday night, like clockwork. Precisely at eight o'clock the outer door would open, and in would walk a tall, ugly man with a shock of bright red hair and a mouth full of stained teeth, and right on his heels would be a wiry man with a face like a rat terrier.

Anyone who didn't know Lansky would be likely to dismiss him as just another old country boy, but Dusty knew better. The lack of polish and unsophisticated exterior covered a mind as sharp and bright as a diamond.

"Yeah . . . I guess we don't have long to wait."

But on Monday night at eight o'clock, Chester Lansky didn't walk into Mitchell's. Instead, about eight-thirty, Toby Perkins strolled in alone, plopped down on his usual stool and said, "Hey, Dusty. Gimme a beer."

"Hello, Toby," Dusty said. "Where's Chester tonight?"

"Had to go out of town. His daughter Carol had her baby."

"I'll bet he was happy. What'd she have?" Spence asked.

"Boy. Ten pounds." Perkins accepted the beer Spence handed him.

Spence whistled.

"Yeah, guess she had a rough time," Perkins said. "Here's to the kid." He raised his bottle.

After the toast, Perkins eyed Dusty, a sly look in his dark eyes. "How's the album doin'?"

Tension balled into a tight knot in Dusty's stomach. "It's only been out a few days."

Perkins stared at him. "Read that review in the *Herald*."

Dusty returned the look unflinchingly. He shrugged.

"What do they know?" Spence said.

"Did Chester see it?" Dusty asked, hating himself for asking, but not able to stop himself.

"Dunno. Told him it was there."

You would, Dusty thought. He knew Perkins tolerated him because Chester Lansky and Dusty's father had been good friends. For some reason, Toby Perkins didn't like him, and Dusty could never figure out why. He'd never cared, but now he wondered if that dislike could hurt him. He decided not to pursue the subject. It wouldn't do to let Perkins know how concerned he was about Lansky's reaction to the review.

But Perkins persisted, small eyes gleaming. "I forgot to ask him if he read it when I talked to him this mornin'. He told me about Carol, and we talked about some other things that was more pressin'...like how money's gettin' tight, and all..."

Dusty's eyes narrowed as he studied the other man. The little bastard wouldn't tell him anything even if he knew whether Lansky had changed his mind about backing him. Perkins would enjoy letting him squirm for a while.

At that moment, if Dusty could've strangled V. M. Patterson, he would have. With icy certainty, he knew Chester Lansky had read the review and that he was even now having second thoughts about backing a "mediocre talent."

Spence, who was behind the bar, turned away. The look in Dusty's eyes was scary; he sure would hate to be in the shoes of anyone toward whom that look *was* directed.

Victoria pushed open the swinging door to the editorial offices of the *Herald* and made her way across the huge room until she reached the features department. She waved to a few people on her way to her desk but didn't stop to talk to anyone. Working three days a week for four hours a day didn't leave her much time for socializing or becoming a real part of things at the newspaper, but the extra income was an absolute necessity if she hoped to be able to send Julie away to college.

Victoria had even less time today than she normally did. She usually arrived promptly at one o'clock on Tuesdays, Thursdays and Saturdays. Today, however, she was running over an hour late because she'd had to stay at the university after her last class to administer a makeup exam to a student who'd been out with mono. So here it was, Tuesday afternoon at two-fifteen, and she'd have to try to cram four hours of work into less than three hours. She never stayed late unless it was an emergency. Victoria didn't like Julie to come home to an empty house. Victoria remembered all too well how tempting it could be to do something forbidden when your parents weren't around.

An hour later, she leaned back in her chair, stretched and read the last sentence she'd typed.

"Uh, Victoria?"

She looked up. Frank Carbone, a sports columnist who'd tried to date her a couple of times, grinned at her as he leaned against the partition of her cubicle, his dark eyes twinkling with mischief.

"Hello, Frank," she said.

"Hi. You real busy?"

"Sort of. Why?"

"A friend of mine is waiting outside. He wanted to meet you, and I arranged for him to be brought in. Do you mind?"

Victoria frowned, suddenly uneasy. For a reason she couldn't explain, she felt he was up to no good. He was notorious for his practical jokes. In fact, his penchant for horseplay was one of the reasons she'd never been interested in going out with him. She eyed him warily. "Frank, I really am very busy today."

"It'll only take a minute. As a favor to me, okay?"

She hated scenes. With a sigh, she nodded her agreement.

Carbone winked and said, "I'll be right back." A few seconds later he appeared and said, "*This* is V. M. Patterson." After pointing at her, he moved aside.

Victoria's heart leaped wildly.

Standing before her, green-gold eyes blazing, was the man she'd never thought to see again. Dusty Mitchell stared at her, and slowly, recognition flared in his eyes.

A small part of her mind, the part that wasn't mortified and wishing she could disappear, took note of his dark green shirt with the sleeves rolled up to expose tanned, muscular arms covered with fine golden hairs and the form-fitting jeans that molded to the muscles of his thighs.

"There must be some mistake," he said.

Victoria swallowed. She couldn't have spoken if she'd wanted to.

His eyes dropped to her desk. She knew what he saw. Amidst the clutter of papers and magazines and album covers and compact disks was a small wooden name plate that had the name V. M. Patterson cut into it in large white letters.

Dusty slowly raised his head.

Victoria's heart pounded so hard she was certain he could hear it. His generous mouth tightened into a hard, angry line. His blazing eyes narrowed, and she saw his fists clench at his sides. When he finally spoke, each word lashed at Victoria like the cutting edge of a whip.

"Now I understand why you were hoping never to hear from me again," he said. "Was it amusing to dupe the dumb cowboy? Did you have a good laugh about it with all your society friends? Well, now it's my turn, lady. I've got a few things to say to you." He smiled, but the smile wasn't the warm, friendly grin of Saturday night. This was a twisted caricature that made Victoria shiver.

"And you're going to listen to every word!"

Chapter Three

Victoria trembled as he moved closer, stopping within inches of her desk. He towered over her, and she could see how rapidly he was breathing.

"What's the matter," he taunted, a furious glint in his smoldering eyes. "Surely you're not afraid?"

Victoria wet her lips. She still couldn't speak. Her heart was pounding wildly. As their eyes locked, she shrank against her chair.

Dusty backed up a few steps, and an expression of something like disgust passed over his strong features. "You know," he said, "if it was just what you'd written...that wouldn't be so bad. After all, we're all entitled to our own opinions, aren't we?"

Victoria stared at him. His eyes had darkened to jade. His mouth twisted, the same mouth that had once kissed her so tenderly.

"I was angry about that," he continued, "I'll admit it, but mostly because what you wrote probably cost me a potential backer."

Victoria wished she could disappear. Just dissolve into nothing so she wouldn't have to sit and look at this man and the dislike she saw in his eyes. Funny how eyes that blazed with green fire could be so cold . . . could chill her straight through to her heart.

"What really ticks me off is the way you lied to me, strung me along. I can't believe I was taken in by your innocent look." He clenched his fists. "You knew all the time who I was, yet you led me on, let me think there was something special happening between us."

"That's not true!" Victoria said. "I had no idea who you were! And I was not leading you on. I—"

"Yeah, sure. You must think I'm really stupid. You saw my picture on the cover of the album when you wrote that review, and your *best friend*, Sissy Farraday, told you she'd invited me to her party. There was no way you couldn't have known who I was. Hell, now I understand everything."

"That's not—"

"Don't try denying it. I know damn well you and your friend cooked it up together. Why, she probably even knew what you'd written. No wonder she was grinning like a cat with a bowl of cream when I asked her for your name and telephone number. She probably couldn't wait to hear how I'd make a fool of myself! And all the while I was thinking how nice she was . . . how honest. Isn't that a joke?"

"She *is* nice. She *is* honest. You've twisted everything. It wasn't that way at all."

"Save your breath, sweetheart. I might have believed you the other night, but you won't take me in again. I'm not that stupid."

Victoria shook her head in frustration. Oh, why wouldn't he listen? The albums she reviewed didn't come in their commercial covers. They were sent to the paper in plain white covers with an accompanying press release from the production company. And Sissy hadn't told her any of her plans for the party except that it was a masquerade. Sissy knew Victoria wasn't interested and didn't have time to discuss all the hundreds of details that went into the planning of such a party.

"Do you two amuse yourselves like this often? Think up ways to play games with other people?" Disgust twisted his mouth.

Victoria felt as if someone had grabbed her heart and squeezed. Her hands shook as she reached out to touch Dusty's forearm.

He jerked his arm away as if she'd tried to burn him. He stared at her, his eyes fiery and fierce. "You sure had me fooled. I thought you were classy...beautiful...a real lady. Huh!"

Victoria was on the verge of tears.

"Well," he said, "I was completely taken in. I fell for your innocent look and big blue eyes. You did a real good job. You can be proud of yourself. You have a great story to tell around the pool or at lunch at Tony's or whatever it is you do to fill up your days...besides playing at being a reporter."

"Look, you've got it all wrong. I know it looks bad, but that's—"

"Save it! I'm not interested. I've said what I came to say, and as far as I'm concerned, it's over. Finished. I have no intention of thinking about it—or you—ever again."

Victoria shivered. She hugged herself and wished there was something, anything, she could say. But the look in his eyes told her he'd never believe her.

His eyes narrowed. "Why are you shivering? Are you cold?" Then he laughed, an ugly sound. "Yeah, baby, you're cold all right. Right through to your frozen little heart." He grimaced. "I can't believe how wrong I was about you. I thought you were Cinderella, but you're really one of the ugly stepsisters."

And without another word or a glance, he turned and stalked away. Victoria heard him stride rapidly through the swinging door. She'd never forget the look in his eyes as he'd called her an ugly stepsister. Sharp pain stabbed at her heart, and she blinked back tears.

She'd hurt him. If he had only been angry with her, she could have dealt with the situation. But she had hurt him deeply, and she knew he'd never forgive her.

An aching sense of loss overwhelmed her, leaving her drained. He'd never forgive her, and she'd never forget him.

"What's the matter, Mom?"

Victoria looked up from the book she'd been staring at for the past hour without comprehending a single word she'd read. She brushed her dark hair from her forehead. "Nothing."

"There's something wrong," her daughter insisted. "You haven't turned a page for at least thirty minutes."

Victoria's eyes rested on Julie with pleasure. Tonight she was dressed in her favorite outfit: faded jeans and a long pink T-shirt that reached almost to her knees. Her slender feet were bare, and her toenails gleamed with a soft shell-pink polish she'd just finished applying. Her light gray eyes, exactly the same shade as her father's, were puzzled. Her dark, curly hair was held back from her face by a silver barrette, framing a small, heart-shaped face, the same face Victoria saw in photos of her grandmother. Except for the color of Julie's hair, nothing about her was like Victoria. Sometimes, standing beside her dainty daughter, Victoria wondered how she'd ever produced her.

"Something happened today that upset me, and I haven't been able to forget it," she said.

"Gosh, what happened?" Julie pulled her feet up to her chest and hugged her knees.

She seemed genuinely interested. Victoria hesitated, then said, "Well, I wrote an uncomplimentary review about a local singer's new album, and he was furious when he read it. Today he came to the paper and told me off." There was no reason to mention the party at Sissy's, not to Julie. How could she possibly explain her behavior the other night to her daughter?

"Who was he? What did he say? What did you write about him?"

The questions tumbled out of Julie's mouth, and Victoria almost smiled. "I don't think you know him. I had never heard of him before I got the album to review. But if you want to read what I wrote, I cut it out just like I cut out all my reviews, and it's on my desk in the wire basket."

Julie bounded off her chair and raced out of the room. Within moments, she was back. Gracefully, she folded herself into her chair and crossed her legs Indian fashion, chewing her lip as she read the article. When she raised her eyes, Victoria saw amazement.

"Gosh, Mom, I can't believe you didn't like Dusty Mitchell's album. He's good! Why, this one song, 'Close Your Eyes,' is being given a lot of play on KKBQ. Skipper Welch loves it."

Victoria knew Skipper Welch was the evening DJ on Julie's favorite radio station. "I liked that song. I...oh, I don't know. I don't know why I wrote what I did. I don't know how I feel about the music. I don't know anything." Suddenly she didn't want to talk about it anymore. She laid aside her book and stood. "I'm going out to make a cup of tea. Want some?"

Julie looked at her as if she were crazy. "You know I hate tea."

Just then, the telephone rang, and Julie, the review forgotten, jumped up and raced to answer it. At her daughter's, "Oh, hi Kate," Victoria bent down to pick up the review, which had drifted to the floor. For a moment she felt like wadding up the clipping and throwing it away so she'd never have to see it again; but she didn't. She folded the paper and tucked it into her shirt pocket.

As she walked out to the kitchen, Julie said, her hand over the phone, "Mom, will you hang this phone up when you hear me pick it up in my bedroom?"

Victoria nodded and watched as Julie's slim form disappeared down the hall. When she heard Julie say, "Okay," she gently replaced the receiver. Julie seemed to spend most of her time on the phone or in her bedroom. Doing what, Victoria had no idea. There was a time when Julie had really enjoyed being with her, but for the past six months, Victoria had noticed a decided difference. Now Julie only seemed interested in her friends and what they had to say. In fact, tonight's show of interest in Victoria had been a real surprise.

Victoria sighed. It was so hard to be a single parent. Sometimes she felt overwhelmed by her responsibilities. Sometimes she felt so tempted to take the easy way out—to say yes to Julie when she knew no was the right answer.

The whistle of the teakettle cut into her thoughts, the hiss of the boiling water reminding her of Dusty Mitchell and his simmering fury. The memory of the scene in her office pushed aside all her other thoughts, and suddenly all she could see were Dusty's eyes, filled with white-hot anger and something else. Something that chilled Victoria. Distaste and loathing. He'd looked at her as if he couldn't stand the sight of her.

Dusty stared at his bottle of beer. The sounds of the busy bar swirled around him, but he ignored them. He'd come straight over to the club after he'd stormed out of the *Herald*'s offices, and he'd been sitting at the bar ever since, nursing his beer and his anger.

"Wanna tell me about it?"

Dusty looked up. Spence stood in front of him, concern etched into his round face.

"Come on, it'll do you good to get it off your chest," Spence said.

"I don't feel like talking about it."

Spence's eyes narrowed. "You still brooding over that review?"

Dusty sighed. He might as well tell Spence about today. He knew he was going to tell him sooner or later. The whole scene had been simmering in his mind for hours. He had to tell someone.

"Sort of," he said. "I went over to the *Herald* today and had a run-in with the Ice Maiden."

"Ice Maiden?"

"V. M. Patterson, better known as Victoria Jones, a cold bitch who gets her kicks out of making fools out of unsuspecting men."

"You mean the guy who wrote that review is really a girl?"

"A woman." Dusty laughed, but even to him it was a bitter sound. "Quite a woman. To look at her, you'd think she was a real lady. I thought she was a class act when I first met her, but of course, that was before I knew she was V. M. Patterson."

"When you first met her?" Spence echoed.

Dusty nodded. "Give me another beer, will you?" He handed Spence his empty bottle.

Spence reached into the cooler under the bar and withdrew another bottle for Dusty. Someone fed money into the jukebox, and the strains of Hank Williams singing "Your Cheating Heart" filled the air. Dusty winced. The plaintive song expressed his feelings exactly.

"Now, will you please explain all this to me?" Spence prompted.

"I met Miss Victoria Jones on Saturday night at the ball."

"The ball . . ."

"Yeah. That's what I said. The ball. You know," he added as he saw the confused look in Spence's eyes. "The masquerade ball at Sissy Farraday's house...mansion...in River Oaks."

Spence's mouth formed a mute oh.

"Well," Dusty continued after taking a long swallow of his beer, "Miss Victoria Jones looked like someone who had just stepped out of the pages of a fairy tale. In fact, she was dressed as Cinderella, and she looked . . . beautiful. You should see her, Spence. She's really something. Tall, slim, curves in all the right places. Dark brown hair. The most gorgeous eyes you ever saw. They're dark blue, almost violet." His chest tightened as he remembered how he'd felt holding her in his arms, how soft her mouth had been when he'd kissed her, how strong had been the urge to protect her, to take care of her.

He pushed the images away. She'd been playing a game with him. "Well, she certainly took me in. She never told me her name, just said she was Cinderella. We spent the entire evening together, and I thought . . . well, never mind what I thought. The entire time she was just stringing me along, setting me up, laughing at me behind my back." His anger boiled up again, and he slammed his fist down on the bar. Several people jumped, and glasses rattled.

"Dusty . . ." Spence cautioned.

"God, I can't believe how stupid I was! She's some actress."

"How'd you know she was the one that wrote the review?"

"I didn't. I went charging into the paper to get a few things straight with V. M. Patterson, and there she was, sitting as cool as you please behind that desk, with those wide eyes staring at me like, 'Who let you in?' I wanted to strangle her pretty little neck."

He clenched his teeth, and his fist tightened around the beer bottle. It was damned frustrating how she'd gotten under his skin. He'd told her he didn't intend to think about her anymore, and here he was, thinking about nothing else for hours.

"What really gets me is the way she wouldn't admit anything. She kept telling me I had it all wrong, like I was a complete imbecile. She tried to make me look like I was in the wrong instead of her. Said she had no idea who I was the night of the party.''

"Maybe she was telling the truth."

"Ha! Her kind don't know the meaning of the word."

"Now you don't know that, Dusty."

"I know it as sure as I know my own name. She knew who I was, and she was laughing up her sleeve at how easy it was to pretend to be interested in me, to get me thinking she really liked me. And I played right into her hands, because that's what I *wanted* to think."

"Now you know how it feels."

"What?" Dusty stared at Spence. The other man's blue eyes were thoughtful. "What the hell are you talking about?"

"Well, you've gotta admit that this woman is the first one who's ever managed to get the upper hand with you. Usually, the shoe's on the other foot."

Dusty couldn't believe his ears. Spence was supposed to be his friend. Why was he siding with *her*?

"It's kind of funny, isn't it?" Spence said. "Women have flocked after you for years, each one thinking she'd lasso you for herself, and you've been brushing them all off like they were so many bothersome flies. No telling how many hearts you've broken. Not one of them has ever even come close to stirring your interest past a few dates. This Victoria Jones...well, she must really be something. I'd like to meet her. See what kind of woman it takes to get Dusty Mitchell all riled up."

Dusty stared at Spence. "I can't believe I'm hearing this. What about that review? You think it was perfectly okay for her to write what she did, too?"

"Well, she was only doing her job. I know the review was pretty bad, but I've read a lot worse. Anyone in the entertainment business has to put up with this kind of thing, Dusty. It's not really important."

"Not important! It could ruin my career! Look at Chester Lansky."

"What about him?"

"You heard what Toby Perkins said last night. Lansky's sure to withdraw his offer of support."

"Dusty," Spence said slowly. "You're jumping to conclusions. Perkins didn't say anything like that."

"He didn't have to. I saw the smirk on his face."

"He always looks like that," Spence said. Then he grinned. "He was probably born with that ugly look."

Dusty drummed his fingers on the bar. He knew Spence was trying to cheer him up, but he also knew it was a wasted effort. He didn't feel like being cheered up.

"You know," Spence said, "your pride is hurt more than anything. You're upset because you think you made a fool of yourself over that woman, not about what she wrote."

Victoria felt like choking Sissy. Sometimes her refusal to be serious infuriated Victoria; other times Sissy's light-hearted approach to life was the quality Victoria enjoyed most because it contrasted so sharply to her own lack of frivolity.

"Will you please be serious, just this once?"

Sissy grinned, her eyes as blue and clear as the spring sky. She tossed her blond hair and stretched her shapely legs, propping them on the corner of a wrought-iron table.

It was a perfect Friday afternoon, one week after the party. Sissy and Victoria had just had a rousing game of tennis, and they were relaxing by Sissy's pool. Victoria's classes had been over since noon, and she'd come straight to Sissy's house. A little of her gloom had lifted since Tuesday, partly because this was the start of spring break for both her and Julie, and Victoria was looking forward to the respite. She'd even wangled a week off from the *Herald*, although she still felt guilty about the loss of income.

The balmy air caressed Victoria's still-heated skin. The exercise had been good for her. She didn't get enough of it. When you worked two jobs and had a teenage daughter and a house to take care of, there wasn't much time left over.

"Come on, Sissy," she said. "What can I do to make it up to him?" She had asked the question before, but Sissy hadn't answered.

Sissy's eyes narrowed, and she chewed on a blade of grass. "Let me get this straight. You're feeling guilty because you wrote a nasty review about the big hunk you've got the hots for, and now you want to fix it so he's not mad at you anymore."

"Sissy!"

Sissy flashed her an evil grin. "Well . . . what part of that statement isn't true?"

"You know good and well which part isn't true. I have not, as you so crassly put it, got the hots for Dusty Mitchell."

"Oh, yeah? Says who?"

"Says me," retorted Victoria. But she remembered the curling feeling in her stomach when his rich voice had whispered to her, when his strong arms had held her close against his broad chest. She remembered the weak feeling in her knees when he'd kissed her, and she could feel herself blushing.

"Hey, I'm not saying there's a thing wrong with you feeling that way, Tory, and you know it. You're so darned uptight about everything. So afraid to let yourself go. You can't spend the rest of your life squashing down honest emotions because of what happened with Chris. You can't let one mistake color how you act forever."

"I don't think I do that, Sissy. Just because I don't jump into bed with every attractive guy I meet doesn't mean I'm inhibited or cold. I'm just selective. I'd even like to get married again, if I can find a man who's solid and mature, someone who won't walk out on his responsibilities . . . or drown his insecurities in alcohol. . . ."

"Who's talking about marriage? I'm talking about sex, kiddo. Wonderful, exciting, delicious s-e-x." Sissy grinned again as the flush on Victoria's face deepened. "Honestly, Tory, you act like sex is a four-letter word."

Victoria squirmed. "I never said I didn't like sex. I'm just not crazy about talking about it. Anyway, I can't have sex with someone just for the fun of it. I'm not made that way. With me, it has to be serious. I have to love him. It has to mean something."

"I agree. It should mean something. But does it have to mean marriage?"

"I know you think I'm old-fashioned, maybe even a prude, but I'm not looking for excitement or momentary satisfaction. I want stability in my life. I've had enough turmoil to last me a lifetime."

Sissy sighed. She couldn't argue with that. Victoria had had such a rough time when Chris died. Sissy often wondered what it had been like for Victoria—only twenty-two years old, with a two-year-old child—to be alone except for a mother who had never been too interested in playing a mother's role and who lived over a thousand miles away. Sissy had been on her honeymoon when the accident happened, so Tory hadn't even had her friendship and support to count on. Stephen had taken Sissy on a cruise of the Greek islands; it had been six weeks after Chris's death before Sissy even knew about it.

By then Victoria was a frozen shell of the person she had once been: a warm, loving girl who had given her friendship and affection easily and trustingly. Now Victoria was cool and reserved, and she kept a locked door around her heart. She'd adopted rigid rules of behavior that encompassed everyone in her sphere. Too rigid, Sissy thought. But despite all that, Sissy loved Victoria, and she knew the feeling was reciprocated. And Sissy kept hoping someone would come along and break through that door. Maybe Dusty Mitchell might be that someone. Despite what Victoria said.

"All right, Tory. I give up. Let's get back to your original question. What you can do to make it up to Dusty Mitchell for what happened." Sissy tented her fingers and rested her chin on them. "I know. Didn't you tell me that

Dusty said he'd probably lose his backer because of your review?''

"Yes."

"Well, that's it, then. I'll back Dusty. I'll tell him that you told me about what happened, and I'll tell him I'm interested in investing in his career."

"Oh, no." Victoria shook her head vehemently. She should have known that gleam in Sissy's eyes boded ill for her.

"It's my money, Tory. And you know I've been looking for a project I can sink my teeth into. This is perfect! I love his music!"

"Oh, Sissy, I don't know."

"Give me one good reason I shouldn't."

"I'm afraid he'll get even more upset if you approach him. I told you he thought you and I had hatched up some kind of scheme to make him look like a fool. What if he thinks we're conspiring against him?"

Sissy rolled her eyes. "All right, if it'll make you feel any better, I'll arrange for some financing for him without him knowing I'm involved."

Sissy's plan sounded okay, but for some reason Victoria still felt uneasy. She frowned.

"*Now* what are you frowning about?"

"I don't know. I just have a bad feeling about this. Maybe we should forget the whole thing."

"Oh, no, you don't. First you get me all excited about something, then you try to back off. It's a great plan. Although there is one thing wrong with it."

"What's that?" Victoria stood up. It was time she started home.

"He won't know it was you who's responsible for helping him."

Picking up her tennis racket, Victoria said, "That's exactly the way I want it."

"But why? What good will it be to make amends if he doesn't know you're doing it?" Sissy stood up, too, and as she did, her two Persian cats, who had been dozing by the side of the pool, stood and stretched, their bushy tails standing straight up like two exclamation points.

"I'll know. That's what counts."

As Victoria started to walk toward the front of the house where she'd parked her car in the big circular drive, Sissy followed. Victoria gave an appreciative glance at the blooming azalea bushes lining the drive.

"You're nuts, Tory," Sissy said as they hugged goodbye. "But I love you, anyway."

Victoria climbed into her old station wagon and shut the door. Sissy leaned against the open passenger side window. "I'll start the wheels turning right away," she said.

"Just promise me you won't bring either of our names into it," Victoria said.

"I promise."

As Victoria drove home, she wondered if she had done the right thing. Maybe she should just forget about Dusty Mitchell, make no attempt to help him. But she knew she'd never be able to forget him if she didn't do something. Actually, Sissy's plan was perfect, and once she'd secured some backing for Dusty, Victoria could relegate him to the cobwebbed corners of her memory, where he belonged.

Chapter Four

Dusty was relieved when the week was over. By the following Monday morning he could think about Victoria Jones without wanting to strangle her. Instead, the image of her shocked face as he'd lashed out at her had started giving him twinges of remorse. The bewildered, unhappy look in her soft eyes haunted him. Could he have been wrong about her? Had she been telling him the truth?

Dusty laid his guitar on the sofa and walked to the apartment's windows. He gazed out at the Southwest Freeway for a long moment. It was well past the morning rush hour, but all four lanes of the freeway heading toward downtown Houston were heavy with whizzing cars.

What would Victoria be doing right now? he wondered. Was she just waking up? Was her maid bringing her morning coffee in bed? Dusty could imagine how she'd look dressed in a satin nightgown, propped against a satin pillow. Her skin would be creamy, and her cheeks flushed a soft pink. The beautiful deep blue eyes would still be sleep-fogged, and her dark hair would curl around her smooth shoulders. Her breasts would be slowly rising and falling...

Damn. He had to stop this. His accelerated heartbeat annoyed him. Victoria Jones was completely wrong for him. Furthermore, he never wanted to see her again. So why was he wasting time thinking about her?

Purposefully, he strode to his guitar. He bent to pick it up, and just as he did, the telephone shrilled. Dusty straightened, then walked to the bar that divided his living room from his kitchen and lifted the receiver.

"Hello."

"Dusty Mitchell, please," said a brisk female voice.

"Speaking."

"Please hold for Mr. Rylander."

Pleasant country music filled his ears. Mr. Rylander? He didn't know anyone named Rylander. Or did he? The name seemed familiar, but Dusty couldn't place it. For a second, he considered hanging up. He wasn't interested in time shares or aluminum siding or mutual funds. But he was curious. If this Rylander was a salesman, he certainly had a lot of nerve. It took guts to have your secretary place a call and put a future client on hold.

"Mr. Mitchell?" said a booming voice. "Vernon P. Rylander from VeePee Productions in Nashville. How the hell are ya?"

VeePee Productions. Of course! He'd just read an article about the company, about its phenomenal success, and about its flamboyant owner who was the envy of the music business for his uncanny ability to scoop up new talent for his Nashville company. After only three years in the business, VeePee Productions had more gold on its walls than most production companies had after ten.

Dusty grinned. "I'm fine, Mr. Rylander."

"Call me Vern," Rylander said.

Dusty's mouth went dry. Was this the call he'd dreamed about? Was it actually happening? He resisted crossing his fingers.

"You know who I am?"

"Everyone in the music business knows who you are, Mr. Ryland— Vern."

Vernon Rylander laughed, the sound hearty and friendly, and Dusty's tensed muscles relaxed.

"Yeah, I sure have made 'em all sit up and take notice, boy. Make no mistake about that. And you know why, don't you?" Without waiting for Dusty's answer, he said, "It's because I'm a damn good judge of talent, and when I hear someone I like, I sign 'em up so fast it'd make your head spin."

Dusty gripped the receiver tighter.

"I just finished listenin' to your album about five minutes ago."

Dusty closed his eyes. Elation, excitement, fear coursed through him.

"And I sure liked what I heard," Rylander continued. "I liked it one hell of a lot."

Dusty wanted to shout; he wanted to laugh out loud.

"You got talent, boy. Lots of talent."

"Thank you." He was proud of himself. No one would ever guess he was ready to burst.

"Don't thank me, boy. Thank your Creator."

Dusty laughed. "I do. Every day."

"That's what I like to hear," Rylander said. Then in a softer voice, he continued. "I want to offer you a contract."

Dusty's voice was steady. "That's great . . . Vern."

Vernon Rylander chuckled. "Good. Good. Now let's get down to business, son."

Dusty was glad Rylander had promoted him from *boy* to *son*. He hated to be called *boy*. On the other hand, Rylander could call him Cookie if he wanted to offer him a contract, and Dusty wouldn't object.

Twenty minutes later, Dusty sank onto the sofa and wondered if he'd dreamed the telephone call or if it had all really happened.

It had finally happened. He'd always known he was talented, and he'd hoped that, with determination and work, someday, someone like Rylander would recognize his talent. But he'd also known he needed luck. And lately he'd wondered if his luck had turned bad. That review and his anticipated loss of the backing of Chester Lansky had put doubts in his mind, even if he hadn't wanted to admit it to himself until now.

He jumped up. The doubts disappeared as if they'd never been. Who needed Chester Lansky? Who needed Victoria Jones? Dusty Mitchell, future star of the country and pop music world, didn't need anybody. Starting today, the sky was the limit. Why, with Rylander and VeePee Productions behind him, the moon, the stars, might be the limit. He might be the next Kenny Rogers!

"Spence! I've gotta call Spence...and Maggie and David," he said aloud. "I'll show you, Victoria Jones. *Mediocre*. We'll see who's mediocre." He wished he could call Miss Jones up, too. But just as quickly as the thought formed, he pushed it away. Victoria Jones, her review, her deceit—all belonged to the past. Vernon Rylander and VeePee Productions, and everything wonderful they represented—they belonged to the future.

He grinned. Life was good. He had everything he'd ever dreamed about, just his for the taking. He didn't need Victoria Jones. Now or ever.

Victoria hadn't been able to banish Dusty Mitchell from her thoughts. Finally, on Monday morning, she yielded to her second impulsive gesture in less than two weeks and decided to go out and buy a copy of his album. She hid her desire to do so by pretending to herself that she'd treat Julie to a shopping excursion and lunch at the Galleria. Feeling virtuous and only slightly sheepish, she knocked on her daughter's door. Hearing no answering sound, she pushed the door open and said softly to the huddled form on the twin-size bed, "You awake, hon?"

A muffled moan emerged from under the pink flowered sheets and matching comforter.

"It's nine o'clock, and I thought if you wanted to I'd take you shopping today. We can have lunch out and maybe even take in a movie later." Victoria's voice rose temptingly as she said *lunch out* and *movie*.

First Julie's head, then her soft gray eyes, peeked over the edge of the bed covers. "Where?" she asked.

"Where, what?"

"Mother! Where, shopping and where, lunch?"

Victoria ignored the crankiness in her daughter's voice and kept her own voice determinedly even and pleasant when she answered. "The Galleria and Shanghai Express." Why did she feel as if she were bribing Julie?

"The Galleria?" Now Julie's pert face was fully exposed, and the note of crankiness had disappeared. "Is it my birthday or something?" She grinned.

Victoria couldn't help but grin back. "No. It's just that it's the first day of our vacation, and we both deserve to do something special, don't you think?"

Julie shoved back the covers and swung her bare legs out of bed. "How soon do you want to leave?"

"How long will it take you to get ready?"

"An hour, at least."

"Then we'll leave in an hour."

Two hours later, Victoria and Julie strolled leisurely around the first level of the Galleria. They paused to watch the ice skaters swirling around the indoor rink comprising the center of the enormous three-level original section of the elegant shopping center.

Just as they turned to move on, two boys, one tall with thick black hair, one short and stocky with sandy-colored hair, walked toward them.

"Oh, gosh, it's Ryan Richardson," Julie said in a breathy whisper.

Victoria looked down. Julie's small face had two bright spots of color on her cheeks. Her eyes sparkled like smoky diamonds.

"Oh, hi, Julie," said the tall, dark-haired boy. His blue eyes were friendly as he smiled in greeting. Victoria thought he was one of the handsomest boys she'd ever seen, and she could see the effect he was having on her daughter.

"Hi, Ryan. Hi, Kurt," Julie said.

The two boys paused a moment, then continued on their way, laughing and talking. Julie's starry eyes followed them.

Before she could stop herself, Victoria said, "Richardson. Is he related to Kate?"

Julie nodded, eyes still watching the backs of the two boys as they threaded their way through the shoppers. They disappeared into a video store, and Julie finally turned her attention to Victoria. "He's Kate's brother."

"How old is he?"

"Sixteen."

Good heavens, Victoria thought. He was much too old for Julie. She nearly voiced the thought, but her good sense finally won out over the impulse. Better not to say anything. Julie obviously had a crush on him, but the boy, although friendly to his sister's friend, was probably not interested in girls her age.

Victoria couldn't help feeling sorry for Julie. Her daughter had about as much chance with Ryan Richardson as Victoria had with Dusty Mitchell. The unwelcome thought angered her. Why couldn't she forget the man? She didn't want to get involved with him. Did she? As it had done for the past two weeks, his name brought back vivid memories of how it had felt to be in his arms, to feel his mouth brush hers, to see his glittering eyes admiring her, to...

Stop this! she told herself. Thinking like this was unproductive, unrealistic, masochistic even. Why torture herself with how wonderful the evening at Sissy's had been?

Julie didn't know any better than to develop an infatuation for an entirely unsuitable boy, but I do, she thought. I know exactly what I want and need in my life, and I also know what Julie needs. She doesn't need to get married young, before she knows what life is all about. I'm not going to let her make the same mistakes I made. She's going to go away to a good college and prepare herself for a career where she can support herself, and someday, preferably when she's in her late twenties or early thirties and mature, she'll meet the right man.

Victoria squared her shoulders. "Come on, honey. Let's go look at clothes. I feel like buying both of us something special." She forced a smile to her lips. After one glance in the direction of the video store, Julie smiled back.

Victoria was glad she'd worn comfortable shoes. She'd done more walking today than she'd done in months. But Julie's happy, flushed face and bright eyes were ample reward. Victoria looked at her watch.

"It's almost five o'clock, Julie. Let's go get rid of these packages, then we can decide if we want to see a movie or not."

"Okay."

As they walked toward the parking garage, Victoria saw a record shop. She hesitated. Did she want Julie to know she was buying Dusty's album?

Julie kept walking.

"Uh . . . Julie . . ."

She turned around.

"I . . . I want to run in there for a minute." Victoria inclined her head in the direction of the record shop.

"Okay."

As they approached the shop, Victoria could see it was quite crowded. Uncertainty gripped her.

Julie was already halfway through the door.

Victoria hesitated, then followed her daughter inside.

The first thing she heard was a blast of Beach Boys music.

The first thing she saw was Dusty Mitchell's face.

His album was prominently displayed on a rack facing the open doorway. Her stomach muscles tightened as she looked at the glossy cover featuring a full-face photo with the Houston skyline as a backdrop. God, he was wonderful looking. And those eyes. Their dark green depths looked as if they were looking straight at her. Pain balled inside her chest.

Julie had headed straight toward the top-forty display.

Like a sleepwalker, Victoria's hand reached out and touched the face of the top album. Then, before she could think, before she could change her mind, she clutched the album in her hand. Hurriedly, she walked over to the counter where several people were waiting patiently to pay for their selections. Victoria knew it was childish, but she didn't want Julie to know she was buying the album. She craned her neck and could just see the top of Julie's dark head as she bent over one of the display racks.

The cash register zinged. Victoria tapped her foot. The woman ahead of her was wearing a strong perfume, and as she moved to lay her purchase on the high counter, Victoria felt stifled by the cloying scent.

"What're you buying, Mom?"

Victoria jumped. "Oh . . . nothing."

"Nothing? What's this?" Julie reached out and took the album. She studied it for a second, then looked up. Her gray eyes sparkled. "I thought you hated his music."

"I—"

"May I help you, ma'am?"

Julie grinned and laid the album on the countertop. "She wants this."

Victoria squirmed. She felt like a kid caught writing love notes in class.

The skinny clerk picked up the album. He turned it over. "You didn't get it signed?"

"Signed?"

"Yeah, you know, autographed. Dusty Mitchell has been here all day. Signing albums. Back there." The clerk pointed toward the back of the store.

Victoria's heart leapt into her throat.

"Really?" Julie squealed.

Victoria turned to look, heart thumping wildly. Just as she turned her head, she could see Dusty Mitchell striding up the aisle toward the front of the store.

Her mouth went dry. She had an insane desire to leave the album, clutch her packages and run. She wished she could disappear.

"Oh, Mom. Let's get him to sign it!"

"Julie..." Victoria said between clenched teeth. She turned. Maybe he wouldn't see her. "How much do I owe you?" she blurted. *Please, God. Don't let him see me.*

"Hey, Dusty," called the clerk.

Victoria couldn't breathe. If only she were invisible. If only she hadn't come into this store. If only she were dead.

"This lady just bought your album. Why'n't you sign it for her?"

Julie was practically dancing next to her. Victoria refused to turn. She felt as if a freight train were roaring down the track and she was tied in front of its chugging engine.

"Sure," she heard him say behind her. Her heart pounded in her chest. She could feel her face heating. Her stupid body had totally betrayed her.

"Mom..." Julie nudged her.

Victoria closed her eyes.

"Mom!" Julie said again.

Opening her eyes, Victoria took a deep breath and willed herself to turn around slowly. "Hello, Mr. Mitchell," she said. She could feel her cheeks burning. Embarrassment and pain warred within her. Why did this have to happen?

His green eyes widened in surprise. For one terrible moment Victoria was afraid he was going to say something awful. But then his mouth twisted into a sardonic smile, and he inclined his head, his eyes gleaming and hard. He reached for the album. "Hello, Miss Jones. You're the last person I expected to see here today."

Victoria wet her lips. Her voice seemed to have deserted her, too.

"Mom..." Julie took the album from Victoria's lifeless fingers and handed it to Dusty. "I'm Juliette Jones. I love your music."

Julie's eager voice jolted Victoria from her state of shock. What was wrong with her? She was a grown woman who had survived the terrible death of her husband, worked two jobs to educate herself and raised a daughter on her own. Surely she could handle this situation. After all, it wasn't the end of the world, was it? Why, even Julie had more aplomb and poise than Victoria had been exhibiting.

"Hi, there, Juliette Jones." Now his smile was real and warm as he responded to Julie's admiring tone of voice and bright eyes. He pulled a black felt marker from the breast pocket of his plaid shirt and scrawled his signature across the face of the album. Still smiling, he handed the album back to Julie.

"Thank you." Julie turned and looked expectantly at Victoria. Victoria swallowed.

"Yes, thank you," she said.

"My pleasure." The smile faded and his eyes darkened to deep jade. His square jaw tightened as he stared at her.

Victoria cringed at the dislike she saw in his expression. She forced herself to keep an even tone of voice and managed a small smile. "Julie will really enjoy telling her friends that you autographed her album." Before Julie could say anything, Victoria gently nudged her daughter toward the door of the shop. "We must be going. Thanks again. Goodbye." She hurried out of the store, a protesting Julie close behind.

"Mom! Why couldn't we have talked to him awhile? He was nice! And why'd you lie to him? You're always preach-

ing to me about lying. Why didn't you tell him you bought
the album for yourself?''

"Julie," Victoria said between gritted teeth. "Quit asking so many questions. Let's just get away from here."

Julie finally gave up, and later, after they'd deposited
their packages in the back of the station wagon and were
comfortably seated in the plush Galleria theater waiting for
the feature to begin, Victoria haltingly explained her reasons for implying that the album was Julie's.

"I didn't want him to think I might change my mind and
write another review, that's all."

Victoria wondered if Julie believed her. Even to Victoria's ears, the excuse sounded like what it was—a fabri-
cation. Julie's look remained skeptical although she said,
"Well, maybe you *will* change your mind after you listen to
his music. He's good."

"We'll see," Victoria said. But she wasn't thinking about
Dusty's music right then. As the lights dimmed and the
background music began, all she could see was the green fire
in his eyes as he looked at her in the music store—a look in
stark contrast to the tender, caressing looks he'd given her
the night they'd met.

That night Victoria waited until she was sure Julie was
asleep before she played Dusty's album. She plugged in her
earphones, settled into her favorite chair, closed her eyes and
gave herself up to the music.

A funny thing happened. The music teacher in her heard
all the faults in the music and was able to analyze exactly
how banal it was. The woman in her felt the emotion in the
music and the lyrics and wasn't able to stop herself from
feeling the same warm glow and stomach-turned-inside-out
feeling she'd had the night of Sissy's party.

Dusty Mitchell's rich, husky voice surrounded her; the
music and her pulse combined in an erotic rhythm until
Victoria couldn't stand the feelings anymore. She yanked off
the headphones and turned off the stereo. The memory of

his blazing eyes and the dislike he hadn't tried to hide flooded back. Suddenly, hot tears formed, and Victoria swallowed against the lump in her throat. What was wrong with her? Why had she allowed the man to get to her like this?

Her feelings, usually so calm and controlled, felt as turbulent as a roller coaster ride, and Victoria didn't like it. She blinked back the tears, infuriated with herself. She never cried. And she certainly had no intention of crying over a man. Any man. Even a man as appealing as Dusty Mitchell.

She shouldn't have bought the album. She was just torturing herself. The best thing she could do was stick it in the back of the closet and not play it again. Just like she intended to push the memory of Dusty Mitchell and his sexy smile to the back of her mind and not think of him anymore.

The next morning, after a sleepless, soul-searching night, Victoria knew she had something to do before she could put Dusty Mitchell out of her life.

She owed him an apology. It was plain and simple.

Then, and only then, could she relegate him to the past. All through the night she'd relived everything he had said, replaying each look, each gesture of that awful scene at the paper.

Victoria cared what other people thought of her, especially people she admired and respected. Respected. Yes. She *did* respect Dusty. Although he really wasn't her type, he was pursuing his dream, and she had to admire determination and hard work. She knew it took a lot of both to achieve even the moderate success he'd attained. He deserved her respect. He also deserved an apology.

Chapter Five

Dusty stared at the yellow roses. It took him at least a minute for the shock to subside and curiosity to set in. A small white card was nestled in the green tissue paper surrounding the fragrant flowers. Mystified, he opened the envelope.

Dear Dusty,
Please accept these roses as a token of my sincere regret for having hurt your feelings. I know you don't believe me, but I had no idea who you were the night of Sissy's party. All I knew was that you were a charming, very nice man with whom I spent several wonderful hours.

I'm also sorry about my review. After buying your album and listening to it several times, I've come to appreciate the music as well as your talent.

I know these flowers won't make up for what I did,

but perhaps they'll show you that I'm sincere in my apology and wish you only the best in your career.

Victoria Jones

Dusty read the note twice. Then he walked to the window and stared outside for a long time. Admiration, a desire to believe her, reluctant respect and guilt all churned in his mind like the ingredients for a cake. He hadn't been very nice to her the last two times he saw her. He had said some real nasty things, things that probably weren't true.

The sincerity in her note was impossible to deny. Victoria's intelligence, her sense of fair play, her class—all shone through in what she had written. And Dusty really admired people who could admit they were wrong. That took guts. Victoria Jones was not only beautiful and classy—she had guts.

Although part of him knew she'd been right when she'd said they came from two different worlds, the tug of admiration and interest refused to disappear. The memory of the harsh words between them—the sad look in her eyes when he'd given her that tongue-lashing seemed permanently imprinted on his brain, and for the rest of the day he caught himself thinking about Victoria time and time again. Even Spence commented on it.

"You sure seem off in the clouds today," Spence said. "Guess you haven't come down to earth since you talked to Rylander yesterday, huh?"

Dusty nodded. Spence was partially right, but although he was still floating from Rylander's call, Victoria's note had dominated his thoughts all day. He wanted to tell Spence about the note and flowers, but something held him back.

That night, as he walked into his apartment, the first thing he saw were the roses. Their perfume filled the air. Their beauty and simplicity drew his eyes. Their elegance charmed him. He smiled. They were very like the lady who had sent them. She, too, had beauty, simplicity and elegance.

Dusty almost laughed aloud as the thought formed. Damn. Victoria Jones had very effectively managed to make every other woman he knew seem second-rate. The time he'd spent with her at Sissy Farraday's masquerade ball had seemingly spoiled every other woman for him. Her face, her voice, her smile, her eyes: all appeared in his mind when he least expected them to. No matter how many times he told himself to forget her, that she wasn't for him, he couldn't seem to do it.

What the hell, he thought. Tomorrow he'd do what he'd wanted to do all along. He'd call her. She deserved an apology, too. She wasn't the only one who'd made a mistake, and if she was big enough to admit hers, he was big enough to admit his. Besides, he wanted to tell her about the offer from Vernon Rylander.

Then Dusty *did* laugh out loud. He might as well be completely honest with himself. He wanted to talk to Victoria again, no matter what the reason.

At ten o'clock the next morning Dusty dialed Victoria's number. He wondered if she'd be there or if she would be at the paper. A rueful smile twisted his mouth as he realized he'd memorized the number. What significance would Freud attach to that little fact?

After two rings, a young voice said, "Hello?"

Dusty frowned. He'd expected a maid to answer but knew immediately the girl at the other end was the bright-eyed charmer he'd met at the record store: Victoria's daughter. He wondered, as he had since he'd realized she had a daughter, if Victoria was divorced or a widow.

"Hello," he said. "May I speak with Victoria, please?"

"Uh...she can't come to the phone right now. Who's calling, please?"

"This is Dusty Mitchell."

"Mr. Mitchell! Oh, hi! I guess it's all right to tell *you*," she said. "My mother isn't here right now. She had some errands to run. I always tell people she can't come to the phone when I don't know who they are. Mom doesn't like me to say I'm home alone.''

"And she's right. It's dangerous to tell strangers your mother isn't around. What time do you expect her back?''

"She should be home pretty soon. Do you want me to ask her to call you?''

Impulsively, Dusty said, "No. I think I'll just come on over there and wait for her.'' The urge to see Victoria again was too strong to deny. He wanted to see the look on her face when he apologized. He wanted to see that dimple at the corner of her mouth when she smiled.

Julie gave him the address, and twenty minutes later Dusty parked his Bronco in front of a modest frame house on Purdue in one of the older sections of Houston. What was Victoria Jones doing living somewhere like this? The house looked to be at least forty or fifty years old with no distinguishing features except an enormous mimosa tree that dominated the front yard and two pots of some kind of purple flowers flanking the front door. The color of the flowers reminded Dusty of the color of Victoria's eyes.

The house was well-tended but small, and Dusty's confusion increased as he got out of the car and walked up the drive. The neighborhood wasn't one inhabited by the kinds of people who had attended Sissy Farraday's masquerade ball. This was a middle-class neighborhood. This wasn't the kind of neighborhood he'd ever expected to find Victoria in.

He knocked on the white painted door. After a few minutes he heard a chain being released. Julie's pert face appeared in the open doorway. "Hi,'' she said. She held a half-eaten Granny Smith apple in her hand. Juice dotted her small chin, and she grinned and wiped it away with the back of her hand. "She's still not back. Do you want to come in?''

"No, that's okay." He didn't know if Victoria would like it if she came home and found him in her house with her teenage daughter. "I'll just wait out here. It's a nice day. I can use the air.''

The words had no sooner left his mouth than he heard the sound of an approaching car. Just as he turned to look, gravel crunched under the tires of an older-model light blue station wagon. The door opened and Victoria, dressed in faded blue jeans and a red and white University of Houston T-shirt, emerged.

Dusty was definitely puzzled. Where was the sleek BMW he'd expected to see? How many more of his assumptions about her would prove to be wrong?

She stood outside the car, an uncertain look on her face. Then she slowly walked toward him, her long legs moving gracefully.

"Hi, Mom," Julie said brightly. "Dusty stopped by to see you." She disappeared into the house, leaving a stunned Victoria on her own with Dusty.

"Hello, Mr. Mitchell," she said.

Her low, musical voice was everything Dusty remembered. She looked just as lovely today as she'd looked in her satin ball gown. The T-shirt and jeans molded to her slim body in the nicest possible way. Her shining hair was brushed away from her face and held by two silver clips. A large tan leather purse hung from one shoulder. Her periwinkle eyes were limpid in the golden morning light. There was a faint pink glow on her creamy skin. She wore no makeup except a light sheen of rosy lipstick. She looked fresh and clean and healthy. Dusty had a strong urge to gather her into his arms and kiss her. He wanted to see her eyes soften. He wanted to taste the sweetness of her mouth, inhale her scented hair. He wondered if it still smelled like spring flowers.

There was an uncertain look in her eyes.

"Hi," he said. "I got the flowers and the note." He smiled, hoping she'd smile back.

When Dusty smiled, Victoria's heart flip-flopped. All her doubts about his reasons for coming to her house vanished like mist. A shaft of pure happiness jolted through her. Without conscious thought, she smiled.

He looked wonderful. His thick hair shone in the bright morning light, gleaming like polished brass. His jeans hugged his hips and thighs, and his dark blue shirt was open at the collar. His eyes swept her approvingly, and warmth seeped through her body. Suddenly she was very glad she'd sent the flowers and note.

"I'm glad to see you," she said, meaning it. For the first time in days she felt good.

"I wanted to thank you and talk to you," he said. His smile was disarming, and his eyes were friendly.

"First I have to get my groceries into the house," she said, remembering the bags she'd left in the wagon.

With Dusty's help, it only took five minutes to carry all the laden sacks into the house.

Victoria wasn't sure what to say as Dusty put the last sack on the kitchen table. To cover her confusion, she said, "How would you like a cup of coffee or something while I put away these things?"

"Coffee sounds good," he said. He walked to the glass patio door and looked into the backyard while Victoria hurriedly filled the coffee maker and turned it on. She surreptitiously studied his profile as she took the groceries from the bags and put them away. Her house had a combination family room and kitchen that was divided by a long serving bar, and from where she stood, Dusty was clearly visible.

Heavens, he was magnificent, she thought. His sheer size was almost intimidating, but Victoria had always liked big men. Chris had been big, too. But in Chris, Victoria had confused size with strength. Chris had been weak in all the important ways. Somehow she knew Dusty wasn't weak. Not in any way.

The smell of fresh coffee permeated the room, and he turned from the door. As he walked to the kitchen, Victoria's stomach fluttered. It had been a long time since a man had shared a cup of coffee with her in the intimacy of her home.

"How do you take your coffee?" she asked.

"Black."

She handed him one of the steaming mugs, and his hand brushed hers. A spark of awareness shot through her. She could feel his eyes on her as she moved past him into the family room.

"Sit down," she said, indicating her favorite chair, a large recliner. She sat on the couch. She felt awkward and unsure of herself.

For a minute or two, neither of them said anything. Dusty sipped at his coffee, then set the mug on the table next to his chair. "Look," he said. "I owe you an apology, too."

"No, you don't," Victoria said hurriedly.

"Yes, I do. I was too hard on you when I came to the paper."

"You had good reason to act the way you did."

"That's no excuse," he said.

Victoria smiled. He was awfully nice, and she was a sucker for nice men. In fact, Dusty Mitchell was altogether too appealing. Nice, good-looking and sexy. Warning signs flashed in her mind, even as she admired him. "I accept your apology," she said.

"It was stupid for me to blame you because I thought I'd lost my backer. If he'd really believed in me, one bad review wouldn't have made any difference, anyway."

"I'm really sorry about that." Victoria took another sip of coffee. Even if there was no future in a relationship with Dusty, she was happy he no longer hated her. "I hope what I wrote didn't have anything to do with it."

"It doesn't matter one way or the other now." He grinned. "I've got something better. I've got a contract with a big-time music producer in Nashville."

"Really? That's wonderful!" Victoria's mind raced in sudden alarm. Sissy had certainly worked fast.

"Yeah," he agreed. "It is. I couldn't ask for a better break. It's almost too good to be true."

"I'm happy for you." She watched the play of emotions on his face, the excited light in his eyes. Guilt nagged at her, but it was silly to worry, wasn't it? He was delighted with the turn of events. In fact, he probably wouldn't even care if he knew she'd had something to do with his good fortune.

"I always knew it would happen someday," he said.

"When did all this come about?" Victoria tried to squash her feelings of uneasiness. She hadn't done anything wrong. The look of pleasure and pride on his face was proof of that.

"He called me yesterday morning. You know, I've always wondered how I'd feel when my chance came. I spent a lot of time daydreaming about exactly when and how it would happen."

She smiled. "I understand. I daydreamed a lot myself when I was struggling to make it through school."

"So you know how I feel. And you know what else I discovered?"

"What?"

"No amount of daydreaming can prepare you for the reality of a dream coming true. I've been walking around in a daze ever since I got the call. But the best part of all this is that I don't owe a damn thing to anyone. I did this on my own." His eyes gleamed with fierce intensity. "That's the other thing that's so satisfying. Before, although I knew I was good, I also knew that for everyone who ever becomes successful in the music business, there are hundreds of others equally talented who never make it. There's a hell of a lot of luck involved."

"Yes, I...I guess there would be," echoed Victoria. Luck and string-pulling, she thought, although he'd never know that.

"The guy who called me, Vernon Rylander, he represents some of the biggest stars in the music business. In fact, they've nicknamed his company Home of the Stars. So I'm really on my way. Nothing can stop me. And I don't owe anyone." He grinned ruefully. "You probably think I'm nuts, but I don't like owing people. My family and I...we're real independent. We take care of our own, but we don't like other people doing things for us."

Victoria's chest tightened as she fought down her feelings of guilt. He *had* made it on his talent. Just because Sissy had called Vernon Rylander and asked him to listen to Dusty's album didn't mean Rylander would have taken Dusty on if he didn't think Dusty would succeed. After all, Rylander had a reputation in the music business. He wouldn't jeopardize it. No matter how much he valued Sissy's friendship.

There was absolutely no reason for Victoria to feel guilty. Dusty would never know about her or Sissy's involvement in his offer. They had done nothing wrong.

"I think it's wonderful," she said. "I know you're going to do well."

"Thanks. I know it, too." He picked up his coffee mug and drained it. Then he leaned back in his chair. His voice was softer as he said, "I'm glad you were off today. I'm glad we got things straightened out between us."

A wayward lock of hair had fallen forward, and he reached up and brushed it back. Victoria's eyes followed the gesture. His hands were large and strong-looking, with long fingers and blunt nails. But Victoria knew how gentle those hands could be, how they had brushed against her cheek, trailed down her neck, lifted her hair.... Suddenly breathless, she answered, trying to keep her voice light. "Yes, I'm on spring break this week. So is Julie."

At that moment, as if she had been waiting for her mother to mention her name, Julie entered the room followed by her dog, Dolly, who tagged along slowly behind her. Spying Dusty, Dolly wagged her tail happily and pattered over to him, sitting at his feet and looking up hopefully.

He reached down and scratched the dog's head. "Hi, there, girl," he said. Then, with eyebrows knitted together, he said, "Spring break? I don't understand. Does the newspaper give spring break to their employees?"

Victoria laughed softly, the tension of the last few moments lifting. "No. Not that I know of. I'm a teacher at the University of Houston. I teach music. I only write reviews part-time . . . to make a little extra money for Julie's college fund."

"Yeah, Mom works all the time," Julie said.

"Don't complain. I don't hear you complaining when I buy you something new," Victoria said, but she wasn't really annoyed. Nothing could annoy her today.

"How do you happen to know Sissy Farraday?" he said. "She said you two were good friends."

"Sissy and I go way back. We went to kindergarten together. She used to live right across the street from me. We lived in Bellaire. Then Sissy met Stephen Farraday and married into the River Oaks crowd. But we've always remained friends, even though she's rich, and I'm not."

"Mom, I'm hungry," Julie announced. "What's for lunch?"

Victoria shrugged. "I don't know. I thought maybe I'd make some tacos." Tacos were Julie's favorite.

"Oh, good. Do you like tacos?" Julie asked Dusty.

"Love 'em," he said. "And I'm starving."

"Dus—Mr. Mitchell can stay for lunch, can't he, Mom?" said Julie.

"Julie . . ." Victoria said. But she wanted him to stay. "Maybe Mr. Mitchell has something to do."

"Not a thing," he said, his green eyes alight with amusement. "I'd love to stay and have tacos with you two pretty girls."

Julie preened. "See, Mom?"

Victoria knew the smile plastered on her face looked silly, but she was inordinately pleased that Dusty seemed to want to be with them. Even though she knew it wasn't a good idea to get any more involved with him, she was *still* pleased.

"There's only one thing . . ." he said.

Victoria had started to get up, but at his words, she sank down.

"No more of this Mr. Mitchell stuff. The name is Dusty, and I want both of you to call me that." His husky voice slid over Victoria like warm honey.

Dusty, Julie and Dolly all followed Victoria to the kitchen, and as Dusty chopped onions and tomatoes and Victoria cooked the ground meat and Julie shredded lettuce and cheese, Victoria once more shoved down the sense of uneasiness. There was no reason for her to feel uneasy. So what if Dusty Mitchell, someone she'd known less than two weeks, someone completely unsuitable for her, seemed to fit into her life and her kitchen as snugly as he fit into his jeans?

Chapter Six

"These are the best tacos I've ever eaten," Dusty said as he polished off his fourth one.

Victoria smiled. Some part of her responded to the elemental satisfaction of feeding an appreciative man. "Thanks. Have another one."

He rolled his eyes at Julie. "I think your mother is trying to make me get fat."

"No, she just hates leftovers," Julie said.

Dusty's green eyes settled on Victoria. "That's because she's a mother. All mothers hate leftovers. In fact, it's an unwritten rule. To be a mother, it's your responsibility to see that nothing, not one crumb, is left over. Even if you can't get up from the table because you're so stuffed, you have to eat everything."

Julie giggled, and Victoria laughed. "I plead guilty, although it's not often I even have to worry about leftovers, because I don't do that much cooking. It's only because we're on vacation this week that I bought so many groceries."

"That's right," he said. "You two are free all week. Say, if you haven't got any plans for tomorrow, how about driving out to my family's ranch with me?" His eyes sparkled with enthusiasm, and he grinned happily, obviously pleased with his idea.

Victoria's chest tightened under his gaze. Why was it that when he looked at her in just that way she seemed to have trouble breathing?

"Oh, Mom, could we?" Julie's eyes, big and shiny as silver dollars, pleaded with her. "Please?"

Victoria knew she should refuse. Prolonging the inevitable was foolish. Deep in her heart she knew there was absolutely no chance she and Dusty could ever have an ongoing relationship. But, oh, she wanted to go. She wanted to go more than she'd wanted anything in a long time.

"The ranch is great," Dusty said, his voice husky and persuasive. "The air is ten times fresher and cleaner than here in the city, and my mother and brother love to have company." He turned to Julie. "Do you like to ride? We've got just the horse for you, a beautiful palomino named Gold Dust." Then he laughed. "She was named after me."

Julie burst into delighted giggles, and Victoria chuckled along with her.

"I *love* to ride. So does Mom," said Julie, with a wistful look at Victoria.

Oh, fiddle, thought Victoria. I know exactly what I should do, but if I do it I'm going to sound like the meanest Scrooge that ever lived. She ignored the little voice inside her that said, *That's right. Lie to yourself. Pretend you're going because Julie wants to go.*

Dusty's green eyes and Julie's gray ones both held question marks. "Come on, Victoria. We'll have a lot of fun. The ranch is near Wimberley, and the drive is beautiful this time of year. You'll get to see all the bluebonnets."

Victoria sighed. Horses and bluebonnets . . . the beautiful Texas state flower . . . what more could she ask for? The little voice sniped at her. *And Dusty. Don't forget Dusty . . .*

"You've talked me into it," she said.

"Hurray," said Julie. "Can we leave early?"

"As early as you like," Dusty answered. His eyes were soft as they turned to Victoria.

A flutter of anticipation stirred deep within her as Dusty smiled: a slow, sexy smile full of promise. Still holding her eyes, he said, "Don't have breakfast. We'll leave early and stop somewhere along the way to eat."

Julie could hardly contain herself. For a moment, Victoria wished she were a kid, too, so she could let go and act excited, but only for a moment. The promise in Dusty's eyes wouldn't be there for a kid.

"Well, now that we've settled that, I guess I'd better be going." He stood up. The sunlight pouring through the kitchen windows lit the fine golden hairs on his forearms and hands.

Victoria tingled at the sudden vivid picture she had of those hands caressing her, those arms enfolding her and pulling her close. What would it be like to abandon herself . . . to have him hold her against his naked chest . . . stroke her heated skin . . . kiss her deeply . . . touch all her secret places . . . Her mouth suddenly went dry as a shudder raced through her.

Julie, still chattering, obviously didn't see Dusty's golden gaze deepen as he watched Victoria's face, didn't hear him say softly, "I'm looking forward to tomorrow."

Victoria nodded, wetting her lips. The undercurrents were so powerful between them, she was amazed Julie couldn't feel them. It took all her strength of will to tear her eyes away from his. "What time do you want us to be ready?" she asked as she walked him to the front door and fought to get her topsy-turvy emotions on an even keel.

"I'll be here at seven. Is that all right?"

"Yes. That's fine."

"Can we bring Dolly with us?" Julie asked, coming up behind them.

"If you want to," he answered. "Does she like to ride in cars?"

"Uh-huh. She's good. She just sits and looks out the window."

After settling the details of the upcoming trip, Dusty left. For the rest of the day, and even after she got into bed that night, Victoria held a two-way conversation with herself. First she'd tell herself the next day's excursion would be harmless fun for her and Julie and nothing more. Then her chiding inner voice would say, *Sure, and my name's Meryl Streep. Who do you think you're kidding?*

Finally, about midnight, she dropped all pretense. I want to go tomorrow because I want to see Dusty Mitchell again, she thought. It's as simple as that.

Then she closed her eyes and went to sleep.

The drive to the ranch took them along Interstate 10, then they branched off toward Luling, San Marcos and Wimberley. All along the roadside, the low hills were covered with the rich color of the bluebonnets, interspersed with scarlet Indian paintbrush and the blush of buttercups. Everywhere she looked Victoria saw a feast for the eyes in the Texas landscape, dotted with live oak trees and the deep green of tall pines.

Victoria glanced over at Dusty. He looked as comfortable behind the wheel of his Bronco as he'd looked strumming his guitar. She knew he'd look just as at home sitting astride a horse. As a matter of fact, she could see Dusty fitting in almost anywhere.

Today he was dressed in jeans and boots accompanied by a cream-colored shirt with its long sleeves rolled up to his mid-forearms. Victoria and Julie also wore jeans and boots, and Julie's outfit was topped with a blue Western shirt trimmed with fringe. Victoria, who felt a bit self-conscious in Western wear, had settled for a plain oxford-cloth white shirt, but in a moment of weakness, had tied a jaunty purple silk scarf around her neck. She didn't own a cowboy hat, but both Julie and Dusty sported theirs, although Dusty had removed his while driving.

"Too hot," he'd confessed sheepishly. "That's what most city folks, especially city folks from up North, don't realize. In the summertime, real cowboys hardly ever wear the traditional felt cowboy hat anymore."

"Really?" Victoria said. "Why, I thought all you cowboys would rather die than be caught without your boots and hats."

Dusty grinned. "I didn't say they didn't wear hats. They do, because otherwise they'd get too sunburned. But they wear straw hats or baseball caps."

"Baseball caps!"

Dusty laughed at her expression. Even Julie's attention had been caught by the exchange.

"Yep. Cowboys discovered that baseball caps were much cooler and more practical than cowboy hats. Plus they stay on their heads better."

"That's really funny. I've lived in Texas all my life, and I never knew that."

"Just goes to show how much you have to learn."

"I beg your pardon," she said in mock indignation. "Don't forget that I'm a teacher."

"Yeah," Julie piped in, "and teachers think they know everything."

"We do," Victoria said, fighting a giggle. She couldn't remember when she'd indulged in such silly banter with a man, and it felt good.

"Hm," Dusty said with narrowed eyes. "Sounds like a challenge to me. Looks like I'm going to have to find more things you don't know...and teach 'em to you."

Victoria's eyes slanted sideways. Dusty turned slightly, and she saw his mouth curve into a lazy smile. Her breath caught as his eyes captured hers.

"Hey, cowboy," she said softly. "Keep your eyes on the road."

He winked, then turned back to his driving, but the smile remained. For the rest of the trip Victoria tingled inside each time she thought about the seductive promise in his voice.

They arrived at the ranch about eleven-thirty. As they pulled into the unpaved drive leading through a stand of scrub pines, the sprawling white frame house came into view. There was a wide covered porch all around one side and the front of the house. As the Bronco's wheels crunched on the gravel and dirt driveway, a tall blond woman appeared on the front porch. She waved.

Dusty tooted the horn. "There's Maggie," he said, and the warmth in his voice told Victoria how much he cared for his mother.

"You call your mother by her first name?" Julie asked, awe apparent in the question.

Dusty nodded. "Yep. A couple of months after my father died— I was nine years old— I told her since I was the man of the house I didn't want to call her Mommy anymore, that I was going to call her Maggie."

"And she didn't get mad?"

"Nope. She understood how I felt, because I'm a lot like her."

Victoria's heart twisted at the thought of a small boy who should have had many more years of carefree childhood but who had felt obligated to be a man instead.

"Anyway, the name stuck," he said. "Come on, let's go meet her."

The three of them, trailed by Dolly, climbed out of the truck. As Dusty's mother stepped down off the porch to walk toward them, the screen door squeaked open, and a blond man in a wheelchair wheeled himself out the door and onto the porch, a big smile on his face. He looked exactly like Dusty, except his face was thinner and paler.

Dusty enfolded his mother in his arms and the two hugged, then kissed. Not seeming the least bit embarrassed by this display of affection, Dusty put his arm around his mother and said, "Maggie, I'd like you to meet two friends of mine. This pretty lady is Victoria Jones, and *this* pretty girl is her daughter, Juliette, more commonly known as Julie." His green eyes sparkled in the dappled morning sunlight.

Grin widening, he said, "And *this* feisty woman here is my mother, Margaret Mary Mitchell, known as Maggie to friend and foe alike."

"How do you do, Mrs. Mitchell," said Victoria. She stuck out her hand, and Maggie Mitchell gripped it firmly. Her eyes were a dark, steady brown, and her face had the same strong lines and planes as Dusty's. Now that Victoria was closer, she could see many strands of white and gray threaded among the gold of her hair.

"The name's Maggie," she said. She studied Victoria quietly for a few seconds, then turned to Julie, gravely shaking her hand. "Welcome to the M & M Ranch."

"Named for Maggie and my father, whose first name was Mike," Dusty explained to Julie.

The man in the wheelchair said, "Hey! Did you all forget about me?"

"Shoot, how could we? You wouldn't let us," Dusty said. Grabbing Victoria's hand, he strode rapidly to the porch. "Victoria, meet my younger brother, David, more commonly known as a pain in the neck."

David grimaced. "Ever since I broke my neck, I've been even more of a pain."

"You were always a pain," Dusty countered, grinning widely.

The two brothers shook hands, laughing and punching one another. "That's pretty funny, coming from you," David said. Then he looked up, and Victoria's heart caught in her throat. His eyes were every bit as green and vivid and compelling as Dusty's. What had happened to put him in a wheelchair? she wondered. Had he really broken his neck?

"Aren't you going to introduce me to your beautiful friend?" he said.

"I don't know if I can trust you around her," Dusty answered.

"You probably can't," David retorted.

Victoria laughed. She extended her hand. "I'm Victoria Jones, a friend of Dusty's, and I'm very happy to meet you."

"How'd this no-account brother of mine hook up with someone as classy as you?"

"Hey, watch it!" Dusty said. "Let her find out I'm no-account on her own."

"Are you?" Victoria said, entering into the spirit of the exchange between the brothers.

In answer Dusty reached out and tweaked her nose. "That's for me to know and you to find out."

Maggie Mitchell shook her head. "Don't pay a bit of attention to these two. Ever since they were little tykes they've been trying to drive me crazy."

"And we succeeded, too," Dusty said.

They all laughed, and Victoria couldn't suppress a twinge of envy at the obvious affection and easy naturalness of the Mitchell family's relationships with each other. She thought of her own family: her father, Victor, had died a year before she graduated from high school, but he had never been a major part of her life. He and her mother had divorced when Victoria was only eight years old, and he'd moved to California where he'd married again. Victoria had only seen him sporadically. He'd been a cold man, more interested in his test tubes and laboratory then he'd ever been in a small, intense daughter who was shy and a bit afraid of him.

Eleanor Patterson, Victoria's mother, had also remarried. Her new husband, an engineer with grown children of his own, had been from the northeast, and soon after Victoria married Chris, her mother and her new husband had moved to Princeton, New Jersey. Victoria and her mother hadn't been as close as Victoria would have liked, and somehow, after Eleanor Patterson remarried and became Eleanor Stuart, she no longer seemed like someone Victoria could count on.

Maybe that's why I was so quick to latch on to Chris, Victoria thought. I was looking for someone to count on, someone of my very own.

"Are you three hungry?" Maggie asked as they entered the enormous sunny kitchen.

"Does a bear snooze in the woods?" Dusty said.

Maggie's mouth quirked up. "He usually says something else. He's being on his good behavior today. He must really like you."

Victoria grinned. "We ate a huge breakfast," she said.

"That was hours ago," said Dusty.

"Yeah, Mom. I'm hungry," said Julie.

Victoria lifted her shoulders in a what-can-I-do-I'm-outnumbered gesture.

"I've got a pot of beef stew on the stove," Maggie announced. "And corn bread in the oven."

"Beef stew and corn bread. Maggie, you sure do know how to make a man happy," said Dusty.

By the time they ate the stew and corn bread and thick wedges of blackberry pie, Victoria thought she'd burst. "If I ate like this all the time, I'd be too wide to fit through that doorway," she said as she patted her stomach. "I hope I can still heft myself up on a horse."

"I'll be glad to help," said Dusty, with a wicked gleam in his eye.

Victoria knew her cheeks were flaming.

"Don't pay any mind to Dusty's lines, Victoria," David said, his eyes shining with amusement. "He probably deserves a slap."

Maggie shook her head, then stood. "Enough nonsense. I'll get this stuff cleaned up. Dusty, you can take the girls for a ride and show them our place."

"I'll help, Maggie," offered Victoria.

"While you help my mother, I'll take Julie out to the corral. She can help me pick out a horse for you," Dusty said.

Followed by Dolly, Dusty and Julie went outside. Assisted by David, who stacked dirty plates in his lap, then wheeled himself to the counter where he carefully placed them, Maggie and Victoria made short work of washing and drying the dishes. The windows were all open, and the mild spring air blew into the kitchen. The sheer white tie-back curtains fluttered in the breeze.

"I like this kitchen," Victoria said, looking around at the solid oak furniture, the old-fashioned gas stove, the red-brick fireplace flanked by copper pots, the scarred rocking chair in the corner, the two calico cats sitting on the hearth and the polished hardwood floor covered by rag rugs. The colors were a mixture of yellows and reds and greens, a bright patchwork that made Victoria feel at home.

"It's not fancy, but it's plain and comfortable. We like it," Maggie said in her no-nonsense voice. She wiped her hands on the sides of her jeans. Her dark eyes studied Victoria. "How'd you meet Dusty? You don't seem like the kind of girl to frequent bars."

Victoria frowned, then realized that Dusty had probably done a lot of singing in local clubs. Maggie Mitchell probably thought Victoria was a groupie.

"No, I don't frequent bars at all. I'm a music teacher at the University of Houston. I teach composition and theory."

"Did Dusty take a class or something? He never mentioned it."

"Mom, Dusty doesn't tell you *everything*," interjected David. He winked at Victoria.

"Dusty and I met at a masquerade ball given by one of my friends," Victoria said, ignoring David's wink.

Maggie nodded and gave Victoria a speculative look.

"We only met a short time ago," Victoria rushed to explain, made uneasy by Maggie's quiet appraisal and David's assumption that she and Dusty were close.

Maggie nodded once more. She looked out the window. "Here comes Julie. I guess they're probably ready for you." Then she turned to Victoria. "You're the first girl Dusty has ever brought home."

Victoria was taken aback as she absorbed Maggie's quiet statement. But before she could think of an appropriate answer, Julie burst into the room. "Come on, Mom. What are you doing? We're ready. Dusty's waiting."

Dusty's waiting.

As Victoria followed her daughter into the bright golden day, those words echoed in her mind; they held as much promise as Dusty's eyes had held yesterday and in the car today.

An hour later, as Victoria sat astride the piebald mare named Lucinda that Dusty and Julie had selected for her, she took a deep breath and looked around her. For miles, as far as she could see, was an expanse of land that could have belonged to an earlier age, except for the telltale telephone poles visible in the distance. Cattle grazed on thick patches of grass. The low hills were covered by native mesquite trees, purple sage and mountain laurel, all tented by a cornflower blue sky and wisps of feathery clouds.

As the three riders paused on the crest of a low hill, Dusty's horse, a big liver chestnut, stamped impatiently.

"Beautiful, isn't it?" Dusty said. He turned toward her, and his eyes, shaded by the wide brim of his hat, studied her face. Victoria heard the rough emotion in his voice, and a frisson of pleasure zigzagged through her. "Yes," she said. "It is."

"You should have seen it years ago. The year my dad died we had more than two dozen hands working the ranch and over fifteen thousand head of cattle. Now all we've got are one hand and Maggie and Luke."

Deep regret tinged his voice. "Are you sorry it's changed so much?" she asked.

He shrugged, the movement causing his shirt to tighten over his back and shoulders. "In a way. 'Course, I didn't want to stay out here and work the ranch. So I can't complain about it too much. Maggie did what she had to do. When I left, she thought it was more important to be here for David than to hang onto all that land. And it's ironic, because as it turned out, the company that bought the land bought it for the mineral rights, which belonged to us, too. And they turned out to be worth a lot more than working the land and raising cattle ever would have brought in. Now Maggie and David won't ever have to worry." He turned and squinted against the sun. "Want to keep going, or are you getting tired?" he asked, directing the question more to Julie than to Victoria.

"I'm not tired," Julie said as the prancing palomino beneath her tossed her head and whinnied softly. "Let's keep going."

"Don't forget, it'll take just as long to get back as it took to get to this point," Dusty warned. "If it's been as long as you said it was since you and your mother have ridden, you're going to be real sore tomorrow."

"Perhaps we'd better turn back," Victoria said. The day, although mild, felt hot, and Victoria knew her face would probably be sunburned tomorrow. She should have listened to Maggie when she'd offered her the use of a hat.

As if he had read her mind, Dusty said, "Your face is beginning to turn pink. You've had too much sun today."

"Oh, well . . ." Victoria said.

Julie had already turned and was cantering ahead.

"You obviously need someone to look after you...make sure you do sensible things," he continued, his eyes soft as they scanned her face.

"I look after myself perfectly well." Victoria knew her voice had taken on an edge, but her ability to care for herself and Julie was a point of pride with her. Her independence had been hard won, and she didn't intend to let anyone question or criticize it.

"Every woman needs a man around," he insisted, eyes beginning to twinkle.

"That's not true. Some women *want* a man around, but they certainly don't *need* one. I've managed to support myself and my daughter for eleven years without the help of anyone, and I think I've done very well." Victoria inadvertently tugged on the reins, and Lucinda tossed her head and whinnied.

"I didn't say you needed a man to support you. I said every woman needs a man, just like every man needs a woman. Hell, Victoria, you've gotta admit that without one another, the whole human race would come to a screeching halt." His voice was serious, despite his crooked smile.

Suddenly, all the fight left Victoria. In many ways, he was right. And hadn't she wished for years that she would meet someone with whom she could build a stable, loving family life? Someone she could depend on to be there for her? Wasn't that really what Dusty was talking about?

"Well?" he said.

"Well, what?"

"You never answered my question. Without one another, wouldn't the human race disappear?"

Victoria laughed. "I don't think we're in any danger of that happening anytime soon." She nudged her horse, and Lucinda responded immediately. "Come on," she shouted over her shoulder, "I'll race you back."

As the three riders raced into the stable yard, Victoria saw a very tall, thin man unloading some boxes from the back of a battered pickup truck.

"Hey, Luke!" called Dusty.

The man stopped in midstride, set down the box he'd just lifted and walked slowly over to meet them. All three dismounted, and Dusty and the man called Luke shook hands warmly.

"Good to see you, son," said Luke, his tanned face creasing into a wide smile. "Maggie told me about your contract. Congratulations."

"Great, isn't it? It's the chance I've been waiting for."

"You worked hard enough. You deserve it," Luke said quietly.

"Thanks, Luke."

Some of Victoria's happiness faded at the reminder of her duplicity. She prayed Dusty never found out about her role in his success. The more she learned about him, the more she realized just how furious he would be if he knew.

Dusty turned to Victoria and Julie. "This is Luke Capshaw. He's an old friend of the family. He's got the spread next to ours, but he always finds time to give Maggie a hand."

"She doesn't really need much help, but I like to pretend she does," Luke said. Then he looked at Victoria and Julie. "Dusty always did manage to find the prettiest girls around, and you two are no exception."

"Are all the men around here adept at flattery?" Victoria asked.

"Only the smart ones," Luke said.

Later, with Julie happily engrossed in a game of checkers with Maggie, and Dolly quietly lying on the floor beside Julie's chair, David said, "Dusty, I'm going to take Victoria to the studio." He turned to her. "I've got something I'd like to show you."

Victoria stood up. "Are you coming, too?" she asked Dusty.

"No, I'm too comfortable. You go on." He stretched his long legs in front of him as he sank deeper into the overstuffed chair. He lifted a frosty glass of lemonade and sighed contentedly.

Victoria slowly followed David down the hallway and around a corner. He expertly wheeled himself into a bright corner room with half a dozen unshaded windows. There was a low drawing table in the corner of the room, with a large sheet of paper taped to its surface. There were several long tables in the room, and every surface, as well as every inch of wall space, was covered with framed and unframed watercolors. The colors of the paintings were vibrant and rich, unlike most of the watercolors Victoria had seen in the past. There was a predominance of primary colors, and the strokes were bold.

Victoria slowly walked around the room, stopping first at one painting, then another. Several were so vivid and compelling, she didn't want to move on. Almost without exception, they were paintings of people: old men and women, children and their mothers, boys playing basketball. All of them were filled with movement and color and strength. David wheeled himself behind her, not saying anything.

Finally she turned to the uncompleted painting on the drawing table. This was the picture of a woman's face. After a few seconds, Victoria realized this was a partially completed painting of Maggie. David had captured her serene strength with just a few brush strokes. The liquid warmth of her deep, dark eyes seemed to be looking straight at Victoria from the surface of the painting.

"This is wonderful," Victoria said, breaking the silence between them.

David smiled. "Thank you."

"I love all of them, but this one . . . this is particularly wonderful."

"Yes," he agreed quietly. "It's one of my favorites, too."

"You're a very talented artist."

David shrugged, but his eyes told her he was pleased. "It's something I started to work at after I came to terms with my . . . situation."

"Have you tried to sell any of your paintings?" Victoria thought they were certainly good enough to sell.

"A few. There are a lot of artists who live around Wimberley, and people come from all over the state to buy their stuff. I've shown a few of my paintings there, and they've sold pretty well. But what I really want to do is move to

Houston and study with a teacher there.'' His eyes darkened with intensity, and his strong-looking hands clenched the arms of his wheelchair. ''You see, I'm good. I know that. But I could be great. If I could study with Borghini for even a year, it would make all the difference. I could find a good gallery, and I could support myself.''

Victoria touched his shoulder in an instinctive gesture of comfort. ''I know exactly what you mean,'' she said softly. ''I felt the same way years ago when my husband died. I knew I could go to Kansas and live with my in-laws if I had to. They asked me to come. But it was very important to me to be able to take care of myself. And I did it.''

David looked up. ''How expensive are apartments in Houston? I'm trying to figure out how long I can manage on the money I have saved.''

''There're all different price ranges,'' Victoria said. ''There's bound to be something you can afford. Why don't you have Dusty look around for you?''

''I asked him to, but he doesn't think moving to Houston is a good idea for me.''

Victoria heard the bitterness that had crept into David's voice. ''Why not?''

''Because he thinks I'm helpless! He thinks I should be contented to stay out here on the ranch forever where he and my mother can take care of me.'' David pushed his wheelchair over to one of the windows and stared out. ''I'm sick of being taken care of. That's what Dusty doesn't understand.''

Without thinking, Victoria said, ''I know someone who would be overjoyed to help you get set up in Houston. I have this friend who loves to take artistic people under her wing...sponsor them and help them get established. If you're interested, I'll have her call you.''

David wheeled his chair around. His eyes were eager. ''Would you do that for me?''

''Of course. I'd be glad to.'' She looked again at the partially finished painting of Maggie on the drawing board. The dark eyes held Victoria's gaze. A twinge of uneasiness needled her.

"Victoria?"

Victoria turned to face David once more. The eagerness was still there, but now it was tempered with caution. "What's wrong?" she asked.

"Nothing really. It . . . it's just that Dusty won't like it if you help me do something he doesn't want me to do. I don't want to cause any trouble between the two of you. If you want to change your mind, I'll understand."

"Look, David. Dusty and I only met a short time ago, and we're just friends. This won't cause trouble between us because we're not having a relationship, or anything like that, so quit worrying."

"Well . . . if you're sure . . ."

"I'm sure."

David's voice still held doubt. "If you should change your mind or anything . . ."

She sighed. "I won't change my mind. The name of my friend is Sissy Farraday, and I'll call her tomorrow. Write down your phone number for me so I can give it to her."

David smiled, and the smile lit up his entire face. "Okay. But don't say I didn't warn you. I hope you won't be sorry."

Chapter Seven

Victoria leaned her head against the headrest and listened to Dusty hum along with Roy Orbison. By unspoken agreement, Dusty and Victoria had been quiet since they'd left the ranch. The inside of the truck was like a dark cocoon. The soft music wrapped around Victoria, and she closed her mind to all thought and just gave herself up to the feeling of contentment stealing over her.

It was close to midnight when they pulled into Victoria's driveway. She had decided not to invite Dusty in. Long forgotten feelings had assaulted her throughout the day. She had some hard thinking to do before she spent any time alone with him. She smiled to herself. *If* she spent any time alone with him.

Dusty opened the back door of the Bronco and gently shook Julie. "Time to wake up, Sleeping Beauty," he said.

Victoria smiled to herself. Sleeping Beauty and Cinderella. And she was the woman who no longer believed in fairy tales.

Following a yawning Julie and a groggy Dolly into the house, Victoria turned to thank Dusty, but before she could form the words, he said, "I sure could use a cup of coffee." His husky voice slid over her like soft spring rain.

With a mumbled "'Night, Mom, 'night, Dusty," Julie stumbled sleepily in the direction of her bedroom with Dolly close at her heels. Victoria gave Dusty a tremulous smile. Part of her wanted him to go; part of her wanted him to stay.

"I'm awfully tired, too," she said.

"I won't stay long. I promise." His voice was a low rumble.

"Well, all right. I guess a cup of coffee *does* sound good." She turned toward the kitchen. "Please turn that lamp up, will you? It's too dark in here."

He followed her out to the kitchen. As Victoria measured coffee into the filter, she could feel him close behind her. She switched on the coffee maker, took a deep breath and slowly turned. Only inches separated them. Her foolish heart began to pound faster as she realized he'd intentionally trapped her against the counter where the only escape necessitated touching him.

Staring at his chest where fine golden hairs peeked from his open shirt collar, Victoria wet her lips. She froze as she watched his right hand move up slowly. The tips of his fingers traced her cheekbone, slowly trailing down until his warm palm rested against her throat. He nudged her chin up so that their eyes met. Victoria couldn't stop a convulsive shudder.

His eyes glowed in the dimness of the kitchen where Victoria hadn't turned on the overhead lights. His hand continued to caress her neck, moving up and under her hair. "It was a wonderful day," he murmured, leaning down and gently kissing the corner of her mouth.

Victoria's breath caught. She knew she should push him away. Friendship was the most that could ever be between them, yet she had no willpower. Her bones had turned to butter, and her muscles had turned to mush. Her wayward heart continued its hectic beat, gaining in tempo as Dusty's warm, moist mouth nuzzled and nibbled, first grazing her ear, then dropping to her exposed neck. His breath feathered her skin.

Moving like a sleepwalker, Victoria raised her hands, placing them against Dusty's chest. She could feel the reverberation of his strong heart beating against her palms, and she turned her head slightly so that her lips touched his.

As her mouth opened under his, and the kiss deepened, Victoria ceased thinking; she completely lost herself to his plundering kiss. Only the flavor and fire of his mouth, the strength and splendor of his body, the smell of sun and sweat emanating from his skin, held any meaning for her. As his arms tightened and his hands slowly explored the planes and hollows of her back, she gave herself up to the spinning sensations, holding him tightly as she returned his kiss with all the pent-up passion from ten years of holding her emotions in check.

A deep shudder ran through her as he drew her closer. She raised her arms and wrapped them around his neck. Her body molded against his like the matching piece of a jigsaw puzzle, each curve and contour an exact fit.

The coffee maker gurgled behind her as the last of the water plopped into the pot. Reality, sanity, returned, and suddenly Victoria realized where she was and exactly what she was doing.

"Dusty," she gasped as she pushed at his chest. "Stop. Stop."

"Victoria—" he protested as he tried to hold her in the circle of his arms. His mouth moved down again, but Victoria turned her head, and the kiss caught her ear. As a jolt of raw desire shot through her, fear entered her mind. What was she thinking of? Hadn't she just this morning told herself that Dusty Mitchell was entirely wrong for her? Why was it that all he had to do was get within two feet of her and she turned into a mindless piece of putty?

Summoning every bit of her strength, Victoria willed herself to speak in a steady voice. "Please, Dusty. I want you to stop."

At her words, he dropped his hands and moved back. "I hear the words, darlin', but your body's telling me something different," he said, his voice low and quiet. "Are you sure you want to stop?"

Victoria knew he was right; she *had* responded to him. But she couldn't do this. At least not yet. Not until she thought about it. Not unless she was absolutely sure it was what she wanted.

She took a shaky breath. "Yes." Heart pounding, she turned her back to him, switched off the coffee maker and opened the cupboard to remove two mugs. It was very quiet in the house. From somewhere far in the distance a siren wailed. The smell of fresh coffee wafted upward as she poured it.

"I'm sorry," Victoria said without turning around, her voice muffled. "I shouldn't have let you kiss me at all. It was a mistake." She knew he was probably angry with her because she had given him mixed signals. She could feel his eyes upon her. She felt like kicking herself.

Dusty stared at her rigid body. Why had she suddenly changed her mind? She'd wanted his kiss as much as he'd wanted to give it—as much as he'd wanted hers.

Stepping forward, he put his hands on her shoulders. She flinched. Dusty stepped back as if she'd slapped him. Was she afraid of him?

Back stiff, she added creamer and sweetener to one of the mugs of coffee. Without looking at him, she handed him a steaming mug and said, "Let's go sit in the den."

Silently, he followed her. Settling himself into the recliner, he fought his rising anger. No sense getting angry without giving her a chance to explain.

She sat on the couch, curling her long legs under her. She raised her mug and sipped, her luminous eyes studying him over the rim of the cup. Her dark hair had worked itself loose from the heavy coil she had fashioned it into for the day's outing. Silky strands framed her face, and an unbidden tenderness slowly pushed away his anger.

There was something about her—a vulnerability under her normal composure—that touched him. Each time he was near her he sensed the uncertainty, the intense capability for giving and sharing love that lay buried under her veneer of calm control and independence.

The silence deepened between them. The grandfather clock standing against one wall of the den chimed softly as its hands moved to mark the hour. The house creaked as a gust of wind rattled the patio door. Dusty watched her as she fiddled with her mug, tracing a circle around its rim with one long finger.

Finally, sighing deeply, she put her mug on the end table next to her and said, "Thank you for taking us out to the ranch today, Dusty. It was a wonderful day. I enjoyed meeting your family."

He smiled. "The pleasure was all mine." She didn't smile in return. Instead she studied him gravely, her eyes dark and serious.

"Tell me about David," she said.

The quiet statement brought a familiar sadness to Dusty. It had been sixteen years since the accident, but the pain and sorrow of that night, although dimmed over the years, had never been forgotten.

"It's a simple story," he said. "David was eighteen, I was twenty. It was right after spring roundup. I was still working on the ranch then. Anyway, we'd been working hard for days. We drove over to Austin for the evening with a bunch of our friends. Like typical kids we hit a few of the clubs on Sixth Street, raised some hell, drank some beer. We weren't drunk or anything like that, but we'd had enough that we were a little reckless."

"What happened?"

Dusty looked at Victoria. Her lovely eyes were shadowed, and her voice had a tremor in it. He hesitated for a moment, then continued. "We got back to the ranch about midnight. Maggie was asleep. It was a warm night, and there was a full moon. I'll never forget that moon. We were singing and acting crazy, and David got this idea that he and I should go riding. I really didn't want to go, but he insisted. When he went down to the corral and got Black Knight, a half-broke two-year-old, I nearly had a fit. Black Knight's behavior was erratic, and only the best riders could handle him."

"Wasn't David a good rider?"

"Yes, but it was late, we'd been drinking, and under the best of circumstances riding Black Knight was dangerous. Well, I tried to persuade David to forget it, but David was stubborn, and I didn't feel like arguing with him. To be honest, I wasn't thinking real straight myself, so I let him talk me into the ride. There's really not much more to tell. Black Knight threw David, and David landed wrong. He severed his spinal cord—broke his neck—and now he's paralyzed from the waist down. He'll never walk again."

Dusty closed his eyes. The memory evoked by those stark words hammered once more in his brain. When the specialist in Houston had told Maggie, Dusty had been standing next to her. He'd never forget that scene in the hospital corridor outside the surgery. The metallic smell of antiseptic. The singsong voice of the loudspeaker system. It all seemed like a dream, like it was happening to someone else.

Maggie had been stoic, taking the news like the tough survivor she was, but Dusty knew how the doctor's words hurt, because they'd hurt him, too. And he'd known deep in his heart that he should have stopped David. He was older; he'd been in charge of the family since his father's death. It had been his responsibility to take care of David and Maggie, and he'd blown it.

That was the day he'd grown up. That was the day he'd vowed that he'd never shirk his responsibility again. And he never had.

"I should've talked him out of it. I've always felt guilty about my part in his accident."

"It wasn't your fault," she murmured. "But I understand how you feel, because I've always felt the same way."

Dusty frowned. "What do you mean?"

"My husband was an alcoholic. He was drunk when his car hit another car head-on. He killed a young mother and her child as well as himself." The words were said so low that Dusty had to lean forward to hear them.

"Oh, God, I'm sorry," he said. Her shining head was bowed. Strange, he thought, how we never know what's under the surface of another person's mask. Victoria presented to the world a picture of a lovely, poised, self-assured woman. He'd thought she was a child of privilege, pampered and spoiled. He'd thought she'd never known a moment's unhappiness or worry, that everything she'd ever wanted had been hers simply for the asking. Who could guess that hidden beneath the creamy skin and shining eyes lay the heart of someone who had suffered soul-destroying pain? She'd been wounded as deeply as he had been—maybe more deeply.

Her head remained bowed, and Dusty wanted to go to her, but he forced himself to stay put. "It must have been very hard for you."

"It was terrible," she said softly.

"How old were you?" Dusty's chest tightened as he watched her shoulders sag.

"Twenty-two."

Twenty-two. Just a kid. He saw her body trembling. Then he was next to her, his arm around her. He felt tension under his palm as he rubbed her shoulder awkwardly. For what seemed a long time, but was probably only seconds, she resisted, then all at once, she turned toward him, buried her head against his chest and cried with heartbreaking, wrenching sobs.

"Oh, babe, I'm sorry," he murmured against the sweetness of her hair. His arms tightened, and he rubbed her back in slow circles and let her cry. He had a feeling she didn't often allow herself the luxury of tears.

Finally, with a great, shuddering sigh, she lifted her head. Her eyes were puffy and red-rimmed, streaks of tears marring her smooth skin. Shakily, she said, "I'm sorry. I never cry. I didn't even cry when it happened. I...I don't know what came over me." Then, as if just now realizing he was holding her, she stiffened and pulled back. "I'm so embarrassed. I don't usually fall to pieces like this."

Dusty wanted to keep her close, but he knew he couldn't rush her. She'd been hurt too deeply. It would take time—time and patience—to break down the walls she'd erected between her heart and love. Before she'd be ready for a relationship with him, she'd have to learn to trust him.

"Isn't it ironic?" she said, pulling a tissue from the pocket of her jeans and wiping her cheeks. She blew her nose.

"Isn't what ironic?" he said gently.

Her eyes, still wet, looked like twin amethysts as she raised them to his face. "David's accident. Chris's death. They were both caused by alcohol."

"Well...that's not quite true," he said.

"It *is* true. If David hadn't been drinking, if Chris hadn't been drinking, neither accident would have happened!"

"You don't know that. Maybe some other combination of circumstances would have brought about the same result."

She shook her head vehemently. "No. It was alcohol."

"That's like saying David's accident was caused by the horse, or Chris's accident was caused by the car. David's accident was caused because some stupid kids didn't use good sense, and Chris's death was caused by his abuse of alcohol. There's nothing wrong with alcohol itself."

"There's nothing right with it," she said stubbornly.

"That's like saying there's nothing right with drugs. Drugs, used the way they should be, to lessen pain and help sick people, are wonderful. It's the abuse of drugs that's terrible."

"I know what you're saying makes sense, but I can't help how I feel. I made a pact with myself the day after Chris's funeral. I vowed I'd never touch alcohol again and that I'd do everything I could to encourage other people to banish it from their lives."

Dusty thought of Mitchell's. For a fleeting moment, he was tempted to say something about the bar, but the look in her eyes stopped him. Careful, he thought. This isn't the moment. Not if you want to see her again.

He knew her feelings about alcohol bordered on the irrational, but he also knew she had a pretty damn good reason for feeling the way she did. Her life had been turned upside-down. She'd lost her husband in a tragic and violent way. She was bound to have some emotional scars.

And she was partially right, alcohol had played a large part in the ruin of her husband's life, but Dusty believed that strength of character enabled some people to face their weaknesses and seek help, whereas innate weakness allowed others to find excuses and never try to help themselves. However, he didn't think Victoria was ready for his philosophy.

No, he'd better not tell her about the bar tonight. He hated deceiving her, but she wasn't ready for the information. She'd shy away from him like a skittish colt.

He sighed heavily. "You've had a rough time, haven't you?" He reached for her hand, and after only a moment's hesitation, she allowed him to hold it. The warmth of the contact between them felt right. His decision felt right. First he had to win her confidence and her trust.

"Look," he said. "It's late, and you're tired. Why don't you go to bed and get a good night's sleep. I'm sorry I reminded you of your husband's death. I know it was a painful time for you, but just look what you've made of your life. You've accomplished so much, and all by yourself. You're a strong woman, and you've survived. You have a beautiful daughter, a good job, friends. You have a lot to be proud of."

At his words, her eyes softened, and Dusty was reminded of the velvet petals of pansies.

"I do, don't I?" she said. Her lips curved into a tentative smile, and she gave a shaky sigh.

"Yes, you do," he echoed softly. He stood, pulling her to her feet. And even though he'd told himself to go slowly, not to force her, he couldn't resist lowering his head and kissing her one last time. Her soft lips tasted slightly salty. A great tenderness filled Dusty as her full lips parted and the warmth and sweetness of her mouth invaded his senses. In that moment, all he wanted was to take care of her. He wanted to give her back her dreams and the innocence she'd lost that night so long ago.

Because he loved her. Shaken, he held her close and stroked her hair as his thoughts spun crazily.

He loved her. My God, what now?

The next week was a jumble of sights and sounds and feelings that Victoria hadn't experienced in years. She drifted through the week in a haze of warmth and happiness. Victoria spent almost all her time with Dusty. He took her and Julie to Surfside Beach where they spent one long, lazy day looking for shells and toasting themselves in the balmy spring sunshine.

They spent one sunny afternoon trekking through the Arboretum, then stuffed themselves with Mexican food at Cyclone Anaya's in the Heights.

They laughed as they watched Dusty roll two gutter balls one afternoon at Fame City, the huge covered amusement arcade that Julie and all her friends adored. Victoria felt like a kid as she played the pinball machines and broke 150 in bowling.

"Say, you're not bad," Dusty praised her. "Sure you don't bowl on the sly?"

"I haven't bowled since high school."

"Yeah, sure," he said, but he grinned.

They ate buttered popcorn at the Spectrum and hot nachos at a Rockets game in the Summit. They spent one day downtown exploring the tunnels and buying souvenirs in the shops. When Dusty suggested they eat red beans and rice at Treebeards, Victoria groaned.

"Dusty, I've gained at least ten pounds this week," she protested as they walked across Old Market Square to the popular Cajun restaurant.

"On you, it looks good," he said, his eyes bold. Their dark intensity made Victoria's face grow hot as his gaze swept over her body with lazy warmth and promise.

The nights were even more wonderful. While Julie was occupied with her friends, Dusty and Victoria did things she'd only dreamed about. They went to the Rainbow Lodge for dinner and watched the squirrels and chipmunks walk right up to the plate-glass windows and peer in. The lovely, romantic atmosphere of the old Victorian house and grounds and the view of Buffalo Bayou outside the windows stirred Victoria's senses. With Dusty sitting across from her, his eyes filled with admiration for her in her red silk dress, she shivered with delight.

When she laughingly said, "Don't you ever work, Dusty? How are you managing to take so much time off?" he brushed her question aside.

"I'm independently wealthy, what else?" He grinned.

She smiled happily. Of course. He would have gotten a share from the sale of the ranch, too.

Fascinated, they watched the water cascade down the water wall next to the Transco tower. They ate huge fried shrimp stuffed with crabmeat at the Atchafalaya River Café and thick steaks at Bud Bigelow's.

And one perfect evening, after grilling chicken on her barbecue, Victoria played the piano for Dusty. He leaned against the top of her old spinet and watched. Victoria played all her favorites, ending with Chopin's "Waltz in A Minor," its poetic brilliance stirring an ache in Victoria's heart.

"Beautiful," Dusty said as the last lovely notes died away.

Victoria's breathing quickened at the undisguised warmth in his eyes.

Only one incident marred the otherwise perfect week. The night they ate dinner at the Atchafalaya Café, as they lingered over their coffee, the conversation turned to David.

"He's got some fool idea of moving to Houston," Dusty said.

"What's wrong with that?" Victoria tried to ignore the guilty feeling nudging her as she remembered her phone call to Sissy the day after she'd visited the ranch. "He's very talented, Dusty. Surely you, of all people, should understand his desire to be a success. To do what he loves."

"Houston's no place for David." Dusty's jaw moved into a stubborn line.

A flutter of apprehension crept up Victoria's spine. "But David's a grown man. You can't stop him from coming here if he wants to."

Dusty's eyes narrowed. "Maybe I can't stop him, but I sure as hell won't encourage him...or make it easy for him. Not when I know it's the wrong thing to do."

Victoria wanted to say, "You can't take care of him forever. It's no kindness to him. He has to learn to survive alone. What if something happened to you? Then what?" But she didn't. She didn't want to argue or make Dusty angry. Not tonight. Not when the week had been so perfect.

For the entire week, Victoria had felt like Cinderella. Nothing had spoiled her happiness. At first she'd been worried, too. Worried about the kisses they'd shared the night Dusty told her about David and she told him about Chris, but Dusty had been a perfect gentleman throughout the week. Yes, they'd held hands and danced close together, and he'd caressed her with his eyes and put his arm lightly around her shoulders, and he'd even kissed her goodnight, but he'd seemed to be holding himself back, almost as if he knew there could never be anything more between them. The kisses he'd given her had been sweet and soft, and they'd never deepened as that first one had.

First one? Second one, Victoria corrected herself. The first one was the sweet kiss they'd exchanged the night they'd met. The second one was the one that had been scary. Scary because it had been so intense. Victoria knew she couldn't allow herself to be drawn into that kind of passion with Dusty. Passion like that only belonged in a relationship that had a prayer of developing further. Otherwise you just got deeply hurt because it couldn't last.

But Dusty had seemed to realize all this, too. Victoria was grateful to him for not pushing her into something she didn't want. What they had was better than passion, anyway, she reasoned. They were building a friendship and a trust in one another. Yes, it was much better. Friendship lasted. Passion didn't.

But on Saturday night, the last free night she had before she had to think about getting up the next morning to go to work, when Dusty kissed her lightly, letting his lips linger on hers for just a fraction of a second longer than he had all week, Victoria's insides curled. A tightening sensation began low down, and she closed her eyes. She ached as a sudden rush of longing shot through her. It took all her willpower and self-control to inch away from him. Oh, God. She'd have to be careful. She was kidding herself when she told herself she didn't want him. She did. She wanted him badly. She wanted him more than she'd ever wanted anyone.

She looked up. They were standing in the shelter of her front doorway, and in the light from the street lamp, she could see his glittering eyes and the tension in his jaw.

She swallowed. Did he know what she was feeling? Her heart pounded as their eyes met and locked.

He raised his hand and cupped her chin as his thumb rubbed softly over her lips.

She shuddered and let the tip of her tongue taste him. Need pulsed deep within her. A great, rushing need.

"We'd better say good-night," he murmured. "Before we both forget ourselves."

He *did* know.

He lowered his head, and his lips touched hers once more. His arms pulled her close, tightened around her. Victoria wrapped her arms around him. Her hands found his head, pulled him even closer. Her thoughts whirled as the kiss became everything. She felt as if she were drowning in a sea of sensation so powerful she would never emerge again. She clung to Dusty, feeling the heat of his palms against her back, the strength of his arousal against her abdomen, the pull of his mouth against hers.

Gently disengaging her hands, he dragged his mouth from hers and drew back. Her body cried out against the sudden loss. Her breasts ached for his touch; she almost whimpered in her fierce need.

For one long moment his eyes held hers, and in their depths she saw something she couldn't define. He bent and kissed the tip of her nose. Then he whispered against her parted lips, "Darlin', I want you, but I'm in no hurry. I can wait. When we make love, I want you to be sure. I want you to want it as much as I do. I don't want our lovemaking to be something that happens because we get carried away."

"Dusty—"

"Sh, don't say anything. Just listen." His mouth nuzzled against hers, and Victoria's heart raced. She clutched his shoulders against the dizziness of her desire.

"I want you with your eyes wide open, with no regrets afterward." His moist mouth moved to her neck with tantalizing slowness and gentleness. Victoria's breath felt trapped in her chest. "I want the decision for us to make love to be a conscious one, something you've thought about. Because I'm not looking for casual sex. When you come to me, Victoria, I want it all...your body, your mind and your heart."

She shivered against the onslaught of his mouth against her heated skin. She could feel his mouth curve into a smile against her throat, and he slowly trailed his lips up until they once more captured her mouth in a hard, demanding kiss that caused the blood to pound fiercely in Victoria's ears.

Then he turned, and as his boot heels clicked against the walk, Victoria's heart thudded in time to the sound.

Chapter Eight

She hadn't heard from him on Sunday. By Monday at three o'clock, Victoria's last class of the day spilled into the hall, and she sighed gratefully as she stuffed papers into her satchel. She could finally relax her guard and allow her thoughts to drift to Dusty, a subject she had forced herself not to think about all day.

She wondered if he'd gone out to the ranch again. What he'd said to her on Saturday night as he left her at her doorstep had gone around and around in her mind. Now his words echoed once more.

I want it all ... your body, your mind and your heart.

He wanted her to think about the two of them. Good God, as if she could think about anything else. That was exactly the problem. She couldn't think straight or think logically; all she could think about was Dusty—his eyes, his smile, his voice—how it felt to be held by him, kissed by him, how it felt when he looked at her, when he touched her.

Even now, as she closed her eyes and remembered the feel of his hands against her skin, she shivered.

"Sure wish that dreamy look was directed my way."

Victoria's eyes snapped open. John Webberly, who had been appointed dean of the music department in September, stood in her open doorway. Tall and thin, with dark brown hair that always fell into his face, he had indicated his interest in her dozens of times over the past school year. Victoria had never returned that interest; she'd never encouraged him. Still, he was her boss, and she'd tried to keep their relationship friendly. Laughing slightly, she put her hand over her heart. "Lord, John, you startled me."

"Sorry," he said as he sauntered into the room. "I didn't mean to. What were you thinking about? You looked like you were in another world."

"Oh, nothing that interesting. I was just trying to remember the name of a song I heard this morning." Victoria was surprised at how easily the white lie emerged.

"Did you enjoy your week off?" He sat on the edge of her desk and smiled at her, his eyes sweeping her approvingly, lingering on the swell of her breasts in her pink silk blouse.

Victoria squirmed uncomfortably. She always felt as if he were undressing her when he looked at her, and she didn't like the feeling. "Yes." Maybe if she picked up her satchel, he'd get the hint, and she could leave.

He pushed a lock of hair from his forehead. "I tried to call you several times, but I never got an answer. Did you go out of town?" His pale blue eyes reminded her of washed-out denim.

"No, but I was out a lot," Victoria said. She picked up the satchel. "Listen, John, I'm picking Julie up at school today, and if I don't hurry, I'll be late."

"Oh, I'm sorry." He stood. As she turned to walk out the door, he reached out and touched her arm. It was all she could do to keep from yanking it from his grasp. "Wait just one minute, Victoria. I wanted to ask you something."

Victoria stiffened. She always refused him when he asked her out, but he simply wouldn't give up. "Well . . . one minute . . . then I really have to go."

"I'd like to escort you to the department's dinner dance next month."

The thought of going out with him was abhorrent. She guessed he was attractive, in a rather colorless, intellectual way. But she couldn't help the mental comparison of his thin, almost gawky body with Dusty's larger-than-life, muscled frame; John's sloped shoulders to the broad expanse of smooth male strength in Dusty's; his washed-out blue eyes, pale skin and lank hair to Dusty's vivid green-gold gaze, bronzed coloring and thick, golden-brown waves.

Smothering a sigh, she said, "I'm sorry, John. I . . . I already have a date for the dinner dance."

His face froze, and he dropped his hand. "Oh."

"I really *am* sorry. It was very nice of you to ask me," she said in a rush to cover her embarrassment and uneasiness. "I appreciate the thought. Well, listen, I'd better get going."

She hurried from the room without looking back, but she could feel his eyes on her as she walked rapidly down the hall. She ignored the cacophony from the practice rooms she passed along the way to the first-floor exit.

What was she going to do now? After telling John Webberly she had a date, she couldn't show up at the dinner dance alone as she'd planned to do. She couldn't afford to make an enemy of John.

Reaching the exit, she shouldered open the door and walked rapidly across the tarmac to her car. As she dumped her satchel and purse into the station wagon, she decided she'd ask Dusty to go to the dinner dance with her. She grinned. He'd make quite a stir among her fellow teachers, especially the females. They'd probably all be jealous. And maybe John Webberly would finally get the hint.

It was almost forty-five minutes later before Victoria pulled up in front of the junior high school. Julie was standing under the shade of an ash tree with two other girls. Victoria honked.

"What took you so long?" Julie said with a slight frown as she opened the door and slid across the leather seat.

"The traffic was heavy today," Victoria said as she pulled out of the circular drive into the road. "How was school?"

"All right, I guess," Julie mumbled. She stared out her window.

Victoria sighed. "Last week was fun, wasn't it?"

"Uh-huh," Julie said. Then, a bit more animatedly, she added, "Oh, yeah, I almost forgot. I have something for you." She reached into her notebook and withdrew a folded sheet of newspaper. "Miss Clancey cut this out of the *Chronicle* 'cause she knows we don't take it. She said to give it to you."

Maureen Clancey was Julie's music teacher, and Victoria had become friendly with the older woman after meeting her at one of the parents' days at Julie's school.

"Don't shove that at me, Julie, I'm driving. What is it, anyway?"

"It's an article about Dusty."

"An article about Dusty! Why would Miss Clancey give you an article about Dusty?"

For a minute, Julie didn't answer, then she said sheepishly, "Well, I...I told her about last week...you know...going out to his ranch...you know...."

"Julie!" Victoria couldn't believe that Julie was going around telling her teachers about her private life.

"What are you getting all upset about?"

"Maybe I don't want people knowing who I go out with. What else did you tell Miss Clancey?"

"You know, Mom, you're really weird sometimes," Julie said. "I didn't tell her anything else. I just said that Dusty Mitchell was a friend of yours, and that he'd taken both of us out to visit his family's ranch one day last week. That's all. It's no big deal."

Victoria knew she had overreacted. She knew she should apologize to Julie. Sighing, she finally said, "I'm sorry, Julie. I don't know why I jumped on you. You're right. It's no big deal." She forced a bright note into her voice. "Now, what's the article about?"

"Do you want me to read it to you?"

"No. We're almost home. I'll read it when we get there." She didn't trust her volatile emotions any more. She certainly didn't want Julie to see her reacting to whatever it was that had been written about Dusty.

A couple of minutes later they pulled into their driveway, and Julie rushed out of the car. Victoria followed more slowly. Her strategy worked. By the time she reached the front door Julie was already in her room, but she'd tossed the newspaper clipping onto the coffee table in the den.

Victoria smoothed out the paper. A picture of Dusty singing at a microphone dominated the page. Just looking at his strong masculine features caused Victoria's chest to tighten and her breathing to quicken. Under the photograph was the header, "Local performer signed by Nashville production company." Victoria smiled and began to read the article.

Lately everything seems to be going right for Dusty Mitchell, a local composer-singer who has been around the Houston music scene for many years. Mitchell has been writing songs since he was a teenager, he said, but he didn't get serious about the music business until he was in his early twenties.

The article went on to tell about Dusty's background and album, about the call he'd gotten from Vernon Rylander and what it would probably mean in terms of his career. Victoria grinned. The article was flattering. The writer obviously liked Dusty. She read until the end, where the last sentence seemed to leap out from the page.

If you'd like to hear Mitchell in person, he sings with a local band on Monday, Wednesday and Friday nights at Mitchell's, a club he's owned for the past ten years.

A club he's owned for the past ten years. Victoria couldn't believe it. Dusty hadn't said a word to her about owning a club. And club was just a fancy word for bar, wasn't it? A bar. Dusty owned a bar. Stunned, Victoria let the clipping drop. Why hadn't he told her? Why had he allowed her to think he didn't work? What was it he had said when she'd asked him if he ever worked? *I'm independently wealthy.* He'd been laughing, like it was a joke, but he'd known she thought his answer was serious.

Victoria's breath caught as the realization hit her like a blow to the chest. He'd purposely evaded her question because he hadn't wanted her to know he owned a bar. He hadn't wanted her to know because by the time she asked the question, she'd already told him her feelings about alcohol and drinking.

He lied to me, she thought.

Pain coiled within her as she thought over all the things she'd told him the night they returned from visiting his family. She'd completely exposed herself, told him things she'd never talked about with anyone else, not even Sissy. And she'd told him because she trusted him. And he had betrayed that trust by lying to her.

Victoria swallowed against the lump in her throat. What a fool she was. Hadn't she learned anything from her mistakes? It was really stupid to put your trust in other people. In the end a person could only count on herself. Trusting someone else always led to being let down.

So what should she do now? Forget him? Push him out of her life? Break it off completely? Find someone else? Unbidden, a picture of John Webberly's thin face rose in her mind, and bile rose in her throat.

Oh, God, how could she forget Dusty? Even though she'd been telling herself they had a go-nowhere relationship, that there was no future for them, hadn't Dusty Mitchell, with his sexy smile and lazy charm, managed to invade every corner of her life so that hardly ten minutes went by without her thinking about him? Hadn't her mouth gone dry every time she remembered the feel of his hands on her body, the heat of his mouth as he claimed hers, the smell and taste of him?

My God, even now, with her gut twisted up inside her and anger and pain churning together over his deceit, just thinking about the kisses he'd given her on Saturday night was enough to cause an aching desire to pulse deep within her.

I want him. I want him more than I've ever wanted any man in my entire life. I'm hurt, deeply hurt, that he didn't tell me the truth, but I still want him. I don't know if I can give him up without ever knowing what it's like to be loved by him.

Emotions in turmoil, Victoria jumped up. She walked to the patio doors, opened them and stood looking out the screen door. A plump wren was perched on top of the six-foot cedar fence that ringed her backyard. She stared at the small bird as if it could help her find answers to her question. Finally she took a deep breath and walked to the phone on the kitchen counter. She still didn't know what she'd do about tomorrow, but she sure as hell knew what she was going to do tonight.

"Tory, don't walk so fast," Sissy complained as she trailed a couple of feet behind Victoria and picked her way carefully through the gravel of the parking lot.

"If you didn't wear such high heels, you could keep up with me," Victoria said. The two of them had just parked Sissy's black Jaguar in the parking lot behind Mitchell's and were making their way to the club's entrance in the front of the building.

"Don't take your bad mood out on me," Sissy said. "I'm not the one who lied to you."

"Oh, really? What do you call it then?" Victoria stopped abruptly and swung around to face Sissy, who had just reached the sidewalk. "You know how I feel about alcohol. You also knew about Dusty owning a bar, and you didn't tell me. I call that lying. What do you call it?"

"You know, Tory, you sound very self-righteous for someone who hasn't exactly been on the up and up with Dusty." There was no remorse in Sissy's voice.

For a moment, Victoria was speechless. Then her eyes narrowed as she studied her friend. "That's completely different, and you know it."

Sissy shrugged, the gesture fully visible in the bright glow of a street-lamp positioned at the edge of the driveway. She started to say something, then stopped as a laughing party of four men and women walked past them and into the club. A burst of music greeted them as the door swung open.

Victoria couldn't believe that hiding her part in securing a contract for Dusty with VeePee Productions even compared to what Dusty had done in hiding the way he earned his living. But Sissy's head was tilted defiantly, and a soft breeze lifted her bright hair as she stood staring at Victoria.

"How is it different?" she finally said. "You did something behind Dusty's back when you asked me to try to arrange for a new contract for him without telling him. He did something behind your back by not telling you about the club. Seems like the same thing to me."

"I was trying to help him. I don't call that deceitful. He out-and-out lied because he was afraid to tell me the truth."

"So you're saying that the end justifies the means, is that it?"

"Damn it, Sissy. Quit twisting things around. You know damn well the two situations are not the same, so don't try to make me think I've done something wrong."

"My, my," Sissy said. "You must really be upset if you're swearing. I think the reason you're so mad isn't so much that Dusty lied to you or even that he owns a bar. I think you're upset because he's gotten under your skin and you don't know what to do about it. I think you've just realized that no matter what he does you're not going to be able to get him out of your life, and I think you're scared out of your mind!" Then she tossed her head, moved around Victoria and stomped up to the entrance. She yanked open the door. "Are you coming, or not?"

Stunned by Sissy's accusation, Victoria stared at her. Was Sissy right? Was she afraid of her feelings for Dusty? Was that why she had jumped at Julie today for no good reason? Was that why she was so annoyed with Sissy? Sissy's words echoed in her head, but it was too late to turn back.

With a sigh of resignation, Victoria followed Sissy into the dimly lit bar. The sound of Patsy Cline singing "Crazy" drifted from a jukebox in the corner. A thick haze of smoke hung in the air. Victoria squinted until her eyes adjusted to the darkness. The bar was larger than it looked from the outside, with about thirty tables grouped around the rectangular room. A half-circle bar jutted from the far corner of the room. A lone bartender served the half-dozen people seated on the bar stools. Victoria saw two cocktail waitresses tending to people seated at the tables. She didn't see Dusty anywhere.

Sissy weaved her way past several tables, then turned. "This one okay with you?"

Victoria nodded, and they sat down. She looked around. There was a dart board mounted on the side wall, and two young men dressed in jeans, plaid shirts and boots were playing darts.

"What can I get you?"

The waitress was middle-aged but attractive. She smoothed back her dark hair as she waited for their response.

"I'll have a light beer," Sissy said.

"Do you have Diet Coke?" asked Victoria, holding out her palm to Sissy.

"Sure," the waitress said. "That's one light beer and one Diet Coke, coming up."

Sissy dropped her car keys into Victoria's hand. "I know," she said. "If I'm drinking, I'm not driving."

"That's right."

The song on the jukebox ended, and a young girl got up to feed money into the machine. Soon the smooth voice of Willie Nelson filled the room.

Victoria squinted at her watch. Eight o'clock. Maybe it was too early for Dusty to be here.

The door opened, and Victoria's stomach lurched as a tall man walked in, but when he turned in her direction, she saw he wasn't Dusty. It took long minutes for her heart to slow. Her reaction angered her. Why should she be nervous? She wasn't the one in the wrong here.

"It doesn't look like Dusty's here," Sissy said. The words had no sooner left her mouth than Victoria saw a door open at the side of the bar. Light spilled out. Silhouetted in the open doorway stood Dusty.

Victoria's heart pounded as he slowly looked around the room. She knew the exact moment when he saw her. He was scanning the room casually, then did a double take when he spotted her. Panic flooded her. She had the absurd urge to get up and run outside.

"Ah, the plot thickens," Sissy muttered as Dusty slowly closed the door behind him and walked toward them. "Our hero has come on the scene. What will the angry maiden do now?"

As he slowly approached their table, Dusty's thoughts whirled. What was Victoria doing here? He still couldn't believe it was really her, but there she sat, looking cool and beautiful, and although he still wasn't close enough to see it, he knew there was an accusing look in her gorgeous eyes.

He knew he was in for it. He didn't know how she'd found out about the bar, but he guessed it had been inevitable. He just wished he'd had the chance to tell her himself. She was probably furious with him. What should he do? Should he pretend like this wasn't a big deal, or should he apologize? His high school football coach had always said, "The best defense is a good offense." Dusty closed the distance between them in two long strides.

"Hey, look who's here," he said with a smile. She didn't smile back. What the hell, he thought. Might as well go for it. He leaned over her and kissed her parted lips. She jerked back, but not before Dusty felt her response in her quickened breathing. "It sure is good to see you. I missed you," he said softly. Then he straightened and looked down at her.

She stared at him, anger and pain reflected in her eyes. Uneasy and uncertain how to proceed, he turned toward Sissy. "Welcome to Mitchell's."

Sissy smiled archly. "Thank you. I'm just thrilled to be here. And I'll bet you're really thrilled to see *us*."

Dusty pulled out a chair and propped one leg on it. He kept his voice light and looked at Victoria, but she refused to meet his gaze. "I am."

The waitress walked up just then. She smiled at Dusty, then put Sissy's beer in front of her and Victoria's Coke in front of her. "That'll be three dollars," she said.

"Never mind, Emma," Dusty said. "It's on the house."

"Okay, Dusty." As she walked away, Dusty saw Victoria's eyes follow her. She'll look at anyone except me, he thought. "Are you going to stick around awhile?" he asked.

Sissy shrugged. "Tory's calling the shots tonight. Whatever she wants."

Dusty looked at Victoria. Her head was slightly bowed. He didn't say anything, just waited until she was forced to return his look. The sounds of the bar receded as his eyes locked with hers. She no longer looked angry. Instead he saw confusion and pain. Suddenly his strategy of pretending nothing was wrong seemed childish to Dusty. He was trivializing the importance of what was between them by ignoring her obvious unhappiness.

He removed his booted foot from the chair. Turning to Sissy, he said, "Would you excuse us for a few minutes, Sissy? I want to talk to Victoria."

"Hey, don't mind me. Take all the time you want." Sissy airily dismissed them.

"Come on," he said to Victoria. He reached down and took her hand. Her hand was cold; he felt a slight tremor at his touch. As she stood, he put his arm around her, and he could feel the shudder that raced through her. She came willingly, but Dusty wasn't foolish enough to think this was going to be easy. He knew he'd hurt her. He knew she was upset. And he knew how important the next few minutes would be.

He led her through a doorway, down a short hallway, past his cluttered office to the side exit. With one arm still around her, he released the dead bolt and opened the door.

There was a narrow walkway between the club and the fence separating the club from the restaurant next door. Trash cans were lined up on the bricks Dusty had placed there to keep the area from getting muddy and messy when it rained. It wasn't a romantic spot, but it was dark, and it was private. Only the light from the street filtered through to where they stood—just enough so that when Dusty turned Victoria to face him, he could see the sheen of tears in her eyes.

Tenderness welled up inside him. He hated that he'd hurt her. All he'd wanted to do, from the first moment he'd set eyes on her at the masquerade ball, was take care of her.

He cupped her face in his hands and, although she trembled, she didn't pull back. "I'm sorry, sweetheart. I'm sorry I didn't tell you about the club."

"Why did you lie to me?" she whispered.

Dusty shook his head. "I don't know. I guess I was afraid to tell you. I was afraid you wouldn't want to see me again. I just couldn't take the chance."

She sighed and raised her hands to his, pushing him away. She backed up so that there was some distance between them. "I couldn't believe it when I read that story about you in the *Chronicle*. I just couldn't believe it. Especially after Saturday night . . . the things you said. . . ."

"Victoria..." He reached for her, but she backed up farther and raised her hands in front of her.

"Don't touch me. It's hard for me to think straight when you touch me."

Hope surged through him. Maybe all wasn't lost. Maybe he still had a chance to put things right between them. "All right. I won't touch you. But let me explain, okay? That's all I ask."

"Why should I?"

"Even murderers are given a chance to explain their side of the story," he said.

She turned her face away. He could see by the set of her shoulders how stiffly she was holding herself, as if she couldn't let herself weaken. He wanted nothing more than to gather her in his arms and comfort her, make the hurt go away. But he was the cause of the hurt, and he knew he'd better tread very carefully.

"Dusty, you can tell your side of things, as you put it, but why should I believe anything you say? If you lied to me about the club, how do I know you haven't lied to me about everything else?"

The question rocked him. For a minute, he couldn't answer. Then he said, "What else? What else do you think was a lie?"

She didn't answer. She shrugged her shoulders and bowed her head.

"Answer me, Victoria." He reached out and raised her chin. "What else?"

"Okay. If you really want to know, how do I know all the things you said to me on Saturday night aren't just a smooth line? 'I don't just want casual sex from you. I want your mind. Your heart.' Maybe that's just a clever way to get me into bed. To make me think I'm somebody special in your eyes, when I'll just be a conquest to brag about. Another notch on your belt!"

Dusty dropped his hand, her accusation like a slap in the face. "You don't really believe that," he said.

"I don't know what to believe any more." She turned her face away from him once more.

Dusty clenched his jaw, then his fists. He felt like hitting something. "Well, I guess there's nothing to say to that," he said.

"I guess not," she answered, her words muffled. She pulled a tissue out of her jeans pocket and blew her nose.

For a few minutes they stood there like two strangers sharing space at a bus stop. They didn't look at each other, and they didn't say anything. Noise from the street trickled in, and they could hear muted music from the club, but otherwise it was silent.

Finally, she straightened her shoulders and said quietly. "I'd like to go in now, if you don't mind."

Dusty shrugged. He had no intention of begging. "Whatever you say." He reached over and opened the door, then stepped back so she could go ahead of him. Her shoulders were rigid, her back straight, her head high. She kept her eyes averted. As she angled past him and stepped into the lighted hallway, he caught a whiff of her light, flowery scent, and pain stabbed his gut.

For one wild moment he almost grabbed her. Maybe if he could kiss her senseless, she'd listen to him. But pride prevented him from forcing himself on her, so the moment passed.

As they reached his office, he stopped. "I have work to do. You can find your way alone, can't you?"

Her footsteps faltered for a second, then she kept going. She didn't turn around. "I always have," she said tonelessly. Then she opened the door and disappeared into the club.

Chapter Nine

"What's wrong, Victoria? Don't you feel well?" John Webberly said when they passed each other in the hall on Friday.

"I'm all right," she said listlessly, attempting a smile.

"You don't *look* all right," he insisted. "You look ill. And if you're ill, you shouldn't be here."

"I'm just tired, that's all," she said. She was very close to tears.

"Well, see that you get some rest this weekend then," he said.

She walked blindly down the hall to the first floor, then outside to the parking lot where she loaded her books and papers into her car. The April day was unseasonably hot, hotter than any day so far that spring. Victoria turned the air-conditioning on as high as it would go in an attempt to cool off the station wagon quickly. The steering wheel burned her hands as she backed out of her parking place. She sighed. The wicked Houston summer was on its way.

The tears that had threatened to spill when John Webberly had voiced his concern over her appearance filled her eyes and choked her throat. Why did the breakup with Dusty hurt so much? Why couldn't she stop thinking about him? What was wrong with her? Was she in love with him?

She groped for a tissue in the box she kept on the front seat of the car and dabbed at her eyes. For someone who never cried, she certainly had done enough of it lately. She almost laughed thinking about it. If falling in love was this painful, perhaps she preferred never to fall in love again.

Pulling into the flow of traffic on the street, she drove toward the Gulf Freeway. Within minutes she was accelerating up the ramp and into the fast-moving traffic headed toward downtown Houston.

The skyline looming in front of her reminded her of the background of Dusty's album cover. Victoria bit her lip. Every single thing she looked at or did or heard or read in some way reminded her of Dusty. It was as if he had invaded every particle of her being, every sense—as if he were now a permanent part of her.

If only she could have believed him. If only she thought he cared about her as much as she was beginning to think she cared about him. If only he had called her this week.

Intellectually, she knew he wouldn't call. If she wanted to talk to him again, it would be up to her to call him. After all, she'd said some pretty harsh things to him. But emotionally and irrationally, she still hoped he'd call. Every time the phone rang, she had rushed to it, but it had never been him. The entire endless week had dragged by, minute by awful minute, and he hadn't called. Didn't he know she'd lashed out at him because he'd hurt her?

Victoria grimaced. She had to get a grip on herself. This wasn't the end of the world. It was time to quit acting like the lead actress in a grade-B melodrama. Sighing, she put on her turn signal and moved into the lane that would take her to the Southwest Freeway and home. She was a grown woman with a good education, a career that paid well, a daughter she'd raised single-handedly, lots of friends, and a good life. She'd gotten along perfectly well before Dusty Mitchell had appeared in her life, and she'd get along perfectly well now that he'd disappeared from it. "So grow up. Quit dramatizing and feeling sorry for yourself," she said aloud.

As Victoria pulled into her driveway, she turned off the ignition and sat quietly in the car for a few seconds. Then she picked up her satchel and purse, opened the door and got out. She took a deep breath of the heavily perfumed spring air and squared her shoulders.

She would forget Dusty Mitchell. She'd been right all along. They were complete opposites with different goals, and she was better off without him. In the end, he would've broken her heart anyway.

She would simply put him out of her mind. She could do it. She'd met every other challenge she'd been faced with in her thirty-three years, and she'd meet this one. Even if it killed her.

Dusty tried not to think about Victoria after Monday night, but he wasn't very successful. The least little thing reminded him of her. Even the bar was no longer a refuge. No matter how many times he told himself that breaking off with her was probably for the best—after all, he had all sorts of exciting things on the horizon, and being saddled with a woman would just create lots of problems—he couldn't get her out of his head.

The words she'd hurled at him, the words that had cut him so deeply, seemed permanently imprinted on his brain. *Maybe you didn't mean any of the things you said. Maybe everything was a lie—a clever ploy to get me into bed. Maybe I'll just be another conquest to brag about. Another notch on your belt.* Is that really what she thought of him? Hell, if that's how little esteem he had in her eyes, he was better off without her! Who needed her? Women were all a pain in the neck. You couldn't understand any of them.

They were never satisfied, no matter what you did. They always wanted your blood. But even as Dusty told himself all these things, a picture of Victoria, tears shining in her eyes and unhappy disbelief in her voice, would appear to haunt him.

When Vernon Rylander called him on Tuesday afternoon to ask him if he could fly to Nashville on Wednesday and stay for a week, Dusty said yes with no hesitation.

"You might even have to be here longer, son," Rylander said. "Don't know how long it'll take you to choose your backup and all."

"No problem," Dusty said.

"No problem," echoed Spence when Dusty told him about the call that night. "I'll be here to take care of everything."

"I knew you would." Excitement coursed through Dusty at the thought of all the work he'd be doing on this trip to Nashville in preparation for cutting his new album. He wished he could tell Victoria...no, he wasn't going to think about her any more. That episode of his life was over. Over and done with. He'd thought he was in love with her, but it hadn't worked out.

He jumped as Spence snapped his fingers. "Hey, wake up, I want to talk to you about something," Spence said, grinning.

"Sorry. I guess I was daydreaming. What is it?"

"Well, I've been thinking a lot lately," Spence said as he deftly mixed a Bloody Mary. "And I was wondering, what are you planning to do about the bar?"

"What do you mean?"

"Just what I said. You know, for the past year you've been around here less and less. Shoot, for the past month I've hardly seen you. What's it gonna be like once you cut this record for Rylander? You'll never be here."

Dusty frowned. Spence was right. He'd felt less and less interest in Mitchell's, especially lately. "I really haven't thought about it," he said, "but I will."

"I have a suggestion," Spence said quietly. "Sell the club to me."

As soon as Spence said the words, Dusty knew it would be the right thing to do. Right for Spence, and right for him. He grinned and stuck out his hand. "Partner, I think maybe we can work out a deal."

Dusty stared out the window of the 727 and watched as the land rushed by. Within moments, they lifted off the ground, and soon the pilot banked the plane as he turned toward the northeast and Nashville.

Dusty relaxed and let his thoughts drift to the night before. He and Spence had sat up far into the night as they discussed how and when the sale of Mitchell's would be completed. Finally, at four in the morning, Dusty stood, stretched and said, "I've got to get up pretty early to catch that fight to Nashville, Spence. We'd better call it a night."

"While you're gone, I'll call Marlin, have him start getting the papers ready," Spence said.

Marlin Lamb was Dusty's attorney. "Good. Maybe this can be a done deal by next week."

They shook hands once more, both men satisfied with the decision they'd made. As Dusty drove to his apartment, he wished Victoria knew he was selling the club.

"Oh, hell," he said aloud, "what difference would that make?" She'd made it plain that nothing he said would interest her. She wanted no part of him. It was over, over before it really started, and he might as well accept it. Because he'd never forced himself on any woman. And he didn't intend to start now.

But now, sitting far above the clouds, on his way to the beginning of a new phase in his life, one he was sure would be exciting and wonderful, he couldn't stop himself from thinking about her.

He fantasized about bringing her along on this trip. He'd have loved taking her to Nashville and showing her the sights. They could have stayed in one of the nicer hotels, and she could have gone with him while he auditioned musicians and posed for publicity stills. And when each day was over they could have had romantic dinners together, then gone to their room where they could close the drapes, turn out the lights and....

Dusty's jaw tightened. Damn. This was ridiculous. She didn't want anything more to do with him. Did he need her to hit him over the head with a sledgehammer?

Determined not to think about her or anything else, he closed his eyes. For the rest of the flight he slept.

Dusty spent the next seven days in a grueling schedule of auditioning the musicians that VeePee Productions had lined up for him. In between he met with the company's marketing department, posed for publicity stills and talked with the engineer. Finally, on Wednesday, he chose the six men who would be his backup band when the first tracks of the new album were laid. The only thing remaining for Dusty to do before he left for Houston was a personal interview with Vernon Rylander, set for the next morning. Dusty was anxious to meet Rylander, who had been out of town since Dusty arrived in Nashville.

But now he had a free afternoon. He decided to get outside and walk for a while. He needed fresh air after being cooped up for a week.

Nashville fascinated Dusty, although he hadn't had much time to see the sights. But just walking the streets was an experience that was unforgettable. There were an electricity and excitement in Nashville. Everywhere Dusty looked he saw evidence of the city's number-one product: music. Hundreds of hopefuls crowded the streets of the country music capital of the world. In other cities the sight of a young cowboy toting a guitar might cause heads to turn, but in Nashville this sight was common, especially on Division Street, where many of the recording studios were located. Dusty walked for hours, soaking up the atmosphere and stopping to listen to the street-corner musicians.

The next morning, Dusty entered Vernon Rylander's office at exactly nine o'clock. A pretty blonde sat behind a glass-topped mahogany desk. She smiled at him expectantly.

He smiled back. "I'm Dusty Mitchell. I have an appointment with Mr. Rylander."

"Oh, of course, Mr. Mitchell." She pressed a button on an intercom system and said, "Dusty Mitchell's here, Mr. Rylander."

Dusty heard Rylander's voice boom through the box. "Send him on in, Lisa."

Sunlight flooded the enormous corner office, which was dominated by a massive walnut desk. Dusty's boot heels made no sound as they sank into the thick blue carpeting. Gold and platinum disks interspersed with framed photographs of country music legends were mounted on the two windowless walls. In the opposite corner to the desk were two paisley printed sofas with a coffee table in between. As Dusty approached the desk, a tall man stood up. His rounded stomach protruded over his silver belt buckle, and his thick gray hair curled over his Western-cut coat collar.

Sharp, dark eyes gleamed from under craggy brows. His face was rounded like his belly, and he exuded friendliness as he said jovially, "I sure have been lookin' forward to meetin' you, Dusty, boy. Welcome to VeePee Productions, home of the stars."

They shook hands, and Dusty sat in one of the two chairs placed in front of the desk.

"How'd things go the past week, son?" Rylander asked, picking up some papers from his desk. He held them up. "I see here where you've picked out your backup band. Made some good choices, too."

"Thanks. Your people had great guys lined up for me to listen to. It was hard to make a decision in some of the cases, especially since I knew some of the guys and didn't know others."

"I see where you decided to go with keyboard, rhythm guitar, bass, drums, fiddle and pedal lead steel guitar."

"That's how it ended up."

"Good decision, son. Good decision. It's you they're gonna want to see and hear, not a lot of sound. But there're a couple of things we think you should do to make your music more commercial. Did you talk to Billy about stacking your tracks on 'Close Your Eyes' and 'Dance with Me, Darlin''?''

Dusty nodded. Billy Struthers was the engineer.

"Do you agree with Billy?"

"I guess so," Dusty said. "At first I didn't see why he was suggesting it, but we experimented with those two songs for a while, and I'm willing to try it."

"It'll be a different sound for you, different from backup vocals, but trust me, son, you're gonna like it."

Dusty still felt funny about the idea of stacking his voice to make it appear as if several people were singing at the same time, but he knew Rylander and Struthers knew their business. Even though Dusty had spent years singing gigs in his bar and other clubs around the Houston area, the album he'd had produced locally with help from Chester Lansky had been his first attempt to record, and he hadn't tried anything different. He smiled, thinking of his probably naive wish to remain pure.

Rylander put down the papers he'd been holding and leaned back in his swivel chair. "Those women out there are gonna go nuts over you. Why, with your talent and your looks, I predict you're gonna be a big star."

Pleasure spiraled through Dusty. "I hope you're right, Mr. Rylander."

"Call me Vern!" Rylander boomed. "We're gonna be friends as well as business partners, boy. Get used to it."

Dusty grinned. "Okay, Vern. You're the boss."

With an answering grin, Rylander sat forward again. He shuffled through the papers. "Did you look over your contract?"

"Yes, sir."

"Any problems with it?"

Dusty hesitated. "No, not really."

Rylander looked up. His sharp eyes narrowed. "You don't sound real sure."

"I'm disappointed in the advance."

"I know the advance isn't big," Rylander said, "but we're going to spend most of our budget for this album on promotion and tour support. Plus, as I'm sure you read in the contract, we've lined up one of the best road managers in the business for your promotional tour."

"I thought Dick Girard was good. I remember reading where he was Jay Dalton's road manager on his last tour. I figured if he used him, he must be good." It pleased Dusty that Rylander thought enough of him to book Girard. "You haven't scheduled the tour yet, have you?"

"We're workin' on it. It'll be in the fall sometime. Right now we're tryin' to nail down dates on halls." Rylander took a handkerchief out of his pocket and blew his nose noisily. "Damn sinuses drive me crazy," he said as he stuffed the handkerchief back. "Did Billy tell you we'd blocked out forty hours at Muscle Shoals?"

The pleasure that Dusty had felt when he'd first heard about the opportunity to work in one of the most famous recording studios flooded him once again. The grin that had been plastered on his face so often this past week spread once more. "Yeah," he said.

"I can see by your smile that you're not unhappy about that," Rylander said. "Anyway, son, I'm sorry about the advance, but it's standard for a new performer. We believe in putting the money where it'll do you the most good eventually."

Dusty knew Rylander really meant where it would do both of them the most good, but he also knew that was just good business, for him and for Rylander.

"We've also lined up some top-notch session musicians," Rylander said. "Did Billy tell you about them?"

"Yes, he did."

"Any problems with the list?"

"No. They're great, all of them." Session musicians, or hired guns as Dusty thought of them, were hired to overdub as they listened to tapes that had been recorded earlier. By using session musicians, a studio could save a lot of money. They weren't paid to sit and wait while others were recording. Dusty knew he was lucky to have them, lucky that Rylander and his people were willing to spend the money to get these skilled professionals.

They talked for about an hour more, going over all aspects of Dusty's contract and the taping of the tracks for the album. Rylander explained their distribution system, and Dusty thought how different it sounded from the way he'd paid people in cases of beer to handle his album for him.

As they wound up their discussion, Rylander said he wanted Dusty to write at least two new songs.

"I've listened to all the stuff you've sent me, and I really like eight of the songs. But we're gonna need two more. One more two-step, and a nice love song. That'll give us just the right balance. Think you can do it?"

"I'm sure I can. I've got three weeks, haven't I?"

"Yep." He stood up. "Pleasure meetin' you, son. This is just the beginning of a very profitable relationship. I feel it in my bones."

Dusty stood, too. "My plane leaves at one o'clock, so I guess I'd better get going." He stuck out his hand once more. "I want to thank you for taking a chance on me, Vern. I know you're sticking your neck out. I appreciate your faith in me."

"Hell, boy, wasn't much of a chance, not with Sissy backing—" He stopped, and his face flushed red.

Dusty stared at him. *Sissy backing?* What did he mean? Was he talking about Sissy Farraday?

"Shee-it. Me and my big mouth," Rylander said. He pulled his crumpled handkerchief from his right pants pocket and mopped at his brow. "Listen, son, it don't matter, you know. Just because Sissy Farraday asked me to take you on and guaranteed me against any loss don't matter a hill o' beans, 'cause I like your stuff. I'd have never taken you on if I hadn't. I have my reputation to think of. Remember what I said? VeePee Productions is the home of the stars, and Vernon P. Rylander don't sign up losers.''

Dusty felt as if someone had kicked him in the stomach. In a daze, he said goodbye to Rylander, went to his hotel, packed his stuff and got himself to the airport, where he boarded the 727 that would carry him home.

His mind spun with his new knowledge. Sissy Farraday had arranged for his contract. He'd been so elated, so cocky, thinking he'd done this all by himself, and all the time, he'd been indebted to Sissy Farraday, Victoria's best friend.

Of course Victoria had known about it, too. Maybe it had even been her idea.

He couldn't believe it. He felt like ten kinds of a fool. How many times had he spouted off about doing this on his own? She must have been laughing at him for being so naive. And she'd had the nerve to accuse him of lying. What did she call this? Telling the truth?

Jaw clenched and eyes narrowed, he stared out the window at the landscape far below. Tonight, as soon as he got home, he'd go straight over to her house. She might not want to hear his explanation of why he'd hidden his ownership of the bar, but he sure as hell wanted to hear why she lied to him a second time!

Victoria couldn't wait for her last class to let out. She'd thought last week was bad, but this week had been worse. Julie had gone on a week-long trip to Washington, D.C. with her class. They'd left Saturday afternoon and wouldn't be back until this coming Sunday night.

After Julie left, Victoria knew she would go crazy if she had to stay in the house all weekend long. So she called Sissy.

"Oh, Tory, I'm sorry," Sissy said. "But I'm just on my way out the door. I've got a meeting of my club this afternoon, and tonight I've got a date."

"Oh? Who is it this time?" Victoria couldn't help feeling a twinge of jealousy.

"Oh, nobody that great. Just Burnett Mason. We were both invited to a dinner party, so in a weak moment, I told him I'd go with him. Now I'm half sorry. I'll probably spend the entire evening fighting him off."

Victoria chuckled in spite of herself. Sissy had regaled her with tales of Burnett Mason before. "So why'd you say you'd go with him?"

"Who knows? A momentary aberration. Or maybe it's hormones." She giggled.

"You're too old for a hormone attack," Victoria said.

"Honey, you're never too old for hormone attacks. If you are, you're dead!"

Victoria laughed. Sissy could always make her laugh. "Well, how about tomorrow? Why don't we go somewhere nice for brunch, then take in a movie or something?"

"Uh, I can't, Tory. I've got plans...oh, phooey, I might as well tell you. I'm driving out to the Mitchell ranch in the morning."

"You're what?" Astonishment caused Victoria's voice to rise.

"I promised David Mitchell I'd come out to meet him and look at his work. That's all."

"Oh."

"Well, damn it, Tory. You don't have to say it that way. After all, you're the one who told me to call him. It's not like I'm abandoning you or anything!" Sissy said indignantly.

"No...I know...it's just that..." Victoria knew it was silly to feel betrayed. Sissy was absolutely right. Victoria had asked her to call David Mitchell. But she couldn't help feeling as if her best friend had deserted her and gone into the enemy camp.

"Just because you're furious with Dusty doesn't mean you're furious with David, does it?"

"No, of course not, but—"

"Look, I haven't got time to talk now. I'm going to be late if I don't hurry, but I'll call you Monday. Or better yet, why don't you call me when you get home from school? I'll tell you all about it then."

Victoria had to be content with that, but all day Sunday her mind kept drifting to thoughts of the ranch. And that, of course, led inevitably to thoughts of Dusty and the wonderful day they'd spent there.

Sunday dragged by, even though Victoria decided to treat herself to a Beethoven concert at Jones Hall that afternoon. But even Beethoven's Ninth with accompaniment by the Houston Symphony Chorus couldn't keep her thoughts from straying to Dusty. During the triumphant finale when the chorus sang "Ode to Joy" and brought down the house, Victoria was filled with an aching sadness. A moment like this should be shared with someone she loved. Someone who loved her.

Finally Monday came. Victoria called Sissy, and they talked, and Victoria felt better. Sissy said she loved David Mitchell's work and had promised to help him.

"And he's such a cutie," she said.

"Is that why you're helping him?"

"No, of course not. He's very talented. But finding him a place to live won't be easy. He has special needs in an apartment. He needs a place that he can get in and out of easily. Plus, he needs special equipment in the bathroom—extra-wide doorways, ramps, things like that. I had no idea it was so hard for wheelchair-bound people to find accessible places to live, not to mention work."

Victoria knew Sissy had found a new cause to champion, and she couldn't hold any grudges. Actually, she was happy for David and hoped Sissy would be able to work something out for him. He needed to be on his own, if only to prove to himself that he could do it. And if Dusty didn't like it, tough.

They ended their conversation with Sissy inviting Victoria to come to her house straight after work on Thursday. "We'll have a luscious dinner... you know what a wonderful cook Anna is...and we'll lie around in the hot tub...and we'll watch *Casablanca* on my VCR...and we'll stay up half the night talking. Bring your nightgown. We'll have an old-fashioned pajama party."

All day Thursday she'd been impatient for the day to end. First the morning dragged by, then she had her four-hour stint at the *Herald*. Finally, she thought, as she finished her last review. Less than an hour later she pulled into Sissy's driveway.

It was past six o'clock before Dusty reached his apartment, and he was hot and tired. He hated driving in rush-hour traffic and usually avoided it at all costs. The heavy traffic was bad enough, but it seemed as if for the past five years, every freeway in Houston had been under construction of some kind. No matter where he tried to go he'd run into street crews and closed lanes and concrete barriers. It was enough to make him wish he'd stayed out on the ranch.

He decided to take a quick shower before calling Victoria, because he intended to go over there if he found her home. Thirty minutes later, feeling much better, he picked up the phone. When her number rang ten times with no answer, he shrugged. He'd try later. Maybe he'd go over to the club for a while, talk to Spence, then try to reach her later.

"Tory, did you ever think that maybe you were being just a little bit unfair to Dusty?" Sissy was sitting cross-legged on the love seat in her upstairs sitting room, a glass of iced tea in her hands.

Victoria didn't answer immediately. The question was one she'd asked herself many times over the past week, and each

CINDERELLA GIRL   141

time she'd come up with the same answer. She sighed. "I
don't know. Sometimes I think I was too hard on him, but
then I think, well, if he really cared so much, wouldn't he
have called me?"

Sissy shrugged. "I don't think so. Men put a lot of stock
in their pride, you know. He probably feels you owe him an
apology, that you should call him."

Now Victoria shrugged. "Well, maybe. But it really
doesn't matter whether he calls or not. I don't care one way
or the other." She deliberately made her voice flippant.

Sissy grinned, a knowing glint in her blue eyes. "That's
the right attitude. Who gives a damn?"

"You don't have to say it like that. I *don't* care!" Victoria picked up her iced tea and took a long swallow, avoiding Sissy's eyes.

"Come on, kiddo. This is your very best friend you're
talking to. The same friend who's known you since you were
only three feet high. The same friend who's seen you
through every crisis in your life. The same friend who knows
you like she knows the back of her hand." Sissy's grin had
faded, and now her eyes were earnest and caring. "You
don't have to put on a happy face for me."

Victoria blinked. "Damn you, Sissy. I don't want understanding and sympathy. What I need right now is distrac-
tion and fun!"

Sissy smiled, but it was a sweet smile. "No, you don't.
You need understanding and sympathy."

Victoria closed her eyes and leaned her head back.
"What's wrong with me?" she said dejectedly. "For days
I've been telling myself to forget about him, and he's all I
think about!"

"I know."

"What should I do?" Victoria wailed.

"Do you want the truth?"

"I wouldn't ask if I didn't."

"I think you should call him up and tell him you didn't
mean what you said. I think you should give him another

chance." She wagged her finger. "Believe me, kiddo, men like Dusty Mitchell don't grow on trees."

Victoria considered Sissy's advice. Lord knows, that's what she wanted to do. The thing she couldn't decide was whether that was a really smart thing to do. After all, there was still the matter of his blossoming career, all the traveling he'd be doing, their completely different life-styles. Did she want to become more involved with him, maybe past the point of no return? Could she stand being a musician's widow? Staying home while he gallivanted all over the country? Was that the kind of life she wanted?

"I just don't know, Sissy," she finally said. "Maybe I should leave well enough alone. This is probably for the best."

"Sure," Sissy said. "That's why you're so miserable."

"It'll pass," Victoria said. "Everything does." She sighed. "Now where's that old movie you promised me?"

At eight-thirty Dusty went to his office and called Victoria's number again. Twelve rings. No answer. He shrugged and decided to pay some bills, try to get things in order so that when he and Spence signed the papers for the sale of Mitchell's next week, everything would be ready.

At ten o'clock he stretched, then tried her number again. Still no answer. He frowned in frustration. Where the hell was she? It was a weeknight. She had to get up early to be at school tomorrow. She should be home.

Maybe she was out with someone else.

Jealousy knifed through him, stabbing right into his gut. Even the thought of someone else holding her close, touching her, was enough to twist his insides.

He slammed a ledger shut and hurriedly cleared the desk. He couldn't sit there another minute.

As Ingrid Bergman walked through the fog toward the waiting airplane, Sissy sighed and said, "You know, David Mitchell is really sexy."

"What?" Victoria was still lost in the final heartrending scene of *Casablanca* and had a hard time focusing on Sissy's comment.

"I *said*, David Mitchell is really sexy!" Sissy's eyes flickered like blue flames.

A sense of unease gripped Victoria. "That's an odd thing to say," she replied carefully.

"Why?" Sissy's question seemed deliberately casual.

"I've never heard you call any man *sexy* unless you were sexually attracted to him."

Sissy smiled. "Very astute, Jones. It's not true what they say about you. You really *are* smart."

Victoria threw a pillow at her. Then, after dodging the pillow's swift return, she said, "Quit trying to distract me. Are you saying that you're interested in David Mitchell? *That* way?"

Sissy's small shoulders lifted in a casual shrug. "Maybe. Maybe not. He's terribly attractive."

Sissy had finally found a subject that drove all thoughts of Dusty from Victoria's mind.

"Why are you looking at me like that?" Sissy demanded. "What's wrong with me finding him attractive? Actually, he makes my toes tingle." She grinned sheepishly. "And that's a sure sign."

"Of what?" But Victoria was afraid she already knew.

"Come on, Tory. Don't play dumb. He turns me on." She lifted her chin defiantly. "Okay, if you want me to spell it out. I'd like him to take me to bed."

"That's what I was afraid of," Victoria said.

"For heaven's sake!" Sissy said, jumping up. "There's nothing wrong with that. What's wrong with that?"

"Sissy," Victoria said patiently. "Under normal circumstances, nothing. But David Mitchell's not normal."

"So?"

"So he's very vulnerable."

"What do you think I'm going to do to him? Have my way with him, then dump him? Is that what you think?" Sissy said.

"Of course not." Victoria was sorry she'd said anything, but it was too late now.

"Well, what did you mean?" Two bright spots of color had appeared on Sissy's cheeks.

"I...I just meant that he's lived a very sheltered life. He's been paralyzed since he was eighteen years old, and he could be hurt very easily."

Sissy plopped down on the couch. "I know that, Tory. I'm not stupid or insensitive."

"I didn't say you were. It's just that I wasn't sure you'd think about things like that. You do have a tendency to jump into situations, Sissy, and you know it. Jump first. Think later. That's always been your style." Victoria smiled to soften her words. "It's what has always attracted me to you, you know. You're so different from me. I have to weigh everything, think about everything from every angle. I'm not spontaneous, and I've always envied that quality in you."

"Now you're trying to butter me up."

The words had no sting, and Victoria relaxed slightly. "Every word I just said is true. But because you're like that, impulsive and generous and eager for new experiences...I worry. Especially when someone like David might misunderstand your interest. He's been hurt a lot already."

Sissy put her hands behind her head and stretched. "Tory, for someone as smart as you are, you amaze me sometimes. I know all that. I have no intention of hurting him. Actually, if you were really using your head, you'd know that in his situation it would probably do him a world of good to know that somebody like me found him attractive. He's probably had a lot of doubts about his sexuality, wouldn't you think?"

Maybe Sissy was right. Victoria knew she herself was no expert when it came to sex or how men felt about it.

"You know what your trouble is?" Sissy continued, ignoring Victoria's silence. "You think everything should be perfect, follow certain rules, go according to some kind of plan. And life isn't like that. I learned a long time ago that you've got to grab what you can while you have the chance, because if you don't, it'll pass you by. I think sometimes you just have to rely on your instincts and forget logic." She leaned forward, her voice intense. "If you'd quit analyzing everything to death and just follow your feelings, you'd be a lot happier."

At midnight Dusty said good-night to Spence. Fifteen minutes later he turned the Bronco onto Victoria's tree-lined street. The truck moved slowly through silvery patches of moonlight. Most of the houses were dark. Victoria's was no exception. Only the outside lamp mounted on one side of her front door was lit.

Unless she'd come home in the last fifteen minutes and was already in bed, there was no one home. Dusty swore, hit his brakes and pulled into her driveway. After a few minutes he clenched his teeth and backed out into the street, this time heading toward home.

"But you won't avoid me forever, Miss Victoria Jones," he said aloud. "And when I do find you, you'd better be ready with some answers."

Chapter Ten

By eleven-thirty Friday morning Victoria's classes were over for the day. As the last stragglers shuffled out of Composition II, she sighed with relief. She was tired. She and Sissy had stayed up until nearly two o'clock the night before, and she was feeling the lack of sleep today. Plus her throat hurt.

Lord, I hope I'm not coming down with a cold, she thought. Well, if she was, she could lie on the beach the entire weekend and let the sun bake it out of her. Bless Sissy for offering the use of her beach house for the weekend. Victoria had protested, but Sissy was adamant.

"It'll do you good to get away for the weekend. What will you do here? Just sit around and feel sorry for yourself. How long has it been since you've had any time alone to relax?"

"Too long," Victoria said, unable to remember the last time.

"So quit arguing with me," Sissy said, grinning.

"Well, all right," Victoria agreed reluctantly. Now she was glad she had. Sissy was right. With Julie gone until Sunday night, Victoria would indeed have moped around all weekend. And it looked as if the weather was going to be wonderful. She rose from her desk and walked to the open windows. Her classroom was on the second floor of the music department's main building. She looked out at the sprawling urban campus. She could see the top of the Houston skyline over the glossy, dark leaves of the huge camphor tree growing next to the building. Students dressed in bright spring and summer clothes sat in its shade. In the distance other groups walked on the sidewalks or gathered on the lawns.

Suddenly her heart lurched as a tall man rounded the corner of her building and walked purposefully toward the front door. For a moment, she thought the man was Dusty. Then she shook her head. *Come on, Jones, you've just got him on the brain.* But as soon as the thought crossed her mind, he looked up, and the sun glinted off his dark blond hair.

It *was* Dusty.

Her heart slammed against her chest, and she jumped back from the window. Had he seen her? What was he doing there?

Grabbing her papers and books, she stuffed them into her satchel. He must be looking for her. What other reason could there be for him to be there? Oh, God, she didn't want to see him. She wasn't ready to see him.

After a fast look around to make sure she had all her belongings, she rushed through the open doorway and down the hall toward the steps at the far end. She raced down, and just as she reached the first landing, she saw Dusty place a booted foot on the bottom stair.

She stopped, heart racing like the snare drum she could hear coming from one of the practice rooms nearby.

He started up the steps. She froze. His head was down. He hadn't seen her yet. She could turn and run upstairs, hide in the teacher's lounge or something. But even as the thought formed, she knew running away was ridiculous.

As he rounded the first corner he looked up.

Victoria's breath caught in her throat. His yellow shirt brought out the golden highlights in his hair, and his skin was burnished in the morning sunlight. He filled the stairwell, everything else paling in comparison.

After a moment's hesitation, he took the steps two at a time. The noise from the practice rooms, the laughter and raised voices of the students outside, the last few students brushing by them to make it to their next class: all receded into the background. The two of them could have been on a deserted island instead of standing in the middle of a school building surrounded by hundreds of other people.

"Hello, Victoria." His eyes looked like new leaves in the spring.

"Hello, Dusty." She took a deep breath. It was silly to be so nervous. What could possibly happen? "What are you doing here?" *And why am I so scared yet happy to see you?*

"I called you from six o'clock on last night, and you weren't home. I want to talk to you. I figured coming here was the only way to be sure I didn't miss you again today." He didn't smile.

"I'm not sure there's anything left to talk about." She gripped her satchel tighter. She was having difficulty breathing as his eyes studied her intently. She was sure he could hear her heart pounding. She was sure he knew exactly how her body was reacting to his nearness. *Oh, you're a fool, Victoria Jones.*

He acted as if he hadn't heard her. "Where were you last night?" Frown lines formed a V on his forehead.

Victoria stiffened. "I don't think it's any of your business where I was last night." *Do you think you can just walk back into my life after ignoring me for nearly two weeks and demand to know how I'm spending my time?*

His jaw hardened, and his eyes glinted angrily. He reached out and grasped her shoulder. "We *are* going to talk, whether you want to or not. There are a few things we've got to settle between us.''

"I think we said it all that night at your club."

His hand tightened. "Maybe you think so, but I don't. Not since I found out you and your friend have been playing games again.''

Victoria yanked her shoulder from his grasp. The look in his eyes made her furious. Here she'd been miserable for days, and instead of apologizing for deceiving her and not calling her, he was talking in riddles. "I don't have any idea what you're talking about, and I'll thank you to keep your hands off me!''

Dusty wanted to shake her. Her eyes sparked with angry fire, and her cheeks were flushed. Wisps of hair had escaped the bow at her nape and curled fetchingly around her face. Her full lips quivered in outrage, and her chest heaved as she stood facing him. For a moment he was tempted to smile. She had a temper under that cool exterior. She looked so beautiful he almost forgot how angry he was. He felt like kissing her right there, kissing her until she begged for mercy. Kissing her until she melted and kissed him back. Hot desire coursed through him as his imagination went beyond kissing and he had a sudden vivid image of the two of them intertwined, naked bodies glistening with sweat and sated passion.

As the thought surged through him, the look in her eyes changed. An awareness of what he was feeling and thinking seemed to communicate itself to her, and her eyes flickered in uncertainty, then softened. As he watched, she slowly wet her lips. A rush of longing so intense it was painful gripped Dusty, and he nearly winced. What was it about this woman that caused him to want her so much? Was Spence right? Did his desire have to do with the fact that she always seemed to resist him?

He reached out and touched her cheek, mesmerized by the look in her eyes. She swayed toward him, then abruptly jerked back, her eyes fastened on something behind him.

He turned. Coming up the steps was a tall, thin man. Dusty moved aside to let the man pass, but he stopped and said, "Hello, Victoria."

If she was flustered by the interruption, she hid it well. "Hello, John," she said quietly.

"I don't believe we've met," the man said, turning toward Dusty. "I'm John Webberly, dean of the music school."

His pale eyes were on a level with Dusty's, and as Dusty extended his right hand, saying, "Dusty Mitchell," he knew without being told that John Webberly was a man who wanted Victoria. *But you'll never get her.* Every instinct he possessed told him to put his arm around Victoria, to draw the lines of battle clearly.

Webberly's grip was surprisingly firm, although his hand was cold. So were his eyes, and Dusty knew John Webberly had also recognized a rival. "Are you a student here?" he asked.

Dusty smiled. "No. I'm a friend of Victoria's."

"I see." Webberly turned to Victoria. "Are you on your way home?"

"Actually I came by to take Victoria to lunch," Dusty said smoothly, ignoring the startled look in her eyes. "Nice meeting you." Turning to Victoria, he said, "Here, let me carry that." He took the satchel from her unresisting grip, put his arm around her shoulders as he'd wanted to do and firmly led her down the stairs.

When they reached the bottom level, she shook off his arm. "I've no intention of going to lunch with you."

"Let's talk outside," he said. As they emerged into the warm spring day, he made a sudden resolution. He would handle this as he'd handled every other problem in his life. The encounter with Webberly had crystallized everything in his mind. "Where's your car parked?" he asked.

"In the faculty lot behind the building."

"Mine's over there, in the visitor's lot. Let's take mine."

"Dusty—"

"What's the matter? Are you afraid to be alone with me?"

She flushed, and he knew his shot had hit home, just as he'd intended.

"Of course not!" she said, indignation practically oozing from her.

Her cheeks were flushed a bright pink, and small beads of moisture dotted her nose. Dusty had an insane urge to lick them up one by one. "Prove it then," he said instead. "Let me take you to lunch." He smiled.

His crooked smile was her undoing. She just didn't feel like fighting anymore—her feelings or him. It would be so wonderful to just give in, climb in his truck, go to lunch with him, let him make all the decisions. She was tired, tired of being sensible, tired of being strong. Tired of being alone.

"Come on," he said. "I won't bite you. All I want is to take you someplace nice and quiet for lunch, someplace we can talk. I promise I'll bring you straight back here and get your car when we're finished."

Sissy's advice echoed in her head. *Sometimes you have to just follow your feelings.* "All right," she said.

Victoria hadn't been to Brennan's in years. She had forgotten how pretty the downtown restaurant was. The maître d' seated them at a window table overlooking the flower-filled patio, and as he went off to fill their beverage order, she sighed and said, "It's nice here."

"Yes," Dusty agreed. "It's one of my favorite places. Have you ever been to Brennan's in the French Quarter?"

"No." She knew he was making small talk in a deliberate attempt to relax her and she was grateful for his consideration.

"I'll take you there sometime." A smile curved his mouth; his eyes were brilliant even in the bright room.

Victoria's heart skipped a beat. He was acting as if everything was all right between them. She'd thought he was angry with her when he came to the school. Now he seemed to have forgotten whatever it was that had angered him. All she saw was admiration and...desire...in his eyes. She swallowed. She felt shaky, fragile, as if she might fall to pieces right here in front of all these strangers if Dusty kept looking at her like that.

The waiter returned, setting glasses of iced tea on the table. "Have you decided yet?" he asked politely.

Victoria tried to get her runaway emotions under control as Dusty gave the waiter their orders. When the waiter had gone, Dusty leaned forward in his chair and folded his arms on the table. His face had settled into serious lines.

"I was furious with you yesterday," he said.

Victoria's heart leaped, but she didn't say anything.

"Aren't you curious as to why?" When all she did was nod slowly, he continued. "I was in Nashville this past week."

She frowned and reached for a packet of sweetener to add to her tea. "I don't understand." What was he talking about?

"Don't you?"

"No." Victoria stirred her tea.

"I had a long talk with Vernon Rylander, the head of VeePee Productions. He explained how I happened to be offered a contract with them."

Victoria's head jerked up. Dusty's eyes were hard and bright. She swallowed. "Dusty—"

"I know you were behind Sissy's manipulations."

"Yes, but—"

"Let me finish," he said. "When Rylander first let the information slip, I wanted to kill the both of you."

Oh, God, she'd been afraid of this.

"But I'm not mad anymore."

"You're not?" Surprise caused her voice to squeak.

"Don't sound so amazed. After I got over my gut reaction, I started to think about it. I realized it was silly to let it upset me that much. I thought about it all night, and I think I understand your motives. You were trying to make up for your review, weren't you?''

Victoria nodded. Relief flooded through her, because she could see he really wasn't angry anymore. ''Vernon Rylander wouldn't have signed you up if he didn't think you were good. The only thing Sissy did was use her friendship with him to get him to listen to your tapes.''

Dusty smiled, the lopsided smile that meant he was amused but not taken in. A tendril of uneasiness twisted through Victoria. ''Come on, darlin','' he said softly. ''Don't try to con me. I think it's time we were one hundred percent honest with each other, don't you?''

Victoria didn't answer until the waiter had served their turtle soup, the pause giving her time to think. ''Yes, you're right, we should be honest with each other. But I wasn't trying to con you. What makes you think I was?''

''Because Sissy also told Rylander she'd cover his losses if he took me on and I failed, didn't she?''

Victoria, who had raised a spoonful of turtle soup to her mouth, put the spoonful down untasted. ''She didn't tell me that.'' Had Sissy really done that?

''Didn't she?'' His eyes captured hers. All around them were the quiet sounds of dining in the elegant restaurant: silver clinking, muted voices and laughter. But for the second time that day, the two of them could have been isolated from all humanity. All Victoria's awareness was centered on Dusty.

''No.''

For a long moment, he held her gaze, then finally, he said, ''I believe you.''

Victoria felt as if the sun had suddenly appeared in a gray, gloomy day. She felt as if a ton of weight had been lifted from her shoulders. ''I'm glad.''

''It still bothers me that my big opportunity came because someone else arranged it for me, but this morning it dawned on me that what happens next is solely up to me. If I'm good, I'll be a success, and no one else can take credit for that. If I'm bad, I'll fail, and I won't be able to blame anyone for that, either."

"That's right," she agreed. Thank goodness he was taking this attitude. Even though she had pretended otherwise, she had really been worried about his reaction if he ever found out about Sissy's intervention on his behalf.

"So," he continued, "now that we've straightened that out, have you finally forgiven me for hiding my ownership of the bar from you?"

She nodded. "Yes."

"What about the rest?"

"The rest?"

His eyes pinned hers. "Victoria, let's not pretend, okay? You know what I'm talking about. Do you still think I was lying to you when I told you how I felt about you? What I wanted our relationship to be?"

His low voice rumbled through her. She shook her head, unable to put her answer into words. Dusty slowly reached across the table and stroked the back of her left hand. Her eyes darted to his as a current of desire jolted her. She caught her breath sharply at what she saw reflected in their depths.

Just then the waiter came to remove their soup plates, and Victoria tried to get her turbulent emotions under control. To cover her confusion, she took a long swallow of tea then looked out the window. A squirrel raced across the brick patio, then scampered up the twisted branches of an oak tree growing in one corner. Sunlight danced over the water in the fountain at the center of the patio.

"Victoria . . ."

Slowly she turned to face him. His eyes were full of tenderness and promise. A sweet urgency tugged at her.

The waiter returned with two plates of Crawfish Kacal. As he set the steaming plates in front of them, he said, "Is there anything else I can get for you?"

"No, thank you. Everything's fine," Dusty murmured, but he didn't look at the waiter. He kept looking at her, and

Victoria was powerless to look away. "Isn't it?" he said as the waiter left.

"I . . . I don't know. Is it?" she said nervously.

Dusty smiled. "I think it is." Once more he reached across the table, covering her hand with his. He squeezed gently. "Now eat your food before it gets cold. We have plenty of time to talk about this later."

Victoria tried, but even the delicious dish couldn't make her forget that Dusty was across the table from her, couldn't wipe away the remembrance of the look in his eyes or the sound of his voice, couldn't banish the jittery anticipation in the pit of her stomach. Finally she gave up and laid her fork down with more than half her lunch left.

"What's the matter? Don't you like it?" Dusty asked as he polished off the last bite of angel-hair pasta and craw-fish.

"It's not that." She watched as he wiped his mouth with his napkin. Something twisted deep inside her.

He stared at her, then laid his napkin down and turned to look for their waiter. Spying him, he lifted his arm in a signal. They didn't talk as they waited for the check. Victoria tried to calm herself by taking deeper breaths and by avoiding his eyes. After what seemed like hours, Dusty signed the charge slip, and they stood up to leave.

As they emerged into the sunny afternoon, Dusty slipped his arm around her, and they walked toward his truck. The Bronco was parked halfway down the block, under the shade of a dogwood tree. The traffic on Smith Street whizzed by, but this side street was quiet. When they reached the truck, he slowly turned her to face him, keeping his arm around her. Victoria's heart pumped wildly as she looked up to meet his glowing eyes. The sun filtering through the leaves of the tree overhead cast a pattern of light and shadow over his strong, square face.

"I've been wanting to kiss you for hours," he said.

Her heart felt as if it were running an obstacle course. Her knees turned to rubber as his head dipped and his warm mouth slanted across hers. Hot desire churned deep within her, and her mouth opened under his. As his tongue delved and his hands slid over her back, she pressed closer. An ache throbbed deep within, an ache that grew stronger and more insistent as his kiss became more demanding and his hands traveled down slowly.

A car horn honked, and someone yelled, "All right!"

Victoria jumped back. She knew her face was flaming. How could she have forgotten she was in the middle of a public street? What was wrong with her, that all this man had to do was touch her, and she forgot everything but him? That she let him do things she knew she shouldn't?

She didn't look at him as he opened the door for her. She fastened her seat belt and stared out her window as he pulled away from the curb and headed toward the university.

When she couldn't stand it anymore, she sneaked a look at him out of the corner of her eye. He grinned, turning toward her, his eyes full of amusement. "Were you embarrassed back there?"

She could feel her cheeks warming again. "You know I was."

"I'm sorry. I didn't mean to embarrass you."

"It's okay," she mumbled. God, why couldn't she be cool and sophisticated? Why did he make her feel as if she were falling apart? Why was it that even now she wanted him to kiss her again, touch her again? How could she be rational, reasonable, about their relationship if her body was so greedy? *So needy, Jones. Needy. That's the word. Eleven years of no sex will do that to a woman.* But even as she tried to tell herself that her reaction was a normal one for a woman who had denied herself for so long, she knew that wasn't exactly true. There had been other men, other opportunities, and she'd never been interested. No, Dusty Mitchell was special, and no amount of lying to herself would change that fact. So she'd better face it and decide what she intended to do about it. And soon.

When they reached the school, Dusty pulled into the faculty parking lot and stopped the Bronco behind her car. He came around to open her door and reached for her hand. As she stepped down, he held onto her hand. "When am I going to see you again?" he asked softly.

"I don't know," she said.

"How about tonight?" His thumb rubbed the back of her hand as he held it. They were hidden from view of the building by the truck.

She raised her eyes. Small beads of sweat had formed on his upper lip. She had an urge to touch one with the tip of her finger, to taste it with her tongue. She tried to slow her breathing, but excitement danced inside her. "I...I can't tonight."

"Why not?"

Now his other hand moved to her neck, and his fingers with their hard calluses trailed up and under her hair, causing her to shiver, then hold her breath as a torrent of desire flooded her body. Her words tumbled out in a rush. "I'm not going to be here this weekend. I'm...I'm going down to Pirate's Beach." She tried to ignore his hand as it caressed her neck, tried to ignore the message her body was sending as his fingers stroked her.

"Where are you going to be staying?" He released her hand, snaking his around her waist, drawing her close. His mouth nuzzled against the corner of her lips, and she could smell his unique scent—a combination of sun, after-shave and male musk. The need and desire that had been so close to the surface of her skin ever since she'd seen him this morning rippled over her.

Victoria could hardly breathe, but some measure of sanity was still left, although it took all her strength and willpower to say, "Dusty, stop. We're in the middle of the faculty parking lot."

"No one can see us," he murmured against her mouth, all heat and moisture and temptation.

Before she came totally unglued, Victoria put her hands against his chest and said, "Dusty. I'm serious. Quit that. Right now. I have a reputation to think of."

He had a sheepish look on his face, but his eyes still held a devilish glint as he backed up a step. "I'm sorry. Of course, you're right. But—"

"Never mind. You don't have to explain." It was bad enough to feel this way about him; she didn't want to talk about it—not here. Not now.

"I just wanted to say that I realize this isn't the time or place."

"That's right." She took a shaky breath. "Now would you mind getting my bag out of your truck?" She had to get away from him. Even now, even here, she wanted to throw herself into his arms. She wanted him to kiss her again, to touch her again. Her breasts were still tight buds of desire, and she wondered if Dusty could see that—could see what he'd done to her. She turned toward the truck.

He hesitated for a moment, then opened the back. After he'd transferred her satchel to her station wagon, he said, "You never answered my question."

Victoria didn't pretend not to know what question he was referring to. "I'm going down to Sissy's beach house for the weekend."

"Oh. Well, that's nice for you and Julie."

She heard the disappointment in his voice, and she suppressed the guilty twinge she felt at allowing him to believe Julie was accompanying her, but she couldn't let him know she was planning to go alone. She didn't know if she had the strength to say no if he asked to go, too. "Yes," she said. "I'm looking forward to a weekend of lying in the sun and relaxing."

"I'd like to go with you."

"That's not a good idea, Dusty."

He opened the car door for her, and she slid inside. The inside of the car felt like a sauna. The car had been sitting in the sun all day long.

He held the door open and leaned on top of it. "Why isn't it a good idea?"

Victoria's gaze lifted. He looked like a bronzed giant against the clear blue sky. She knew what he wanted her to say. She also knew that if she did, it would mean she'd made a decision about him and about their relationship. Time seemed to stand still. She could almost hear her heart beating. "It's not a good idea because I need this time away from you to think."

"What's there to think about? I thought we'd straightened everything out."

"I need to decide how I feel about us, about our relationship."

"Decide? Don't you know yet?"

"No, I don't. I'm confused, and I don't like the feeling."

"You sure didn't act confused when I kissed you. You acted as if you wanted me as much as I want you."

Victoria's heart thudded at the look in his eyes, at the slow, sexy smile that curved his lips.

"See?" he said. "I can see it on your face. You *do* want me. Why are you fighting it so hard?"

"Look, Dusty, this isn't the place to talk about this. Please. Just bear with me, okay? I have to get away. I have to think about you. About my feelings for you. Please don't push me. I promise I'll give you an answer on Sunday night when I get back."

He stared at her for a long moment. His jaw tightened. "I guess I have no choice, do I?"

Victoria shook her head. "No."

"Will you be sure to call me Sunday night when you get back?"

"Yes."

"I guess I'll have to be content with that."

He didn't like her decision. She could see that. But he wasn't going to fight her, which was good, because she wasn't sure she could have stood up to him.

His eyes glittered in the bright sunlight; suddenly, before she could react or resist, he leaned into the car and grasped her head between his large hands and kissed her—hard. Victoria's senses reeled as his hands held her fast and his mouth claimed hers, searing her with its heat.

After what seemed an eternity, he slowly drew back, but his hands still held her head still as he gazed deep into her eyes. "That was something to remember me by," he growled softly.

As if she needed anything, she thought, heart hammering.

He released her, stood up and backed off. He put his hands on his hips, and his long legs were planted apart as he stood there. He looked . . . magnificent.

As Victoria drove off, she watched him in her rearview mirror. Even when he was no longer in sight, she pictured him standing there, waiting.

She almost turned back. She knew Sissy would have. But she didn't. She'd use this weekend to think, to weigh all factors, then she'd make her decision the way she made all her decisions: sensibly, rationally, logically. She would not let her emotions, those untrustworthy feelings, rule her life.

Not ever again.

Chapter Eleven

All the way home Dusty thought about Victoria and the look on her face and in her eyes when she'd said she needed time to think. *Damn it, I'm tired of waiting.* Maybe he'd made a big mistake when he'd told her he didn't want just sex from her, that he wanted everything. Maybe he should have taken what he could get and let the rest work itself out. Instead, he'd given her time to think, and now that's all she wanted to do.

Yes, he'd been stupid. If they'd made love that night, the night he'd outsmarted himself, Victoria would be committed to him by now. At the very least, they wouldn't be torturing each other. Why shouldn't they make love? Hell, when a man and a woman wanted each other, a man and woman who were both unattached, both free, what was stopping them? To his way of thinking, nothing was stopping them.

He smacked the steering wheel with the heel of his hand as the knowledge sank in that he'd acted like a wimp. *Sure,*

Victoria. Of course, Victoria. Anything you say, Victoria.
He'd been letting her call the shots all along.

"That's not your style," he said aloud. Hadn't he always
gone after what he wanted? Ever since he'd been a little kid,
he'd been in charge of his life. In fact, he'd been in charge
of his entire family's life. They'd always relied on him. Sure,
Maggie ran the ranch with Luke's help, but in the end, when
there was something important to decide, she always turned
to Dusty. And David, although he'd been a bit rebellious
lately, had always come to Dusty for advice, too. Even his
foolish idea of moving to Houston had been dropped when
Dusty had disapproved.

*I've never sat back and waited for someone else to make
the decisions that affect me, and I'm not going to now.*

He wouldn't force Victoria to do something she didn't
want to do, but he certainly wouldn't let her decide something that might determine the way he lived for the rest of
his life without reminding her of how she felt about him, of
what they felt for each other. Why make this easy for her?
If she decided against him, against *them*, she'd have to do
it straight out, to his face. And if that meant he had to follow her to Galveston and Pirate's Beach, so be it.

Dusk had settled over the city. A medley of orange, scarlet, rose and purple striped the western sky. Cicadas sang
noisily, and birds chattered to one another as they flew from
tree to tree. As Victoria loaded her supplies into the back of
her station wagon, the sun disappeared in fiery splendor. A
perfect evening for lovers, she thought, then banished the
wayward thought.

Thirty minutes later she was on her way, past downtown
Houston and rolling smoothly south along the Gulf Freeway. The flat land rushed with each mile she covered. Trying
to relax, she turned on the radio until she found Houston's
only classical music station, but its weak signal made for too
much static. She kept turning the dial and finally found a
soft rock station with music she thought she could live with.

As the radio played softly in the background, she allowed her thoughts to return to the afternoon. Even now, hours later and alone, her body tightened with wistful longing as she remembered the feel of Dusty's hands against her skin and the turbulent emotions he'd unleashed with his bold caresses and heated kisses.

There was no doubt in her mind that she wanted him. She wanted him to make love to her, even though the thought of lovemaking after so many years of abstinence was scary. That aside, could she forget her values, her plans, and carry on a casual love affair? That was the big question. She was afraid her awakening physical needs and her emotional needs were too closely interwoven. She wouldn't be able to separate them, and she'd end up getting seriously hurt. She knew she couldn't share herself intimately and then casually say goodbye to Dusty.

Of course, if she and Dusty got married... But there were two things wrong with that idea. First of all, Dusty had never indicated he was interested in marriage. Second, hadn't she been telling herself for weeks that Dusty's lifestyle and hers weren't compatible?

What was she going to do? Decide whether you want him badly enough to take a chance on working out your problems, she told herself.

Sighing, she pushed her dilemma out of her mind. She was nearing Galveston and the causeway. She'd better pay attention because she hadn't been to the beach house for a long time, and she didn't want to take the wrong turn. For the next fifteen minutes she concentrated on driving and finding the turnoff for Pirate's Beach. It was easy to find once she'd turned onto Seawall Boulevard, and soon the station wagon was parked in the carport of Sissy's house, and Victoria was unloading her stuff.

The quarter moon shone brightly, and the waters of the Gulf looked inky and mysterious, the breeze whipping up whitecaps. Victoria loved the house—a weathered gray A-frame sitting on pilings that lifted it above the waterline. The

salty air misted her face, and she closed her eyes and
breathed deeply. She relished the smell of the sea and the
sound of the surf. She looked around with pleasure. Lights
twinkled in the windows of several houses down the beach.
She caught a whiff of charcoal. Someone was cooking out
tonight.

After unloading her things, she carried them up the stairs
to the wraparound porch. The house had always enchanted
Victoria. Built before the area had been developed and the
larger, more ostentatious houses had appeared, it was a bit
isolated from its neighbors. It seemed perfect for two people, with a large living area and a small kitchen separated
from the main area by a low bar. The sea side of the house
was all windows that could be shuttered in the event of a
storm. Victoria refrigerated the perishable food she'd
brought along, then carried her duffel bag to the master
bedroom and unpacked.

There was another, smaller bedroom for guests, but the
master bedroom had a view of the Gulf, and Victoria had no
qualms about using it. Furnished simply, it contained a big
brass bed with a large ceiling fan centered over it, a light oak
dresser, wicker bedside tables with lamps and a large wicker
rocker. The floors were natural wood with braided rugs
scattered around.

Victoria opened the windows to let the fresh gulf breeze
in, turned on one of the lamps, then walked into the at-
tached bathroom. The bathroom was sinful, she thought.
Stephen Farraday, Sissy's ex-husband, had spared no ex-
pense on the extravagant bathroom when he'd built the
house. Snapping on the overhead light, she grinned as her
eyes rested on the remembered oval tub that was large
enough to comfortably hold two people. During the day,
sunshine poured through the skylight centered over the tub.
In addition to the huge navy-blue porcelain tub, there were
a shower stall, double sinks with yards of counter space, an
enclosed commode and a long, low, velvet-cushioned window seat. During the summer, when Sissy came almost every

weekend, there would also be dozens of plants sitting on the floor and around the tub. Victoria had always felt like a hothouse rose surrounded by the greenery and basking in the sunshine.

Decadent.

That was the right word to describe the lush surroundings, but she intended to enjoy the decadence while she could. Spying a crystal bottle full of Sissy's bubble bath on the counter, Victoria grinned again. She looked at her watch. Nine o'clock. Why not?

A hot, perfumed bubble bath and a long soak. It sounded wonderful. Then she'd fix herself some of those huge strawberries with fresh whipped cream, and she'd make limeade with the limes she'd brought too. She'd put on a Mozart tape and wrap herself in one of the thick robes Sissy kept on hand for her guests, then she'd go outside and sit in the porch swing in the moonlight and eat and listen to the music and the soothing surf and empty her mind of everything. Suddenly happier than she'd been in weeks, she began to strip off her clothes.

Dusty sang along with George Strait all the way to Galveston. He hadn't had a bit of trouble getting the address of the beach house out of Sissy. In fact, she seemed almost eager to give it to him, and there was a mischievous look in her eyes.

"So she doesn't know you're coming?"

"No. I decided to surprise her and Julie."

Sissy smiled. "Oh, it'll be a surprise, all right."

But she gave him precise directions, and now here he was, almost there. He'd made good time, but even so, it was close to ten o'clock. He'd hoped to arrive earlier, just in case Victoria and Julie had opted for an early bedtime. But surely they wouldn't be in bed already. Not their first night there. Not when they could sleep late tomorrow morning.

He looked at the little map Sissy had drawn, finding the road leading to the section of the beach where she'd said her house was. Sure enough, there it was. Good, there were lights on inside. They were still awake.

Dusty turned onto the unpaved road, then turned again into the drive leading to the house. Victoria's Plymouth wagon was tucked neatly into the carport, and it looked as if there was room for his Bronco, too. He expertly maneuvered the truck into the space next to her car, then turned off the engine. As he got out of the truck, the rushing sound of the surf greeted him. He took his bag out of the back of the truck, then walked around to the stairs. As he put his foot on the bottom rung, he wondered what Victoria would think when she saw him.

Victoria paused with the spoon in midair. Someone was climbing the steps. Setting the whipped-cream-laden spoon on the plate containing her strawberries, she padded silently to the front door and very quietly latched the screen. She wasn't really frightened. It was probably one of Sissy's neighbors. Someone had seen the lights and come to say hello or something, but still . . . it didn't pay to be too trusting.

She was suddenly very glad she hadn't put on one of the terry-cloth robes. Her periwinkle blue sundress might not cover any more than the robe would have—in fact, it covered a lot less, she thought—but at least it gave her the appearance of being fully dressed. When she'd finally emerged from her long, luxurious and completely relaxing bath, she'd felt different than she'd felt in a long time.

In a way, she'd thought, it was too bad she was alone, because the bubbles and the decadent bathroom had made her aware of herself physically. Of course, the kisses she'd exchanged with Dusty earlier in the day had had a hand in her feelings, too, she was sure of that. But there was no denying the fact that she was feeling very feminine, very sexy. Well, why not? she thought. Why not indulge herself? So she gave in to the urge and pretended she was dressing for her lover who was waiting for her outside in the velvety darkness of the porch.

Slowly, she slipped on a pair of lacy panties, then slid the soft cotton dress over her head. Closing her eyes, she pictured Dusty—the play of sunlight against his bronzed skin, the look of heated desire in his eyes. As she fastened the dress around her neck, she wondered what he'd think if he could see her. She'd never worn the revealing dress anywhere but around the house. She wasn't the kind of woman who felt comfortable in a dress like this one, which left little to the imagination with its plunging neckline and completely bare back.

She stood in front of Sissy's big oval mirror and brushed her hair into a topknot, pinning it loosely. She looked at herself, knowing she looked beautiful and desirable. Sighing deeply, she reached for her thin gold chain—the one that held the tiny gold charm in the shape of a treble clef that had been given to her by a couple of her students—and fastened it around her neck. Barefoot, she walked to the kitchen, enjoying the feel of the dress against her bare, scented skin, and the soft caress of the breeze blowing through the house.

All dressed up and no place to go, she thought wryly. Then she gave herself a little shake, told herself to quit mooning around and pretending and began to fix her snack.

That had been fifteen minutes ago. Now it looked as if she was going to have a visitor.

She flicked on the porch light.

As Dusty reached the top step, the porch light blazed on, and he blinked. "Victoria?" he called. "It's me. Dusty." He hadn't thought about it before, but he didn't want to frighten her.

In two strides, he reached the door, and he could see her startled eyes on the other side of the screen. "Hi," he said. "Did I scare you?"

"Dusty?" Her voice sounded odd—husky and slightly breathless. She stood motionless, staring at him with her big, luminous eyes.

"Aren't you going to let me in?" He laughed to cover his sudden uneasiness. "I drive all the way down here to see the girl, and now she just stands there staring at me."

She reached up, and the porch light disappeared, leaving him in darkness once more. Then she unlatched the screened door and pushed it open. She moved aside as he walked in, and as she did, her dress shifted against her body and her long, bare legs.

Dusty's breath caught as he got his first good look at her. She looked more beautiful than he'd ever seen her look before, even counting the night they'd met. Her skin glistened in the soft light. Her hair was piled on her head, and tendrils escaped all around, giving her a soft, all-woman look.

And that dress.

Dusty swallowed. That dress was really something. The front was little more than two wide panels, with a deep V between that plunged to her waist. Her shoulders and back were bare, as were her legs and slender feet. As he watched, her toes curled, and he knew she felt self-conscious as he stood there blatantly drinking her in.

"Nice dress," he said, his voice coming out gruff and hoarse as he fought the desire pulsing through him.

"Thank you." She wet her lips, and Dusty watched the tip of her pink tongue moving across her full bottom lip. The ache in his groin threatened to be his undoing.

Suddenly she seemed to regain her equilibrium, because she cleared her throat and said briskly, "Now what exactly are you doing here?"

"I . . ." All his carefully worded arguments deserted him. He tried again. "I thought this decision you plan to make this weekend is too important to me—to us—to let you make it on your own." Confidence returning, he said more forcefully, "I think I have a right to have some say-so in the outcome, don't you?"

"So you just took it upon yourself to come down here uninvited?" Color stained her cheeks.

"Do you want me to leave?" He put his bag down and covered the distance between them in one stride. Letting his hands rest gently on her shoulders, he looked into her upturned face, noticing the way her eyelashes swept her cheeks as she closed her eyes, then opened them. The deep blue was troubled, and Dusty's hands tightened. "I don't want to leave, but if you really want me to, I will."

He could feel the tremor that passed through her, see her battling with herself. Finally she spoke. "No. I don't want you to leave."

He smiled. "Good." As casually as he could, he dropped a kiss on her slightly parted mouth, forcing himself to keep it light, although what he really wanted to do was crush her to him and keep her there until she did and said what he wanted her to do and say.

He backed up. He'd better keep his distance. She smelled too good, tasted too good. She was Eve, tempting him. He'd never wanted anyone as much as he wanted her, right now, right this very minute. His hands itched to touch her back, to slide under the front of her sundress and feel the firm, warm flesh hidden from his view. He knew if he did, he could make her lose her tightly guarded control, but he also knew Julie was somewhere nearby and could walk in on them at any moment.

Victoria turned, walking into the kitchen. "I was just fixing a snack. Are you hungry?" Her voice held only the barest trace of breathlessness. Otherwise she seemed perfectly calm.

"Sure." What would she be like in the throes of passion? Would she still be guarded? Or would she lose herself, give in to the feelings he knew were buried under her surface coolness? Would she moan and cry out? Would she touch him, want him? When those walls finally came down, would she be eager and aggressive, or would she be shy and tentative?

"By the way, where *is* Julie?" he asked, walking around the bar and into the kitchen. "Is she at a neighbor's house or something?"

Victoria didn't look at him as she took a bowl out of the cupboard and began spooning large strawberries into it. "She's not here."

"I can see that," Dusty said, chuckling. "But where is she?"

"In Washington."

"In Washington?" Where was Washington? Was that a beach he'd never heard of?

"Washington, D.C." Her answer was matter-of-fact, as if she hadn't almost knocked him off his feet. She ladled whipping cream on top of the strawberries and handed him the bowl and a spoon.

As the knowledge slammed home that he and Victoria were completely alone, their eyes met, and he knew she knew exactly what he was thinking.

Victoria kept telling herself to be calm. After all, what could Dusty do? What *would* Dusty do? Force her to make love if she didn't want to? No, of course not. She knew he wasn't that kind of man. But still, she couldn't even smile, that's how nervous she was. Not that he'd done anything wrong. From the moment she'd told him he could stay, he'd acted like a perfect gentleman, but she knew he was thinking the same thing she was thinking.

They were alone.

They were alone and together in this wonderful, romantic house. And she, Victoria Jones, a staid, cool schoolteacher was sitting here in a revealing, sexy, completely-unlike-her sundress while her heart hammered into her throat every time he looked at her. God, the look in his eyes was enough to melt her insides. She knew he wanted her, knew he was thinking about making love with her, knew that all it would take was one word of encouragement from her, and he'd have her inside and in the bedroom within minutes.

Is that what she wanted? Her body was certainly sending her signals. She felt hot all over, and her insides were jumping around. She closed her eyes for a moment and leaned against the porch railing; she could feel him only inches away from her. The wind had picked up, and clouds scudded across the sky, blocking the moonlight. She listened to the waves breaking on the sand. Unable to resist, she peeked at Dusty.

His strong profile was sharply etched against the purple sky. He was dressed in an open-necked white shirt with rolled-up sleeves and faded blue jeans that hugged his thighs. Oh, God, she wanted him to kiss her. She wanted him to touch her. She almost hurt with the deep longing that assailed her.

"This is a great place," he said.

"Yes. I love it." *If only I could relax and enjoy it.* But her awareness of him, her building hunger, wouldn't let her. Oh, if only he hadn't come here.

"I wouldn't mind owning a house like this," he said.

"I wouldn't, either. It's one of the few possessions of Sissy's that I really envy." *Dusty. Dusty. Do you have any idea what you're doing to me?*

"Maybe after I make my first million, I'll buy one," he said.

"Your *first* million?" She fought to keep her voice light. He mustn't know how he was affecting her. Just then the clouds scurried away, and a shaft of moonlight spotlighted the two of them. Victoria's breath caught at the picture he made. He was so perfect. Even his crooked nose was perfect. It was all she could do to keep from touching his cheek, stroking the smooth skin that stretched across his cheekbones.

"Why not? When you're dreaming, you might as well dream big."

Dream big. The words rocked her. Her own dreams had always been specific, focused on one immediate goal. She'd never dreamed about getting rich or becoming famous. She'd never wanted that for herself. But he did. She had to remember that. He did. It would be a fatal mistake to give in to the wildly churning desire that was building inside her.

"I do more than dream, though," he continued softly, turning toward her, his face now in the shadows so she couldn't see his expression. "I go after what I want."

Victoria's heart skipped a beat as his hand reached out and stroked her shoulder, igniting fires wherever it touched. He moved closer, so close she could smell the spice of his after-shave. "I want you, Victoria," he said, his voice a husky purr.

Her lips parted, her blood pounded, her pulse raced as those three little words chased around and around in her mind. She couldn't move, couldn't even breathe as his hands stroked her bare shoulders, then slid down her arms, inching around and feathering across her bare back. Even as her head warned her to tell him to stop, her breath came in shallow spurts. She knew she should call a halt now, before she lost it, before it was too late.

"Stop," she said weakly, even as she arched her back in mute invitation. Her breasts throbbed as the material of her dress was pulled against their tightened nubs.

His hands stilled. "Do you really want me to?"

"Y—yes."

"Are you sure you don't want me to touch you like this?" His hands whispered over her skin, tracing the outline of her dress from her neck to her collarbone, pausing for heart-stopping seconds, while Victoria's heart nearly stopped. Then his hands continued their agonizing journey, coming to rest against her rib cage. She shuddered as she felt their heat against her bare skin. *Don't stop.*

Her body jerked as his thumbs crept under the cotton panels of her dress and slowly, oh, so slowly, stroked the sides of her breasts, then inched up with tormenting slowness until they found their target. Victoria bit her lip. A fierce pleasure spiraled through her, and her legs tightened against an onslaught of intense need. But even as desire rushed in great waves over her body, intensified by each stroke of Dusty's hands, fear rippled in its wake.

She knew that exposing her body to his eyes and touch, sharing the intimate act of love, also meant exposing her very self with all her inhibitions, imperfections and failings. Could she do that? she wondered even as a small whimper escaped her parted lips—caused by the pleasure-pain he was inflicting with his mouth and hands.

No, her mind shouted as she felt herself falling, coming apart, losing control. But her body seemed to have a mind of its own as it trembled beneath Dusty's hands. Each brush of his thumbs, each sweet pull of his mouth, catapulted her with dizzying speed into unknown territory. The sensations and her reaction to them terrified her. She had held herself so tightly reined in for so long. How could she open up and allow him to see her as she really was? What if she disappointed him? What if she let herself love him, let herself give him everything, let herself fall so far apart that she'd never again be a whole person without him? What if he took it all, then left her to try to put the pieces back together by herself?

"No," she said, fear shooting through her. She couldn't take the chance. She couldn't. Losing him would be her undoing.

"Victoria, don't be afraid. Trust me."

But I am afraid.

Then swiftly, before she even knew what he was about, he reached behind her neck and loosened the ties of her dress, pushing the front panels down. As the moist night air hit her exposed skin, Victoria shuddered. She wanted to cover herself again, but Dusty's hands gripped her shoulders, holding her fast, and his head lowered. His mouth explored the hollow of her throat, his tongue tasting her, then moved lower, turning its heated attention to the breasts that still tingled from the touch of his hands.

No. No. I can't let him do this. I can't do this. But the insistent pull of his mouth kept her captive. Need shot through her—a long-buried need for love, for a touch exactly like this, for the fulfillment that would make her a complete woman. She wanted him. She needed him. She was scared to death.

She moaned as his mouth and tongue drew her. She felt as if she were on a roller coaster, a wild ride that might go anywhere, that might even fall off the track and explode, taking her with it into oblivion. "I can't," she said.

"Yes, you can," he whispered as he raised his head, and his demanding mouth slanted across hers. His hands held her tightly, and his tongue explored the crevices of her mouth: insistent, greedy, asking her for something she wasn't sure she could give him.

Victoria's emotions churned. She lifted her arms and wrapped them around his neck, her hands delving into his thick hair. The smell and taste of him filled her. She clung to him as he crushed her to him. His hands kneaded her back, then dropped to her bottom and pulled her hard against him.

She could feel the heat and size of him through her thin dress, and she strained toward him.

"Victoria," he said, tearing his mouth from hers, his voice hoarse and full of desire. "In a few minutes, it's going to be too late to stop. So if that's really what you want, tell me now."

What *did* she want? Her safe, controlled, secure little world? Nights alone at home, curled up with a book, listening to her beloved classics?

Or did she want Dusty? Dusty, a terrific man who'd asked her to trust him, who wanted to take her along on a dangerous, uncharted course—a course that might lead to chaos—a course that might also lead to glory.

Suddenly she knew. Tomorrow she might be sorry, but at this moment, Dusty and the way he made her feel, the way she felt about him, the unknown world that was beckoning—they were all that mattered.

"I want you," she said.

Within seconds she was being lifted in his strong arms. He kissed her again, a deep, drugging kiss that erased any doubts that might be lingering.

Swiftly, he carried her down the hall, then shouldered open the door to the bedroom and laid her on the bed. Within seconds he had pulled off his boots and was lying beside her.

"Don't be afraid," he murmured against her hair as he gathered her into his arms. "I won't do anything you don't want me to do."

"I'm not afraid," she said. *Liar*. "I just don't want to disappoint you."

"You could never disappoint me."

He began to kiss her, and as he kissed her, his hands stroked her, sliding down and lifting the hem of her dress. "Let's take this off." He lifted her, and she released the zipper at her waist. Then he helped her to remove the dress. Minutes later he had shed his own clothes, and although Victoria's doubts were gone, she was assaulted by a new rush of fear. As if he sensed her feelings, Dusty encircled her in his arms, kissing her gently until her muscles relaxed.

Then he raised himself up on one arm and looked at her. Moonlight spilled into the room from the open shutters, and the sound of the sea surrounded them. Oh, God, Victoria prayed. Please don't let him be disappointed in me. Unbidden, a picture of Chris frowning in displeasure filled her mind. She knew she had never responded very passionately to her husband; what if the same thing happened now?

"You're very beautiful," he said, cupping one breast as his mouth nuzzled the other. Then his warm, wet mouth moved lower, kissing her flat stomach just above her bikini panty line while his fingers brushed lower, burrowing under her panties till they found that secret, yearning place.

Desire rocketed through her, and she gripped his shoulders tightly.

"Relax," he whispered as Victoria's heart thudded against her chest. "Just let yourself go."

I want to. I can't. Oh, she wanted this. Yes, she wanted it. She closed her eyes, squeezing them tight.

His mouth moved up once more, and his finger, nesting in her warm, wet core, began to move. "Now touch me," he said as the roller coaster once more began to move, at first slowly, then gaining speed, going faster and faster.

Keep me safe. She held her breath as her hand moved toward him. He filled her palm, and she heard his sharp intake of breath as she touched him, at first tentatively, then with stronger, surer strokes.

She liked touching him. She liked hearing the sounds he made. She almost forgot what his hand was doing to her as the roller coaster started its ascent. She almost forgot to be afraid.

"Let go," he whispered. "Let me love you." His hot mouth captured hers as she moaned in pleasure, or was it protest, and his tongue mimicked the action of his hand as Victoria's control slipped and she fell faster and faster and faster until she plunged to the bottom and shot up again.

Tremors wracked her body, and a sweet, sweet pleasure exploded inside. Dusty held her tightly, kissing her deeply until the tremors stopped. A wild joy consumed her, and she ran her hands down his back, feeling the muscles rippling beneath his skin. She could feel the power in his body, a power he hadn't yet unleashed, and she wanted that. She wanted him to let go, too. She wanted to make him feel the way he'd made her feel. She wanted them to make that wild journey together.

Her hands moved lower, across his tight rear, then came around to find him once more. He groaned as she stroked him. Soft, moist skin. Hard, hard length. She closed her eyes, her palm closing around him.

"Do you want me?" he said, his voice ragged.

"Yes." He jerked against her hand as she kissed his neck, letting her mouth trail down into the crisp, curly hairs of his chest. Her tongue touched his skin. It tasted faintly salty to her. She tasted him again, and smiled as he shuddered.

"Say it," he said.

"I want you." Her teeth nipped at him.

"Where? Where do you want me?" His hand held her head against his chest, and Victoria took a deep breath, drinking him in. Anticipation built inside her, and she felt that sweet ache once more.

"Inside me. Filling me." Joy that this was so helped her forget she'd ever been afraid, helped her give him assistance as he rolled her panties down, helped her guide him to her. She held him for a long moment so that she could savor his heat and his strength and his power.

Then swiftly, impatiently, he entered her, and as she felt him filling her body, filling that emptiness, driving deep inside her, she knew without any doubt at all that this was right. This man was right for her. He wouldn't let her fall apart without being there to catch her. This wasn't a dangerous journey they were about to embark upon. This was a journey of bliss. *Dusty, Dusty. I love you.*

And then she matched her movements to his, wrapping her legs around his waist, letting herself begin the climb to the top of the next peak. And it was a glorious climb, slow and torturous and wonderful. Victoria's heart climbed along with her body, right along with Dusty. Her heart hammered as she went up and up and up. She could feel his heart hammering right along with hers. And then they were there, at the crest. *Oh, oh.* When she couldn't stand it another second, she let go, and she could feel him letting go, opening up, bursting, just as she was shattering into thousands

of shimmering pieces. Shaking, she held on tight, held him
close to her heart as the force of his passion filled her. Tears
ran down her face, and she knew she was whole in a way
she'd never been whole before.

Chapter Twelve

Dusty knew Victoria had fallen asleep. She was so beautiful, he thought as he watched her. Her eyelashes curled against her skin, and in the ivory moonlight, she looked as fragile and delicate as a sea nymph. Tenderness welled inside as he remembered her trembling reaction to their lovemaking, her tears and the way she'd clung to him afterward, and he'd known that what they'd experienced together had been as emotionally draining for her as it had been for him.

Dusty touched her cheek, and she sighed in her sleep. Softly, so as not to awaken her, he let his lips brush across her parted lips, feeling her moist breath against his mouth. He closed his eyes.

This woman, this wonderful woman, had scared the hell out of him. When he'd felt the tremors in her body, heard her cry, seen her tears, he'd been stunned, filled with a sense of awe and fierce pride. The feeling had been incomparable: an intense joy and pleasure that rocketed through his body and filled his heart. This experience with Victoria had been unlike anything he'd ever experienced before. His feelings were more than physical, and he knew it. He had committed himself to this woman, whether he'd intended to or not. When she'd placed her trust in him, he'd been hooked. And the knowledge shook him.

Watching the moonlight play against her face, Dusty felt her power over him. It made him feel very humble. He'd thought he was so smart all along. He'd wanted to take care of Victoria, wanted to have her on his own terms, wanted to call the shots. Wasn't that why he'd come rushing down here? Hadn't he wanted to be the big, brave man and hit the little woman over the head with a club and drag her off to his lair? Make her see who was boss? Make her do his bidding? Control her?

Dusty almost laughed out loud as he realized that had been exactly what had been in his mind, even if he'd never admitted it or even thought it in so many words. So it was very fitting that instead of all those things happening, he had ended up feeling as if *he'd* been hit over the head with a club. Victoria Jones: a classy lady with big eyes, cool demeanor and sweet mouth, had tied him up just like a roped calf. He would forever be her prisoner and her slave.

Was he really ready for this? He touched her hair, soft and silky looking, fragrant and moist as it lay against her skin. Here he was, on the eve of the biggest break of his life, just starting off on a new and exciting career—was he ready for this?

Well, ready or not, you've done it, he thought. You've broken down her walls, made her face herself and her fears, and now you've got to live with it. He guessed this was like saving someone's life—then they belonged to you forever.

When Victoria opened her eyes, the first pink light of dawn was creeping in the open window. Memories of last night flooded through her. She turned her head. Dusty was sound asleep, one arm thrown over his head, the other resting on her stomach. The blue and white flowered sheet barely covered him, and Victoria smiled. He looked so handsome and so sweet and so sexy lying there.

She thought about how they'd finally gotten up last night and taken the quilt off the bed and snuggled together between the crisp sheets. She thought about how Dusty had touched her and whispered her name in the warm darkness, how the ceiling fan had whirred gently overhead, how her body—now that it had come out of its long hibernation—had responded eagerly. She thought about how she'd cried out when Dusty had brought her to that glorious peak, how she'd clung to him, how she'd longed to hear him say he loved her. Did he love her? Or was last night and what had come before it only the natural mating instincts of two people who were overpoweringly attracted to one another physically?

Victoria hoped not. She didn't really think she was capable of the kind of response Dusty had elicited if all she felt for him was physical. But with her limited experience, how could she be sure? Once more, she thought of Chris. Their lovemaking had been perfunctory. Oh, she'd had satisfaction out of it, she supposed, but it had been nothing like what she'd felt last night. Last night had been glorious, like all the romantic movies and sappy love songs put together. Like rockets and fireworks and volcanoes and every other word she'd ever heard used to describe the experience. And Dusty—tall, bronzed, gorgeous, sexy Dusty—had been the one to make her feel this way.

It was wonderful; it was scary. And now she didn't know what to do. One thing she did know, though. While she was feeling like this was no time to make a rational decision. So for now, maybe her best bet would be to play it light, enjoy the weekend, but make no promises and no commitments.

Quietly, taking care not to wake him, Victoria eased herself out from under the weight of his arm, then slid out of bed. She opened the top drawer of the dresser and quickly rifled through its contents until she found an oversize T-shirt, her normal sleeping attire. Pulling it over her head, she padded silently to the window. The eastern horizon was washed with pale pink and apricot. The silent silver mist of morning covered the calm waters of the Gulf. Sea gulls swooped low over the sand dunes, and a lone walker was visible in the distance.

"Good morning, Cinderella." Dusty's arms circled her from behind.

She smiled and turned her head, looking up at him. His hair was tousled, and his eyes still looked sleep-fogged. A great rush of tenderness enveloped her. He bent to kiss her, and she turned in his arms, lifting hers to hold him close.

"Mm," he said and slid his hands up and under her T-shirt, moving unerringly to her breasts. "You feel so good. So soft."

"You don't feel soft."

He laughed against her mouth. "Be serious."

"I'm always serious. Maybe I'm tired of being serious."

"Oh? That's great. Let's be silly then." He squeezed her bottom.

Victoria giggled, the sound startling even her. She slapped at his hands. "Will you quit that?"

"Let's go back into that nice bed," he said.

"We shouldn't."

"Why not?"

Victoria's breath was shallow and choppy. "I don't know."

"That's the most sensible thing you've said so far today."

And so they went back to the bed, and within moments Dusty brought her to that brink of total abandon, then let her fall, catching her before she dissolved and lifting her up again.

For the rest of the weekend Victoria existed in a circle of shimmering happiness. She drifted in a haze of sexual awareness and contentment. She had never thought of herself as a passionate person. When she'd been married to

Chris she'd never thought about sex when she and Chris weren't making love, never anticipated it, never caught his eye and silently communicated the message that she wanted him, never counted the hours before they could be alone in bed.

Now, just looking at Dusty made her want him. They frolicked in the surf, and when he playfully pulled her under and she retaliated by jumping on his back and knocking him down, it wasn't long before his hands had pulled her bathing suit down, and he took her right there, in the water, as if it didn't matter at all that someone might figure out what they were doing. Gasping, she'd wrapped her legs around him and dug her fingernails into his back with a wild wanting that astounded her.

On Sunday morning, they spent hours in that wonderful, wicked, decadent tub. They laughed like children as they kept filling it with hotter and hotter water, and Dusty spilled the entire contents of Sissy's bubble bath in with them.

"You're going to smell so sweet, men will be chasing you," she teased him.

In answer he grabbed her, pulling her into his lap and up against him. Victoria shuddered at the delicious sensations: the hot, soapy, scented water surrounding her, Dusty's hard body pressed up against her back, his hands sliding over her and into all her secret, hidden places. She trembled with longing as he turned her to face him, holding her as he fitted himself to her, driving deep and looking into her eyes. The golden sunshine shone through the skylight and lit his hair, made his eyes smolder like the hidden fire in emeralds as he held himself still inside her. She closed her eyes.

Afterward he teased her. "You're not Cinderella, I've decided," he said, curling a strand of her wet hair around his fingers as he let more hot water into the tub.

"Oh? Why do you say that?" Her heart still hadn't slowed.

"Don't you know the story of Sleeping Beauty? I fear your education has been sadly lacking."

"I know the story of Sleeping Beauty, but I'm not sure you do."

"Oh, really? Well, you just sit there and I'll tell it to you." He composed his face into serious lines. "Once upon a time there was a beautiful dark-haired girl named Sleeping Beauty. She never wanted to do anything. All she ever wanted to do was sleep. She lay in her bed for years looking cool and beautiful and untouchable. Then one day along came a cowboy."

"A cowboy?"

"You heard me. A singing cowboy."

"A *singing* cowboy?"

Dusty glared at her. "Why do you keep interrupting me? How can I get to the end of my story if you won't let me finish?"

"Sorry," Victoria said meekly.

"Well, the singing cowboy saw Sleeping Beauty, and he liked what he saw. He knew that underneath that cool exterior was a hot wench."

"A hot wench!" Laughing, she splashed water into his face, but he caught her hands and stuck his tongue out at her.

"That's what I said, a hot wench."

Victoria rolled her eyes.

"Anyway, our singing cowboy kissed her. That woke her up, all right. From that moment on, she was insatiable. All she ever wanted was sex, sex, sex. She wouldn't leave the poor guy alone, and for the rest of their lives, he was forced to make love to her. Morning, noon and night. That's all they ever did."

Victoria laughed. "Poor guy. He must have been exhausted."

"All the time. That wench nearly killed him." Dusty stood up, and water rolled down his body.

Victoria's breath caught in her throat. He was the most wonderful-looking man she'd ever seen. She'd thought he looked terrific in his clothes, but naked he was magnificent.

"Yeah," he said as he watched her looking at him, "that's exactly what happened. She drove the poor guy crazy. Nothing else in his life seemed important. The only thing he ever thought about was her."

And then he pulled her up and held her close, capturing her mouth with his, kissing her fiercely, and Victoria forget everything else except this moment and this man and how he made her feel.

That afternoon as they sat on the porch, swinging slowly on the swing, Dusty's arm around her, his mouth nuzzling against her forehead, he said, "There's something I want you to know."

He's going to tell me he loves me. Heart skittering, Victoria said, "Oh?"

"I'm selling the bar."

Surprise rocked her. She fought to keep her voice level. "I hope you didn't make this decision because of me."

"I made it because it's the right thing to do at this point in my life."

Victoria was ashamed of the disappointment she felt. What had she expected him to say? That he loved her, would do anything for her? *Is that what you want?* she asked herself. *Do you really want that much of a hold over him—that he'd sell his business simply because you disapprove of it? Simply because you've shared a couple of days of wonderful lovemaking?* "Who're you selling it to?"

"Spence."

That didn't surprise Victoria. Dusty had told her about Spence and their long-time friendship.

"The deal will be final next week. Then I'll be perfectly free to concentrate on my music and the tour Rylander is planning for me."

Perfectly free. Well, of course he's perfectly free.

She didn't answer him; she didn't trust herself to answer him. She knew if she wasn't ready to commit herself to him completely she shouldn't expect him to commit himself, either. And if that was the case, why did she feel so suddenly empty, so disappointed?

As the billboards multiplied along the Gulf Freeway, Victoria's thoughts turned to Julie and home. Her perfect weekend had ended. Actually it had ended when Dusty left, and it hadn't been as satisfying an ending as the weekend itself had been. She sighed deeply, remembering her parting conversation with him.

"What time will Julie get in?" he'd asked as he threw his bag into his truck, his eyes sparkling in the sunlight.

"About seven o'clock tonight."

He touched the tip of her nose. "I'll call you later."

"No. Don't."

He frowned. "Don't? Why not?"

Victoria bit her lip. Doubts were already assailing her, and he wasn't even gone yet. She looked away. "I . . . I'd rather have this evening alone with Julie."

"I didn't say I wanted to come over. I just said I'd call you." His voice had a hard edge, and when her eyes flicked to his, she saw his jaw had tightened. She knew he was angry.

"Look, Dusty," she began, "I...Julie doesn't even know we're seeing each other again. Please. I don't want her to know we spent the weekend together."

She saw a muscle in his jaw twitch. The long column of his neck looked corded and strong. His chest moved in and out. He didn't say anything. He just stared at her. The sound of the surf and gulls and some children laughing down the beach were like a backdrop to the stage where she and Dusty were the only players. Why didn't he say something?

He finally did. "Just what the hell does that mean?"

She'd made a mess of it. She knew she would. "Not what you seem to think. I just meant that...oh, come on, Dusty. Julie's only thirteen. She's very impressionable. I don't want her to think that I think it's all right to spend the weekend with a man without benefit of marriage."

His eyes narrowed, and he shook his head in disbelief. "I don't believe I'm hearing this. We didn't do anything wrong this weekend, Victoria. Do you think what we did was wrong?"

"No, of course not. It's just that I'm Julie's mother. I don't want her to think—"

"Think what? That you're human? That you have human needs and desires like everyone else? Do you really want Julie to grow up thinking her mother is perfect? That's an impossible example to give her. That's bull!"

Victoria cringed at the look on his face. "Dusty, don't look at me that way."

"Then tell me the truth," he demanded.

"I am."

"You're not."

"I'm trying to."

"Try harder."

A tendril of fear crawled up Victoria's spine. "I just want to be able to tell Julie in my own way, at the right time. I don't want to be forced to discuss this with her tonight. She'll be full of her trip, all excited about it, and I want to be able to devote all my attention to her. That's all."

"You're sorry about the weekend, aren't you?"

"I'm not sorry about the weekend."

"Why is it I don't believe you?"

His eyes reminded her of pictures she'd seen of the color of the sea at the ocean floor—deep green shot with the golden rays of the sun—as they glared at her.

"I . . . I'm worried about the future," she admitted.

She could see his anger dissipate like the fog that had been burned off by the morning sun. He touched her cheek, and she curled into his touch like a cat curling into a warm blanket.

"There's nothing to worry about. We'll work everything out."

"Will we?" She wanted to believe him, wanted to believe they could dissolve their differences. And now, driving home, thinking about what he'd said, she still wanted to believe. But she was really too sensible, too realistic not to know they had enormous hurdles ahead of them. They'd finally parted with her agreeing that he should call her tomorrow. He'd kissed her there in the sunshine, and as the kiss ended, he whispered fiercely, voice rich with feeling.

"Always be honest with me, Victoria. If you are, if *we* are, we can work anything out."

"Yes," she whispered.

He held her at arm's length. "And quit worrying." A smile curved his mouth as he opened the door of his truck. "That's an order."

Dusty walked into his musty apartment and the first thing he did was push the play button on his telephone recorder. The speed of the flashing red light indicated there were several messages for him.

Hey, big brother, where are you? The low voice belonged to David, and Dusty's smile became a grin as he listened. *Guess you're out. Maybe I'll try the bar. Talk to you later, okay?*

He'd have to call David. In fact, if there was nothing going on at the bar that Spence needed him for, maybe he'd even drive out to the ranch tomorrow.

There was a beep and a dial tone, then another beep. Dusty sorted through the mail that had come the day before as he waited for the next message to play.

Dusty, I know you went away for the weekend, said Spence's voice, *but call me when you get back. There're a couple of things we've gotta talk about.*

Another beep, another dial tone, another beep. *Dusty,* boomed the voice of Vernon Rylander, and Dusty stopped opening the envelope he held as he gave his full attention to the message. *Got good news, son. We've moved up your recording date. Got a chance to get some time at Muscle Shoals earlier than we planned. Decided we wanted to release your album before summer. I want you to fly up here Monday. You're scheduled to record on Friday. Call me as soon as you get this message.* Rylander went on to give his home phone number, and Dusty dropped the envelope and grabbed a pencil, hastily jotting the number down.

After his conversation with Rylander was over, he hung up the phone, elated. This was great news. He *had* to tell Victoria. He knew he'd promised not to call tonight, but this news couldn't wait. He wanted to hear her excitement and pride. He wanted to share this moment of triumph and success. He waited through the final beep and rewinding of the tape, then turned the recorder off and picked up the receiver.

"Victoria?" he said when he heard her soft hello.

"Dusty?"

"Yeah, I couldn't wait until tomorrow. I had to call you today. I've just had great news." He quickly recounted his conversation with Rylander.

"That's wonderful."

Although the words were right, her voice was curiously flat. She didn't sound excited or enthusiastic or proud of him. In fact, she sounded as if she couldn't care less. Disappointment coursed through him.

He waited for her to say something else, and when she didn't, he said, "What's the matter?" He thought he'd laid all her fears to rest; he thought when he'd left her that everything was all right between them.

Ignoring his question, she said, "Listen, Dusty. I...I can't talk now. I...I've...been away for the weekend, and Julie just got home from a week-long school trip...and we were just getting ready to drive over to Sissy's to pick up Dolly."

Dusty heard the halting explanation . . . the lie. Ashamed of his impatience, which had necessitated the lie, he said softly, "I'm sorry, darlin'. I forgot about Julie being there. I forgot you wouldn't be free to talk. I forgot about everything, I was so excited. Why don't you call me later tonight after she goes to bed? I'll be here."

Once more she ignored his suggestion. "Good luck on your trip, Dusty," she said. "Call me when you get back."

He wasn't going to get her to do something she didn't want to do; he could see that. "I'll do better than that. I'll call you tomorrow night from Nashville. All right?"

"All right."

As he replaced the receiver, he guessed he'd have to be contented with that. It looked as if he still had his work cut out for him with Victoria. But she was worth it, he told himself. She was everything he'd always wanted in a woman: smart, strong, beautiful, good, honest, passionate, sexy. Besides, it wasn't as if he was really free to make any commitment right now. He really would have to wait until he saw how the album did, how his career did. He no longer had any sort of real income, and even if she *did* have a job, he had always believed a man should be able to support a wife. And Julie. He couldn't forget Julie. If he committed to Victoria, married her, he'd have a ready-made family.

Besides, wasn't anything worth having worth waiting for, working for? If Victoria had come too easily, maybe he wouldn't have appreciated her as much.

Grinning, he picked up the phone once more.

As Victoria quietly replaced the receiver, Julie said, "Did you and Dusty make up?"

"Yes." God, she'd hated lying like that.

"Good. I like him."

Victoria glanced at Julie, who was sprawled on the couch. Her daughter's face had an impish smile. "I like him, too." She walked into the den. "He called to tell me some good

news. He's flying to Nashville tomorrow to record his new
album for VeePee Productions.''

"Whoa," Julie breathed softly. "I'm gonna be able to say
I know somebody famous.''

Victoria smiled. "We'll keep our fingers crossed for him.''
She reached out to help Julie up. "Now, come on, let's go
retrieve our dog. You can finish telling me about Washington on the way to Sissy's.''

When they arrived at Sissy's, she wasn't there. Junella,
her maid, explained that Miss Farraday had gone somewhere for the weekend. "She went to visit some artist out at
some ranch," the maid said. "She left Saturday mornin'
and said she wouldn't be back until tomorrow night." Then
Junella smiled, showing a big gap between her two front
teeth. "Your dog's fine, though. Waitin' for you two to
come back.''

Had Sissy gone to see David Mitchell again? Victoria
wondered. Why, she'd just been there last weekend. A sense
of disquiet gripped her as she remembered the look in Sissy's eyes when she'd said how much she liked David Mitchell. Suddenly Victoria wondered how Dusty would feel
about all this when he found out about it. Would he understand why she had given Sissy David's name—encouraged
her to call him and help him out? A cold lump of dread settled into Victoria's stomach. Would he feel Victoria had
been dishonest by not mentioning that she'd offered to help
David?

She worried all the way to the house. This complication
was one she didn't need. Her and Dusty's relationship was
complicated enough without any added problems. And she
knew how touchy he was when it came to the subject of his
brother. Dusty was overprotective, just as he seemed to be
of everyone he loved.

Julie chattered happily that evening, and Victoria tried to
concentrate on her daughter's conversation, but her
thoughts continued to stray, and worry continued to nag at
her. Worry and guilt. Had she been wrong in helping Da-

vid, in introducing him to Sissy? That day he'd asked her had been so long ago, when she'd first met Dusty. She'd never dreamed her spur-of-the-moment generosity would come back to haunt her. Well, maybe she was worrying for nothing. Maybe nothing would ever come of Sissy's involvement with David Mitchell.

"Mom, are you listening to me?"

Victoria started. "Oh, hon, I'm sorry. I guess I was daydreaming. What did you say?"

Julie's gray eyes were thoughtful. "You haven't been paying attention to me at all."

That's just what I need, Victoria thought. More guilt. Now I'm a bad mother because I'm not paying attention to my daughter. I'm daydreaming about the man I can't get out of my mind. "I really *am* sorry, honey. I'm just tired, I guess."

Julie didn't look as if she believed her, but she didn't pursue the matter. Instead she said, "My birthday's in a couple of weeks."

"Yes, I know."

"Well, I've been thinking. Do you know what I'd like to have for my birthday more than anything in the world?" An eager smile played around her mouth.

"What?"

"I want to redecorate my room!" Julie announced, eyes dancing.

Victoria did a quick mental calculation as she thought of the pink and white frilliness of her daughter's room. "What do you mean by redecorate? New furniture? Or just a new color scheme?"

"A little of both," Julie said. "But it won't cost much money. Tell me now much you planned to spend on my birthday, and I promise I won't go over."

Victoria smiled. Although Julie was still childish in many ways, she'd always been pretty sensible when it came to money. She knew Victoria was on a strict budget, that they didn't have money to throw away.

Victoria named a figure.

Julie's eyes widened. "Great! That's more than I thought. Can I do whatever I want to do?"

"Well..." Victoria hedged. "You don't want to paint the room black or anything, do you?"

Julie giggled. "No, Mom. You don't have to worry. I'm not going to plaster acid rock posters all over the walls or anything like that. I just want a different kind of room. I have it all planned in my mind."

"Well, tell me about it."

Julie shook her head. "I want it to be a surprise. Okay?"

At the look of wistful longing on Julie's face, Victoria couldn't refuse. "Okay," she agreed. "Surprise me." Julie jumped up, and Dolly jumped up, too, startled by Julie's abrupt movement. "I'm going to go call Kate and tell her!" She raced from the room, and a few seconds later her bedroom door slammed.

Victoria shook her head. The enthusiasm of youth. If only redecorating a room could solve all her problems. She closed her eyes and laid her head back. Dusty's face with its square jaw and wide mouth, its slightly crooked nose and vivid green eyes filled her mind. *Oh, Dusty, I pray we can work out a way to be together.* An ache of loneliness constricted her chest. He wasn't even gone yet, and she already missed him. What would it be like to have him traveling for weeks, months at a time? She'd go crazy without him. If she felt this strongly now, before she'd had a chance to get used to having him around, before she started to depend on him, to lean on him, how would she feel later? How would she feel when she needed him and he wasn't there?

But there wasn't any answer to her question. A sense of futility gripped her. Their weekend together hadn't solved anything. It had made her realize she was in love with him, but it hadn't given her any insight into how they could solve their problems. And now, instead of only wondering what it would have been like to be loved by him—now she *knew*.

Oh, God, it was infinitely worse to know. How could she give him up?

Exhausted from thinking, she opened her eyes and rose from her chair. Maybe the only way they could be together was if she quit her job. But she couldn't drag Julie all over the country. Julie was in school. She needed a stable home life.

Suddenly angry, Victoria turned out the lights and walked to her bedroom. There's got to be a way, she told herself. She hadn't given up when Chris had died, and her problems had seemed insurmountable then, too. She hadn't given up all those years she'd worked and gone to school, even though some days she'd thought she couldn't go on another minute. And she wouldn't give up now. There *had* to be a way.

Chapter Thirteen

Dusty couldn't sleep. He kept thinking about his conversation with Vernon Rylander. Then he'd think about Victoria and the weekend. Finally, in disgust, he tossed off the sheet and snapped on the bedside light. Pulling on a pair of shorts and a T-shirt, he walked out to the kitchen and put some water on to heat.

When he'd called Rylander, he'd told the record producer that he hadn't had a chance to write the two songs he'd requested.

"And recording the album so soon...I don't know if I'll be able to come up with two new songs in a couple of days."

"That's okay, son. Just bring the music for some of your older songs. We'll pick two of the best and include them on the album," Rylander assured him. "I think it's more important to get the album out in July. We haven't got anything big coming out then so we can really push your album."

"Okay, Vern."

But Dusty wished he had the two new songs, or at least one. He knew from experience, though, that if he pushed, he'd never get an idea. Ideas came when he least expected them to, and no amount of wishing was going to produce one. However, there were tricks he could try. Sometimes just playing his guitar and singing older songs would give him ideas for new ones.

The kettle whistled, and Dusty fixed himself a cup of instant coffee, then carried the steaming mug into his living room where he set it on the coffee table next to a notebook he used to jot down lyrics and ideas.

Lifting his guitar out of its case, he tested the strings, then tuned it. For the next hour he played and hummed and thought about Victoria.

She was wonderful. In all the ways that counted, she was special. His Cinderella. He smiled, remembering the first time he'd seen her standing in the middle of Sissy's enormous drawing room. She'd looked so beautiful dressed in her purple satin ball gown, her hair a dark cloud surrounding her face, her deep blue eyes the color of the periwinkles that spread like wildfire in the summertime. His Cinderella girl.

My Cinderella . . . my Cinderella girl. . . .

He strummed an E chord, then a D, and began to hum, trying first this chord, then another. Within minutes a melody line had formed, and for the next two hours Dusty painstakingly picked out and fleshed out the song.

By the time he fell asleep at three o'clock that morning, he'd finished the music and made a start on the lyrics. He couldn't wait to see the look on Victoria's face when she heard the song for the first time.

Monday dragged by. Victoria could always tell when the spring semester was winding to a close. More than any other time of year, spring was a hard time for students and instructors. No one wanted to be working at anything when the days were warm and the entire world was bursting with new life.

Finally the day was over, and Victoria headed home. Because she had to pick up some dry cleaning and stop at the music store, she only beat Julie home by about fifteen minutes. Victoria barely had time to change her clothes when Julie yelled, "I'm home," followed by the slam of the front door.

Victoria gritted her teeth. She'd told Julie not to slam doors at least a hundred times, but she continued to do it. She only hears what she wants to hear; that's the problem, Victoria told herself.

Sighing, she headed toward the kitchen. After staring into the freezer, she decided to defrost some ground meat in the microwave and mix up a meat loaf. As she was punching in the codes on the microwave, Julie bounded into the room.

"We planned our schedules for next year today."

"Oh?" Victoria put the meat into the oven and closed the door, then pressed start. The microwave hummed. "What're you going to be taking?"

"You mean besides the regular stuff?" Julie perched onto a bar stool and reached for an orange from the bowl of fruit on the counter.

"Now don't eat too much. You'll spoil your dinner," Victoria warned.

Julie rolled her eyes and tore a hunk of orange peel from the orange. "You didn't answer my question."

"Yes, besides the regular stuff."

"I got to choose two electives, and I chose art and design and home economics."

"Art and design and home economics! Julie, you took art this year. There's no reason to take it again. And home economics is ridiculous. If you want to learn to cook, I'll teach you. You need to be thinking about the rest of your life, about your career. You need to be taking subjects with some meat to them, something that will help you prepare for a career. What earthly good will art and design and home economics do for you?'' She opened the vegetable keeper and took out two large potatoes.

Julie finished peeling the orange and pulled a section of orange free. Juice dribbled over her fingers as she popped it into her mouth. ''Maybe these will.''

''Don't talk with your mouth full,'' Victoria said automatically. ''What do you mean, maybe these will?''

''Just what I said.''

''I know what you said, but what did you mean?'' Victoria put down the potato she was washing and stared at Julie. Julie chewed on another orange section, and the pungent scent filled the kitchen.

''What I mean is that I don't want the kind of career you've been talking about.'' Julie ate another orange section.

''What *do* you want to do?''

''I want to be a fashion designer.''

Shock rendered Victoria speechless. When she finally recovered her equilibrium, she said, ''I can't believe this. How could you all of a sudden decide you want to be a fashion designer? You've never shown any interest in that before.'' But even as she said the words, images of Julie making her own paper dolls and dozens of clever outfits for them to wear flashed through Victoria's mind.

''Yes, I have,'' Julie said. ''I've always known what colors looked good together, and I've always been interested in clothes. I loved dressing my dolls and putting together different outfits. And for years I made paper dolls for me and my friends. You just didn't notice.''

''I noticed, but I didn't think you were any more interested in clothes than any other little girl. There's a big difference between drawing clothes for paper cutouts and dressing up your dolls and being a fashion designer.''

''I know. That's why I particularly want to take home economics. I need to learn to sew as well as draw. When you design clothes, you have to make up the dress as well as design it. In fact, I was hoping you'd let me take sewing lessons this summer to start me off.''

Victoria couldn't believe her ears. Julie had really given this subject some thought, from the sound of it. But a fashion designer! Julie couldn't have any idea how lucky you would have to be to make any sort of decent living designing clothes. Why, the chances of making a good living in the fashion design business didn't compare to the kind of living she could make as an accountant or doctor or lawyer or anything sensible.

"Julie, I don't think this is the kind of decision you can make at your age. Furthermore, I don't think it's an entirely sensible decision, or even a practical one. Why don't we compromise? You can take sewing lessons this summer if you sign up for something like debate for the fall. Debate will help you in any career. And that way you'll keep your options open.''

Julie's mouth settled into a stubborn line. "I don't want to take debate. Debate doesn't interest me.''

Victoria sighed. "Julie, don't be unreasonable.''

"Unreasonable! You're the one who's being unreasonable! You want me to live the kind of life you think I should live, not the kind of life I want to live. You're doing what you wanted to do. Why can't I?'' And with that, she jumped up. "You can't make me take something I don't want to take. And I'll find a way to pay for sewing lessons myself!''

Julie's words rang in the room long after she'd retreated to the privacy of her bedroom. Victoria kept thinking about what her daughter had said and, unbidden, an image of David Mitchell popped into her mind. The way he'd looked when he'd said how much he wanted to move to Houston.

The two situations are not alike, Victoria told herself. Not anything alike. But as she worked bread crumbs into the meat loaf mix, she realized that in many ways, they were. David Mitchell had pleaded for a chance to do what he wanted to do with his life, and Julie was pleading for the same chance.

I can't protect her forever, Victoria thought. I can't make her choices for her, either. She'll have to do that herself. And if she makes the wrong choices, well, that's life. That's how we all grow up and learn.

Later that evening, she apologized to Julie and told her to do what she felt was best for herself.

"Thanks, Mom." Julie's face showed her relief. "I was afraid you were going to give me a hard time about this. I know how much you wanted me to study law."

Victoria smiled helplessly. "I still wish you were going to prepare for a career that has higher earning potential, but I understand how you feel."

"You're not disappointed in me, are you?" Julie's eyes clouded.

"Of course not. I'm proud of you."

Julie grinned and threw her arms around Victoria's neck. As Victoria hugged her daughter, she hoped she'd done the right thing. Once again she wished Julie had a father. What a relief it would be to have someone to share the responsibility of raising Julie. Someone strong and decisive. Someone like Dusty. Funny how her thoughts seemed to turn his direction no matter what she was thinking about. She wondered if he'd keep his promise to call her tonight.

By the time he called, at eleven o'clock, she'd almost given up on him.

"Sorry I'm calling so late," he said. "But Vernon Rylander and his wife invited me out to dinner, and I just got back to my room."

"It's all right. I was grading some papers anyway." Just hearing his voice gave her a breathless, shivery feeling.

"So how was your day?" he asked. "Did you miss me?"

Suffused with longing, she strove to keep her voice light and teasing. "Conceited, aren't you? What makes you think I'd miss you?"

"Oh, nothing. Just because you give me wild, abandoned kisses every time you see me—"

"I do not!" But she couldn't help laughing, even as her body tingled.

He sighed heavily. "Have it your way. You don't miss me."

Smiling happily, she said, "Okay. I *do* miss you."

"And I miss you like crazy," he said huskily. "I can't wait to see you again." Then he chuckled. "Enough of this talk, or I'll have trouble sleeping tonight. Tell me about your day."

She told him about Julie.

"But isn't it your job as her mother to steer her in the right direction?" he asked.

"Yes, but my right direction and her right direction might not be the same thing. I have to allow her to make her own choices."

"You're a good mother," he said. "I don't know if I could be that understanding."

His praise warmed her. "Now tell me about your day," she said.

When they finally ended their conversation, it was almost midnight. He hadn't once mentioned their talk of the afternoon before, and Victoria was grateful. She still wasn't ready to voice her concerns. She felt funny about it because Dusty had never said he loved her, and he'd never hinted at marriage. Maybe he would think she was pushy or reading more into their relationship than there was.

As Victoria turned out her bedroom light and slipped into bed, she decided she needed to talk to another woman. Maybe she'd go to work at the paper a little later tomorrow and see if Sissy could meet her for lunch.

Yes, she thought. That'll kill two birds, anyway. I also want to know why she went out to the Mitchell ranch again.

On the break between her nine o'clock and ten o'clock classes, Victoria called Sissy.

"I'd love to meet you for lunch. Where do you want to go?"

"How about something close to the paper so I won't be too late for work?" Victoria suggested.

"Do you feel like seafood?" Sissy asked.

Victoria laughed. "I always feel like seafood."

"Let's meet at Don's, then."

As Victoria climbed the wooden steps leading to Don's on Post Oak Boulevard she glanced over at the Transco tower, remembering the night she and Dusty had stared entranced at the water cascading down the water wall.

Sissy was waiting for her in the foyer of the restaurant. "They're holding a table for us," she said. She was wearing a dark blue linen dress and blue and white spectator pumps. The outfit looked as if it had cost more than Victoria earned in a month.

Victoria glanced down at her own beige skirt and white blouse and inwardly shrugged. Even though she recognized quality when she saw it, she was perfectly contented with her own modest wardrobe. She smiled. If Julie did become a fashion designer, perhaps she'd expect Victoria to wear more trendy, flashy outfits.

Once Victoria and Sissy had placed their orders, Victoria wondered how to approach the subject of David Mitchell. But she needn't have worried; Sissy didn't require any encouragement. Without preamble, she plunged into a description of her weekend at the ranch.

"Oh, Tory, I think I'm in trouble," she said, blue eyes brilliant.

"Why?"

"I think I'm in love with David."

The quiet statement didn't surprise Victoria. As the words hung in the air between them, she knew she had been expecting something like this ever since Sissy had hinted at her attraction to Dusty's brother.

"What are you going to do about it?" Victoria asked.

Sissy's small shoulders lifted in a helpless shrug. "I don't know. I'm a little scared."

Their waiter returned with two steaming cups of dark gumbo, and Victoria waited until he was gone before answering. "I know exactly how you feel. I'm a little scared, too."

They looked at each for a long moment, then Victoria said, "Is the move to Houston still in the works?"

Sissy's hand stilled over her gumbo, and she returned Victoria's look steadily. "Yes. In fact, I've decided to have an elevator installed and put David in my garage apartment."

Victoria swallowed against a sudden lump of anxiety. At one time Sissy had had a chauffeur who lived in the attractive three-room apartment, but it had stood empty now for over two years. With an elevator for ease of access, it would be perfect for David. There were lots of windows and it was bright and sunny. But Dusty would be very upset about this, Victoria knew. Why had she interfered in David's life? He might have accomplished the move to Houston on his own, anyway, but at least she wouldn't have had any part of it.

"What's the matter? Do you disapprove?"

Victoria's thoughts centered on Sissy. She shook her head. "No . . . it's just that . . . well . . ."

"Well, what?" Sissy demanded.

Victoria heaved a sigh. "I can't help thinking how angry Dusty will be when he finds out about this. I'm afraid he'll be furious with me, and I don't know what to do about it."

Sissy ate a spoonful of gumbo, a thoughtful look on her face. "Maybe you should tell him before he finds out."

Victoria considered the suggestion, then said, "I don't want to attach more importance to it than there already is. If I make an issue of it, Dusty will think that I realized he wouldn't like my intervention, but I intervened anyway."

"Well, didn't you?"

"Not really. When I offered to put you and David in touch with one another, I had just started seeing Dusty. I really didn't know how obsessive he was about his family—especially about David."

"David is a grown man," Sissy said. "Dusty can't protect him forever."

"I know that, and you know that, but I don't think Dusty sees it that way," she said, worry gnawing at her.

"I'm sorry, Tory. I don't envy you being put in this position, but David would've rebelled sooner or later."

"I know, but I'm afraid Dusty won't see it that way."

Their waiter returned, and conversation ceased as he removed the empty gumbo cups and replaced them with a plate of broiled shrimp for Victoria and stuffed flounder for Sissy.

After he left them alone again, Victoria resolved to push her worry out of her mind. Determinedly cheerful, she said, "Let's talk about you."

Sissy grinned. "I'd rather talk about *your* weekend. I think you're deliberately steering away from the subject."

"No, I'm not. It . . . it was . . . wonderful."

The grin got wider. "Wonderful, eh? Well, I want to hear all about it. Every single juicy detail."

Victoria could feel herself blushing, and to cover her confusion, she said, "The weather was beautiful, and Dusty loves the beach as much as I do."

"Who gives a rat's patooty about the weather?" Sissy exclaimed. "What I want to know is, has your self-imposed virginity of ten years finally been banished?"

To Sissy's hoots of laughter, Victoria indignantly refused to answer her question, instead telling her about how nice Dusty was and how considerate. "We had lots of fun," she ended. "He makes me laugh."

"That's good. It would be hell to be married to someone who didn't make you laugh," Sissy declared.

An ache of longing gripped Victoria. "I don't know that marriage is an option with me and Dusty."

Sissy frowned. "I thought you told me you could never carry on a casual affair. Have you suddenly changed your mind?"

Victoria shook her head. "No. It's just that I can't see how Dusty and I can ever work out a permanent arrangement. Plus, I don't even know that Dusty wants to. He's never mentioned marriage to me."

"Honey, most men don't. What women have to do is get them to start thinking about it without their ever knowing you're steering them in that direction."

Victoria couldn't help smiling. The advice was typically Sissy, who always believed she could maneuver anyone into her way of thinking. "Well, whether Dusty is interested in marriage or not, I simply don't see how we could ever work it out."

"Tory, as usual you're creating problems where none exist. All you have to do is go get a marriage license and a minister. It's easy."

"If I were to marry Dusty, I'd never see him, unless I wanted to quit my job and follow him around the country, and I can't do that."

"Why not?"

"Number one, because of Julie. And number two, because I'll never allow myself to be dependent on someone else again, Sissy. It's a fatal mistake for a woman to give up her independence and her ability to make a living. If I did that, and something were to happen between me and Dusty, where would I be then?"

Sissy pursed her lips. "Hmm, we have to think about this. There has to be a more reasonable solution."

Victoria glanced at her watch. "We can think about it, but we can't talk about it anymore, because if I don't leave within the next five minutes, I'm going to be late for work."

Later that day, as Victoria finished her last review and prepared to go home, she recalled Sissy's parting words that afternoon.

"Tory, if you love Dusty and you want him, don't let anything stand in your way—least of all a job. There will always be teaching jobs, but men like Dusty don't come along more than once in a lifetime. And who knows, maybe he'll want you to work. Maybe you could teach one semester and take the others off. Something's bound to work out."

She was still thinking about Sissy's advice two hours later as she broiled two chicken breasts for dinner. Julie had stayed late at school for an end-of-the-year play practice, and their dinner was going to be later than usual.

She turned the chicken breasts, then began washing lettuce leaves for a salad. The phone jangled near her elbow, but she knew Julie would answer it from her room. Sure enough, she must have snatched it up immediately, for there was no second ring. Victoria smiled to herself. She had been just as eager for phone calls when she'd been Julie's age, although she hadn't been nearly as popular as her perky daughter.

Ten minutes later, as she removed the chicken breasts from the oven, Julie's bedroom door slammed and she came racing through the den to the kitchen. "Mom. Guess what!" she shouted.

"What?" Victoria shook a bottle of ranch dressing and poured some over the salad.

Julie skidded to a stop and said breathlessly, "Ryan Richardson just asked me to go to his school's prom with him!"

Victoria screwed the bottle cap on the dressing and slowly turned to face Julie. "Kate's brother?" she asked, stalling for time.

"Yes! Isn't it great? Oh, I'm so excited. I can't wait. Just think! The prom at the high school! My friends are going to die! They won't believe it!"

Each statement was punctuated by a rise in the volume of her voice until she was almost squealing with delight. Her heart-shaped face was pink with happiness, and her eyes were as shiny and bright as gray satin.

"Well," Victoria said, "I guess that *is* exciting, honey, but we need to talk about this. Sit down. Dinner's ready."

Julie plopped into her chair and reached for the salad bowl. "Oh, Mom, I still can't believe it. Ryan Richardson! He's . . . he's . . . perfect. And he's a sophomore! Can I get a new dress? Please? Please?" She stabbed one of the chicken breasts and dumped it onto her plate, her eyes never leaving Victoria's. "I want one of those black and white dresses they're showing everywhere. Can I get that? I've got money saved."

"Julie—"

"And I'll need new shoes, too. Maybe some two-inch heels. If I get one of those dresses I could get black satin pumps." She chattered on, totally oblivious to Victoria's growing consternation.

Victoria thought it pointless to tell Julie that even if she intended to give her permission to Julie to go to the prom with Ryan Richardson, a black and white dress was completely unsuitable for someone as young as Julie—that a pastel shade would be much more appropriate—but since Victoria didn't intend to allow Julie to go, it really didn't make any difference.

Julie cut off a piece of chicken and stuffed it into her mouth. She chewed happily, then said with dreamy eyes, "Oh, Mom. I can't believe he asked me."

Victoria set her fork down, her chicken and salad untouched. "Julie," she began haltingly. How was she going to say this without breaking Julie's heart?

Julie's fork stopped in midair. Something in Victoria's tone of voice must have alerted her to impending trouble, because her forehead creased into a frown. "What?" She laid her fork on her plate. Her eyes clouded. "What?" she demanded more loudly.

Victoria sighed. At that moment she truly hated Chris. Why was she having to do this alone? "Julie, aren't you forgetting something?"

"What?"

"Aren't you forgetting that you and I have an agreement, an agreement that you can't date until you're in senior high school?"

"But Mom, this is different!"

"How is it different?" Victoria asked quietly.

"It's a *prom*! It's special. I might never get asked to go to a prom again."

"Come on, Julie, you're dramatizing. Of course you'll get asked to go to other proms. When you're in senior high school, you'll probably go to dozens of proms."

"But I *have* to go to this prom. I already told Ryan I'd go. I can't call him back and say my mother won't let me go. He'll think I'm a baby."

Victoria braced herself against the look of agony in her daughter's eyes. "You had no right to say you'd go without asking me, Julie," she said quietly.

Julie jumped up, almost knocking her glass of milk over in her haste. "You can't be that mean! You can't! You've got to let me go!" Angry tears welled in her eyes, and two bright spots of color flamed on her cheeks.

Victoria almost weakened. She knew Julie was infatuated with Ryan Richardson, and she knew how earth-shaking this refusal would seem to the youngster, but she also knew it wasn't a good idea for someone as young as Julie to attend a senior high school prom with a boy several years older than her. Especially not on a first date. Especially not when she and Julie already had an agreement— one they'd worked out together.

"I'm sorry, honey. I know how much you want to go, but I simply can't break our rule because you want me to. I think you're too young to date, especially a date like this one, with a much older boy, and to attend a function where everyone else will be older, too. No. I'm afraid you can't go."

Julie's face twisted, and the tears spurted out. "I can't believe it! I can't believe you're being so mean! If you don't let me go, I'll never forgive you! I'll hate you for the rest of my life!"

Chapter Fourteen

Julie didn't come out of her room the entire evening. The only contact Victoria had with her daughter was when the phone rang at nine-thirty. Julie's muffled voice called, "It's for you," and when Victoria picked up the phone in the kitchen, she heard the quiet click that meant Julie had replaced the receiver in her own room. She sighed and said, "Hello?"

"What kind of a greeting is that?" Dusty asked. "You sound like it's the end of the world, or something."

"Oh, hi, Dusty." She couldn't help smiling, even though she wondered if Julie would ever forgive her. "Julie and I had a disagreement earlier, and she's very upset and angry with me." Victoria settled herself onto a bar stool so she could talk to him in comfort.

"Want to tell me about it?"

The caring evident in the gentle question warmed her heart. She quickly recounted the conversation at the dinner table, fighting against the urge to feel sorry for herself. She had to remember she wasn't the only woman in the world trying to raise a teenager alone.

"I guess I'm not sure I understand," Dusty finally said when she finished. "You let her decide what courses to take the other day, and you told me you couldn't make her choices for her. What's different about this?"

"There's a big difference. It's a parent's prerogative to make rules about what's appropriate for a child to do at a certain age. Dating at thirteen or fourteen is completely inappropriate, I think. But making Julie lead the kind of life I want for her—that would be overstepping the bounds of parenthood. I can give her advice and try to show her alternatives, but the choice has to be hers."

"So you told her no, and now she's mad at you."

"Yes."

"Well, she'll get over it."

"I hope so." Forcing herself to push the confrontation with Julie out of her mind, Victoria said, "So what did you do today?"

Voice tinged with excitement, he said, "I'm in Muscle Shoals. We laid down the first tracks today. We also worked on a new number that Vern wants me to include on the album—ironed out some rough patches. It was a good day."

"I thought you weren't going to actually start recording until Friday."

"Those were the original plans, but things are going so well, it looks as if I'll be able to get a flight out of here Friday afternoon and be home for the weekend. My part will be finished, and the rest of the tracks will be taped in at VeePee's studio in Nashville with the session musicians."

"That's great," Victoria said, flustered by the flutter of anticipation his words had caused.

"Great? Is that all you can say? I'm elated and flying high, and my best girl says that's great. That's not what I want to hear, darlin'."

His voice had dropped to a husky caress, and Victoria closed her eyes. She loved when he called her *darlin'* in just that way. It evoked vivid pictures in her mind, and made her toes tingle.

"I was hoping you were missing me like crazy," he said softly. "I know I'm sure missing you."

Victoria's chest tightened. "I . . . I do miss you," she admitted.

"I haven't been able to stop thinking about the weekend," he said. "It was wonderful. You were wonderful."

Heat flooded her body as erotic memories of their lovemaking filled her mind. She knew by the gruffness of his voice that he was picturing the same scenes. Suddenly Victoria was embarrassed and didn't know what to say.

"Hey, darlin', you still there?" he said.

Victoria cleared her throat. "Yes, I'm still here."

"I can't wait to see you," he said softly. "I have something I want to tell you."

Hope exploded within her like a firecracker exploding in the night sky. "Can't you tell me now?"

"No, it's too important. I want us to be together when we talk about this. I want to see your eyes when I tell you."

A delicious shiver of happiness raced through her. Even though she felt their problems were insurmountable, she still wanted him to say he loved her. And somehow she knew that's what it was he wanted to tell her.

"Victoria," he said, breaking into her thoughts.

"W—what?" She felt as if he were caressing her with his voice, and she had trouble catching her breath.

His voice dropped to a sexy rumble. "When you get into bed tonight, think about me, and I'll think about you."

Victoria's heart thudded slowly, heavily, as her body remembered the touch of his hands, the way he'd made her feel, the wild abandon of her responses to him. She trembled as she ached with longing and a deep-seated need to be enfolded in his arms. "I will," she whispered.

"I'll call you again tomorrow night. Good night, darlin'."

By the time Dusty was finished recording the final song on his album Friday afternoon, he was bone tired but exhilarated. This last taping session had gone without a hitch, and it looked as if he'd be able to make the two o'clock flight he'd booked.

Anticipation quickened his movements. He couldn't wait to see Victoria. He said his goodbyes and picked up his suitcases. He'd packed this morning before leaving the hotel and brought the cases with him to the studio. As he walked out to the main lobby and past the receptionist, she stopped him.

"Oh, Dusty, I was just getting ready to call downstairs and leave word for you." She pushed back a strand of red, curly hair and smiled.

Dusty grinned at her. She was pretty, and even though he was wild about a tall, dark-haired beauty, he could still appreciate a pretty woman who was flirting with him.

"Here's a message for you." She handed him a pink telephone message slip.

"Call your mother" and a telephone number were printed on the paper.

Alarm stabbed him. Something must be wrong at home. Maggie would never call him here unless something was wrong.

"You can use the phone in there, if you like," she said, pointing to an empty office across from hers.

"Thanks, Norma." He put his suitcases in a corner of her office and walked across the hall.

Tapping his fingers impatiently as he waited for the connection to be made, Dusty wondered what was wrong. God, he hoped nothing had happened to David.

"Hello," Maggie's brisk voice said after two rings.

"Hi, Maggie. It's me."

"Oh, Dusty, I'm so glad you called."

"What's wrong?"

He heard her heavy sigh. "Everything. David's moving out."

"What! David moving out? What are you talking about?"

"Listen, Dusty, it's a long story, and I'd rather tell it to you in person. When are you coming home?"

"I was just ready to leave. I have a two o'clock flight to Houston."

"Good. Can you come straight out to the ranch? He says he's leaving first thing in the morning. Maybe you can talk some sense into him."

He had wanted to go straight to Victoria's tonight, but he guessed he'd have to take care of this first. "Of course I'll come. I won't even go home. I'll head straight for your place."

It was five o'clock when Dusty climbed into his Bronco at the Park 'n Fly lot, and it was almost eight-thirty before he pulled into the entrance to the ranch. It was still light out, but the sun was low on the western horizon.

He had called Victoria from the airport to tell her he'd been called out to the ranch, but she wasn't at home, so he decided to call her from the ranch. She's got to get a recorder, he thought. He'd have liked to leave a message for her.

Maggie's golden retriever, Amber, came racing around the house as Dusty's boots scraped against the brick sidewalk leading to the porch, and her two calico cats stretched and yawned as they raised themselves from their sleeping position near the front door.

Dusty scratched the dog's head before opening the screened door and going inside. The kitchen was quiet, the table clean, all the dishes from supper put away. His stomach growled, but he ignored it. "Anybody here?" he called.

"We're back here."

Dusty headed in the direction of Maggie's voice. They must be in David's studio.

The door to the studio stood open, and Dusty walked inside. The sight that greeted him confirmed Maggie's statement that David intended to move out of the ranch house. Dozens of paintings were bundled together, tied with heavy string. Maggie sat on the windowsill on the far side of the room as she watched David tying a batch of four paintings together.

Both heads turned at Dusty's approach, and Maggie's dark eyes lit with relief when she saw him. David's green eyes clouded, and he frowned slightly, then turned toward his mother.

"You called him, didn't you?" he said accusingly.

"Yes, I did." There was no apology in Maggie's voice. "I think what you're doing is foolish, and I was hoping your brother could talk some sense into you."

David turned to Dusty. He sat up straighter and lifted his chin. A defiant gleam sparked his eyes. "You're not going to talk me out of this, Dusty. No matter what you say."

"Will someone please explain what the hell is going on?" Concern made his voice harsher than he'd intended it to be.

"It's no big deal," David said. "I'm moving to Houston tomorrow, that's all."

"No big deal!" Dusty exclaimed. "I thought we had that subject all settled the last time we talked about it. I thought you realized how stupid the idea was and had forgotten about it."

"Maybe *you* forgot about it," David said, "but I didn't."

"Where do you think you're going to live in Houston?" Dusty demanded, hands on his hips as he glared at David.

"Why don't you sit down? I don't intend to talk to you when you're towering over me like that. I *won't* be intimidated." David went back to tying up the bunch of pictures he'd been working on when Dusty arrived.

Dusty looked at his mother, and she shrugged and raised her hands in a helpless gesture. What the hell was going on around here? David had never acted this way before. Even when he and Dusty had disagreed in the past, David had always deferred to Dusty's greater experience and knowledge of the world. What had changed?

Rubbing his eyes wearily, Dusty looked around, choosing an empty space on one of David's worktables to sit. "So are you going to tell me about it, or not?"

David set the tied-up bundle next to the others that were similarly bound, then he looked at Dusty. His green eyes glittered as he said, "I have a place to live. You don't have to worry about that."

"Where? Some apartment? That'll never work out, David. You don't know how dangerous Houston can be, and a man in a wheelchair would be easy prey."

"Why don't you ever listen to me, Dusty?" David said, an edge to his voice that Dusty didn't like. "I'm not going to be living in an apartment. Well, at least not the kind of apartment you're thinking of—in some big apartment complex. I'm going to live in an apartment on the grounds of someone's home. It's a perfect place for me. I'll be absolutely safe, plus it'll be a good place to work. And on top of that, it's only five minute from the Montrose area, so I'll be close to the galleries and to Borghini's studio."

"Whose home?" What was happening to David that he'd go and make these arrangements without even telling Dusty? He'd never done anything like that before.

A flicker of some emotion passed over David's face, then vanished. He hesitated, then said, "I believe you know her. Her name is Sissy Farraday."

Sissy Farraday! Dusty felt as if someone had punched him right in the gut. "How the hell did you ever meet Sissy Farraday?" he said through gritted teeth, but he knew. He knew. And the knowledge pierced him like a sharp knife.

David wheeled his chair around and grabbed a couple more of his paintings from the floor.

Dusty stood and closed the distance between them in two strides. He grabbed David's shoulder.

"Dusty—" Maggie cautioned.

He ignored her. David's shoulder was rigid under his hand. "I said, how did you meet her?" he repeated.

David turned around, and Dusty dropped his hand. For a long moment the two brothers stared at each other. Without blinking, David said quietly, "I met her through Victoria."

A feeling of betrayal overwhelmed him. He'd known what David was going to say before he'd ever said it, but the pain wasn't lessened. "I see," he said. He backed up a few steps. "I see."

"Now, look, Dusty, this is not Victoria's fault—"

"Whose fault is it, if it's not hers? Maggie's? Mine? Don't try to con me, little brother, I wasn't born yesterday. I know perfectly well whose fault this is." Rage pounded through him. How dare Victoria interfere in his family's life? How dare she take it upon herself to arrange for David to meet Sissy? To make it easy for him to leave the ranch? She knew damn well Dusty didn't want David to move to Houston, but she cared so little about what he thought that she'd gone ahead and helped David to defy him. Anger, white-hot and furious, flooded him.

How could she betray him like this? He'd fallen in love with her. He'd thought she was wonderful, the most special woman he'd ever known, his Cinderella girl. He'd trusted her, given her his heart, written a song about her—a song that exposed his deepest feelings. He'd even planned to tell her he loved her, to ask her to marry him tonight. He'd decided that he was ready to commit the rest of his life to her. The ring he'd planned to give her was locked in the Bronco's glove compartment.

"Dusty..." David reached out and touched his hand.

The touch of David's hand galvanized Dusty. He jerked his hand away and said through clenched teeth, "I don't suppose you'll change your mind?"

David shook his head. "No. My mind is made up. Sissy will be here about ten in the morning, and I'm following her to Houston."

David had a customized van with a hydraulic lift for ease in entering and exiting, as well as hand controls for driving. He had learned to handle the van expertly.

Dusty's eyes narrowed. He was torn between the desire to stay at the ranch and confront Sissy and the equally strong desire to tear back to Houston and confront Victoria. Within moments he made up his mind. He directed his remark to Maggie. "If he's made up his mind, there's no reason for me to stay. I've got to get back. I'm going to leave."

Maggie sighed wearily and stood up. "I'll walk you out."

Dusty was glad she didn't try to talk him out of leaving. No matter what time he got to Houston, he intended to see Victoria and tell her exactly what he thought of her, and nothing was going to stop him.

At eleven o'clock Victoria decided to go to bed. She might as well face it. Dusty wasn't going to call her. Disappointment filled her as she looked at the small table she'd set in the living room. Fresh flowers sat in a cut crystal vase in the center of the table, and she'd put out her best china and stemware. She had a pot of French onion soup on the stove and a seafood casserole ready to heat in the oven. She'd run around after school today, buying the food and flowers, all excited about seeing him again. Her stomach had been full of butterflies, and her body had tingled all day in anticipation.

She'd even gone through her sheet music, pulling out selections she knew Dusty would enjoy hearing. She'd thought after they had dinner, she could play for him again. She'd spun romantic fantasies about the evening ever since she'd talked to him two days ago.

And he hadn't called.

What had happened? Was he still in Muscle Shoals, or had he flown to Nashville instead of Houston?

Then she began worrying. Maybe something awful had happened to him. What if his plane had crashed? Oh, God. She hadn't watched the news or read the paper, either.

Hands shaking, she turned on the television set and turned to the news. After watching for thirty minutes, she turned off the set and sat dejectedly. Finally she stood up and walked around turning out the lights.

Julie wasn't at home tonight. After two days of giving Victoria the cold shoulder, she had asked if she could spend the night with Laura Barnes, one of her school friends. She was very polite when she asked, but there was no warmth in her voice or her eyes, and her coldness had chilled Victoria. She was obviously still very angry with her mother. Victoria had given her permission, and Julie left about five o'clock.

Victoria had been glad to see her go. Normally she missed Julie when she was out, but today Victoria couldn't stand to feel Julie's displeasure or look at her accusing eyes. Even though Victoria knew she was right about refusing to allow Julie to go to the prom with Ryan Richardson, the weight of her daughter's unhappiness was taking its toll.

But once Julie was gone Victoria was free to let her spirits soar in anticipation of Dusty's arrival. She'd put on one of her prettiest summer dresses, a flowery cotton in shades of blue and green and white, and splashed scent on with a lavish hand.

Oh, well, she thought, as she undressed. The dress she'd selected with such high hopes was returned to its hanger, and Victoria gloomily prepared for bed. Worry still nipped at the edges of her mind. It just wasn't like Dusty to say he'd be home today and not even call her.

Should she call his apartment? But now it was eleven-thirty, awfully late to be calling him. What if he was there? What would she say?

No. She'd better just wait. There was bound to be some reasonable explanation for his not calling.

Climbing into bed, Victoria shut off the bedside lamp and closed her eyes. She took deep breaths. The house was quiet, except for the normal creaks and groans of all old houses. Victoria's bedroom faced the street and every once in awhile, lights swept across her windows as she heard a car move down the street past the house.

Her body had just begun to feel heavy, the heaviness that preceded sleep, when the doorbell rang, accompanied by a pounding on the door. Victoria bolted from the bed, heart hammering wildly. She grabbed for her bathrobe, pulling it around her as she raced to the front door.

Turning on the outside light, she peered through one of the narrow panes of glass that flanked both sides of the front door. A heady rush of joy replaced the fear that jolted her when she'd heard him at the door and, with shaking fingers, she hurriedly undid the dead-bolt lock and yanked the door open.

"Dusty! Oh, I'm so happy to see you!" She threw herself into his arms, happiness making her giddy, so it was a few seconds before she realized his body was rigid and that instead of pulling her close, his strong hands had gripped her arms and were pushing her back.

She stood aside to let him enter. Fear caused her heart to gallop as he strode past her, face stony. Quickly shutting the door, she followed him into the den. She snapped on lights, then said haltingly, "Dusty, what . . . what's wrong?"

His mouth twisted into a sneering smile. "That's what you do best, isn't it? Play the innocent."

Her hands trembled as she instinctively reached out to touch him. But he held himself back, and she let her hands drop to her sides. She swallowed. She was frightened. He looked so cold. He looked like a stranger.

His hands clenched at his sides. When he spoke, he almost spat the words out, and his eyes blazed. "I just can't believe that I've allowed you to take me in one more time."

He snorted, and Victoria winced. Pain balled in her chest like a tight fist.

"It's incredible," he said. "All you had to do was open your eyes wide and tell me you'd always be honest with me, that you wanted me to always be honest with you, and I believed you. Despite the fact that you lied to me before, which probably meant you wouldn't have any qualms about doing it again, I believed you."

"Dusty, I don't understand—"

"Oh, you don't understand," he said mockingly. "I'll just bet you don't understand. What's so hard to understand? My brother is moving to Houston, doing something I think is dangerous and stupid, because you chose to ignore my wishes, chose to ignore the fact that David is *my* brother, and took it upon yourself to help him in this ridiculous idea."

Victoria cringed as each word rained down upon her. Oh, God, it was so much worse than she'd imagined it might be if he were to find out about her role in David's plans. "Dusty, please, I know it looks bad—"

"You're goddamned right, it looks bad. In fact, it couldn't look worse, not if you tried in a million years!" His voice, which could be softer and gentler than a kitten's paw, was hard and tight and edged with steel. His eyes, which could caress her like warm spring rain, were icy and accusing and full of disgust. His mouth, which had claimed hers in passion and sweetness, was curled and twisted into hard, cruel lines.

Hopelessness overwhelmed her, causing her shoulders to slump as the knowledge engulfed her that nothing she said could make a difference to him. Trembling, she tried once more, desperation pushing aside her pride. "Dusty, I never meant to hurt you. When I told Sissy about David, you and I were just beginning to be friends. I truly didn't know how you felt about David moving."

"Don't waste your breath. I came here to let you know that I know all about it, and believe me, I don't really care why you did it or when. I know all I need to know, and I'm not interested in listening to more of your lies. In fact, I'm not interested in listening to you, period." His eyes narrowed to slits as he hurled the words at her. "I never want to see you again."

Chapter Fifteen

The weeks inched by, and somehow Victoria managed to get through them. Soon May turned into June, and the days grew longer and hotter and more humid. The spring semester ended, and the summer session began. Victoria had decided to go easy on herself, so she was only teaching two classes this session; composition and music theory.

She and Julie had fallen into an uneasy truce ever since their disagreement in early May over Ryan Richardson and his invitation to the senior prom. Gradually Julie seemed to get over her disappointment and unhappiness, and Victoria began to hope their relationship would improve.

Julie was lucky and had landed a summer job as a lifeguard for a neighborhood pool, so Victoria didn't have to worry about her when she was at school or working at the *Herald*. Julie was also taking the sewing lessons she had requested. She'd finished decorating her room, and even Victoria was impressed with Julie's sense of style and color. The room was elegant and classy with a combination of turquoise and umber and navy blue, and Julie had accomplished the entire look with very little money.

David Mitchell moved to Houston and soon became a permanent fixture in Sissy's garage apartment. He had apologized to Victoria for causing the breakup between her and Dusty, but she'd brushed aside his hesitant words.

"It wasn't your fault, David. Please don't feel badly about it. Dusty and I . . . well . . . it was just never meant to be, that's all." She ignored the ever-present pain that threatened to push through the wall she'd erected to keep it out of her mind and heart. "I'm only sorry this has caused a rift between you two," she added sadly. "I know how close the two of you were."

David made a halfhearted attempt at a smile, then gave up and shrugged. "Dusty's stubborn, and he doesn't like to be crossed. He'll come around eventually."

"I hope so," Victoria said. Talking about Dusty had put a chink in the wall, and she called on all her willpower to push the painful rawness away. She kept thinking that if she could just get through June, she'd be all right. Surely six weeks was long enough to get over anybody.

Eventually July came, and with it a renewed campaign from John Webberly to get her to go out with him. It was as if he sensed that she was very vulnerable, very much in need of comfort and admiration. A shroud of melancholy had settled over her, and no matter what she did, it refused to be lifted.

After John had asked her to go out several times in two weeks, Victoria finally gave in. Why not? she asked herself. John was nice, and he obviously liked her. And he was comfortable. He didn't make her feel as if she were balancing on the edge of a precipice like Dusty did. He also didn't cause her stomach to turn inside out when he walked into a room, which might be a nice change. So she said she'd go to a chamber music recital that was being given by a group of his friends, and she tried to enjoy herself. But she couldn't concentrate on the music, and she found herself wishing she was home curled up with a good book and a cup of tea.

And then, when they reached her house, and John roughly pulled her into his arms, planting a wet kiss on her mouth before she could say anything, a shock of revulsion shuddered through her body, and Victoria thought she was going to throw up.

John's labored breathing revealed his agitation and excitement when she was finally able to escape his embrace, and his eyes glittered in the light outside her door. He reached for her again, but this time she was too quick for him.

"No, John, please don't. We're friends, but that's all," she said firmly, fighting the urge to wipe her mouth with the back of her hand.

"Come on, Victoria," he said, desire causing the words to slur. "Don't give me that bull. You know how I feel about you."

"I'm sorry, John." Oh, God. Why had she agreed to go out with him? She had known how he felt, but she'd been selfish and unconcerned with his feelings. Because Dusty had hurt her, because she was hurting so badly, she'd used John, thinking that perhaps going out with him, seeing the admiration and desire in his eyes, would make her feel better. She was disgusted with herself.

The evening ended badly, with John angry and full of hurt pride. He stalked off, and Victoria slowly turned and let herself in.

That night she cried herself to sleep, and the next day she called in sick, the first time she'd ever done that. But her eyes were so swollen and puffy, she couldn't let anyone see her.

"Mom, what's wrong?" Julie asked when Victoria finally emerged into the kitchen.

"I think I'm getting a cold," Victoria said.

Julie kept giving her covert glances, and Victoria knew her daughter suspected that a cold wasn't the reason for Victoria's misery.

At the end of July, Dusty's album was released, amid great fanfare, especially in Houston. Everywhere Victoria went she saw his picture. The day he was interviewed on *Good Morning, Houston*, she succumbed to the irresistible urge to tape the show. Then she was afraid to watch it. She knew it would only cause her more pain and heartache. Remembering him was hard enough. Remembering his touch, the way his eyes would soften when he'd looked at her, the way he'd say the word *darlin'*, the way his kisses had made her feel—that was enough to almost kill her. But seeing him on television— Victoria wasn't sure she could stand it. Eventually, however, late one night, when Julie was asleep, Victoria unearthed the tape from where she'd hidden it and inserted it into the VCR.

Numbly, she watched as Dusty smiled and talked and laughed. He was completely charming and devastatingly handsome. It was an agonizing experience to sit and watch him and listen to him and know exactly what she'd lost.

The pain she'd managed to shove away in the far corners of her mind where it couldn't torment her began to seep out like a poisonous gas, creeping closer and closer until she was consumed with it. She felt as if she might disintegrate from the sheer power of her heartache. Hot tears burned in her eyes, and she shivered with a numbing sense of loss.

That night marked a turning point in her life. That night she reached the bottom. After that, the only way to go was up. So gradually, little by little, she began to feel better. Oh, she still hurt, but the pain was bearable. And she intended to keep it that way.

She refused to be exposed to Dusty's album. She purposely didn't listen to the radio so that she wouldn't have to endure hearing him sing. Somehow she knew that hearing his voice singing his songs would be her undoing. She knew that the album was doing phenomenally well, and she was glad. She knew how hard he'd worked for success, and it pleased her to know he'd achieved it.

By the middle of August, she was actually feeling almost happy again. Of course, she avoided all mention of Dusty. Even Sissy, normally not the most subtle person in the world, didn't mention him.

Then one Saturday toward the end of August, Sissy called and invited her to come for dinner. "Come on," she urged when Victoria started to decline the invitation, "you don't have any other plans, do you?"

"No," Victoria admitted.

"Good. There's something I want to talk to you about."

Later, dressed in a cool white sundress and white sandals, Victoria drove to Sissy's. She was surprised to see David Mitchell, highball glass in hand, already ensconced in the sitting room. Her heart lurched as he turned and smiled. A lump grew in her throat, and she blinked. He looked so much like Dusty.

"Hi, Victoria," he said. "It's been a long time."

"Yes, it has," she agreed, shaking his hand, as she tried to get her emotions under control. Accepting a glass of tomato juice from Sissy, Victoria sat in a bentwood rocker. Sissy perched on a stool near David and took a sip of her vodka gimlet.

She looked beautiful tonight, Victoria thought. Sissy's cheeks were rosy, and her eyes sparkled like blue topazes. She wore a linen dress in a rich shade of deepest rose, and her blond hair was piled atop her head.

Sissy and David exchanged a look, then a smile. Victoria's heart twisted.

"Tory..." Sissy reached for David's hand, and he clasped it. "David and I have something to tell you."

The knowledge of what was coming roared through Victoria, and she braced herself.

"We love each other," David said gruffly, and Sissy's eyes softened.

"We're going to be married," Sissy finished. And as she did, David leaned toward her, and she leaned toward him, and they kissed gently.

The lump in Victoria's throat expanded, and it was a long moment before she got herself under control. She was happy for them. She really was. But, oh, it hurt to see them together. Because seeing them together brought back the reality of what she had once had, too.

Somehow Victoria managed to get through the evening, to say all the appropriate things, to wish David and Sissy well and to mean it. After all, they certainly deserved the happiness they'd found.

All the way home she kept telling herself she and Dusty would never have been able to make a permanent relationship out of what they had. But she couldn't convince herself.

And that night, as she lay in bed unable to sleep, replaying everything over and over in her mind, everything she and Dusty had done and said and shared, she knew she never would convince herself. The fact of the matter was that even though it had been almost four months since she'd laid eyes on Dusty Mitchell, she was as much in love with him as she'd ever been, and she was terrified that she always would be.

Dusty looked around his new house with a sense of satisfaction. It suited him perfectly. A rambling ranch house with an enormous stone fireplace that divided the living and dining rooms, it sat on a large tree-covered lot near Buffalo Bayou in the heart of the Memorial area. Six months ago, he would never have dreamed he could afford a house like this one, but sales on the album were so spectacular, he'd decided to use the proceeds from the sale of the bar to buy his new home.

He'd moved in August fifteenth. Now, nearly a month later, everything was done, and all he had to do was sit back and enjoy it. Curiously, though, he wasn't enjoying it as much as he thought he would. Walking to the wall of windows that made up the back of the house, Dusty watched as squirrels raced up and down the tall pines. Sometimes he saw chipmunks or other small animals along the edges of the bayou.

But his pleasure in the house was always fleeting. For a while he'd be happy, then something would remind him of Victoria, and a curtain of gloom would settle around him, and all his pleasure would fade away, to be replaced by a lethargy he couldn't shake.

He'd long since gotten over being angry with her. In fact, that searing anger had faded within days of their confrontation in her house. This dispiritedness, this disinterest and dullness, had replaced it, and now nothing seemed to excite him.

He'd tried everything to forget her. He'd gone out with other women, but that hadn't worked at all. Even the prettiest, sexiest women didn't elicit a response. The most he could say for those evenings he spent with them was that he was bored. Bored. That described his life right now. He was flat-out bored.

Even the success of the album, *Gold Dust*, had failed to bring him the elation he'd thought it would. He was proud of the album, pleased with the success it had attained, but the thrill he'd expected, the sheer delight he'd thought to experience, weren't there.

What the hell was wrong with him? Why couldn't he forget about Victoria? Why did she continue to haunt his dreams as well as most of his waking moments? Why did memories of her make it impossible for him to enjoy his life and his hard-won success?

She had gotten under his skin as no woman ever had before. As no woman ever would again. He made the vow silently. Never, never again. When he finally succeeded in pushing her out of his life, he'd never allow himself to fall for a woman again. He'd go out with them, he'd make love to them, he'd use them, but he'd never let himself become vulnerable. That was the way of fools, and Dusty was no fool. He grimaced at the thought. Well, maybe he had been foolish in trusting Victoria, in believing in her, but he'd learned his lesson. No one had to hit him over the head with a hammer. Once burned, twice shy, isn't that what they said?

Sighing heavily, Dusty wandered to the den. The long day stretched ahead of him. He was supposed to be working on new songs. VeePee Productions was arranging a winter tour that was supposed to start November first. Dusty would be performing in Los Angeles, San Francisco, Dallas, St. Louis, Chicago, New Orleans, Atlanta, Philadelphia, Washington, D.C., Boston and New York. He was supposed to be getting ready for the tour, but his heart wasn't in it.

He missed David, too. It seemed ironic that David should be so close, probably within a fifteen-minute drive, yet they hadn't seen one another or spoken for months. Why was he still punishing himself as well as David by clinging to his pride? Obviously David was doing fine; Maggie had said as much. Dusty knew he should call David and make an attempt to patch things up, but somehow knowing and doing were two different things. Every time he reached for the phone, he couldn't bring himself to dial the number.

So wallow in your misery, he told himself. Then he grinned. Now he was even getting melodramatic. What he needed to do was get out of the house. Go see somebody. Do something.

He grinned. That was it. He'd drop into the bar and see Spence. He hadn't visited the bar in over a week, and Spence's good-natured philosophy of life always gave him a lift when he needed one.

By the time Dusty returned to the house, it was almost midnight. After parking the Bronco in the garage, he walked down the driveway to retrieve the evening paper and get his mail out of the mailbox.

Once inside the house, he tossed the mail on the kitchen table and petted his new puppy, a black Labrador he'd named Rocky. As he scratched behind the dog's ears, he idly sifted through the mail, discarding the junk and putting the few bills aside.

Then he frowned, picking up a thick, creamy envelope. What was this? He opened the flap, then drew out another envelope. This one was not sealed. Curious, he withdrew the contents. A small, flat card and stamped envelope, as well as another bigger card were enclosed. A wedding invitation? Who?

Dusty opened the bigger card. At first the words made no sense.

Mary Louise Farraday
and
David Reed Mitchell
Invite you to share in the joy of their marriage
Four o'clock Saturday afternoon
October Seven
at the Farraday home
Reception to follow

The card fell from his hand as shock shuddered through him. Mary Louise Farraday. Sissy? David and Sissy? David, getting married? Dusty felt as if someone had slammed him against a wall as hard as he could.

He picked up the card again. Had Maggie known about this? Why hadn't she said something to him?

He read the invitation again, repeating the words, trying to make sense of them. Then he saw the message scrawled on the back of the card in David's familiar handwriting.

Big brother, let's call a truce. Sissy's wonderful, and I'm happier than I've ever been. I love you, and I want you to be my best man.

Something squeezed Dusty's heart, and there was a painful constriction in his throat. He put the card back on the table and, like a sleepwalker, he moved silently into the dark living room. Sinking onto the huge sectional sofa, he lay back against the pillows and stared into the darkness.

Rocky jumped up beside him, and Dusty absently cuddled the puppy, too preoccupied to tell him the sofa was a no-no, too in need of warm contact to shoo the dog away.

The card and its message and David's note had produced a curious reaction in Dusty. The shock had given way to something else, something he didn't understand, something that was strangely like loneliness.

"Why didn't you tell me about this?" Dusty said as he held the wedding invitation in front of Maggie's face. It was the Sunday after he had received it, and he was still trying to decide what he wanted to do about it.

"I didn't know about it until last week, and I thought it was David's place to tell you," Maggie said calmly, dark eyes thoughtful. "Have some more mashed potatoes." She held the bowl out to him.

"Damn it, Maggie, I don't want any more mashed potatoes. I want to talk about David." Why did he seem to be losing control of everything?

"What about David?" Maggie helped herself to more roast beef and ladled on some gravy.

"Luke," Dusty said, turning to the man who had been his mother's helper and confidant for years, "can you talk some sense into her? She seems to think this marriage is a good idea."

Luke's cool blue eyes lifted, and he said slowly, "I think it's a good idea, too."

Dusty jumped up. "I don't believe this. What's wrong with everyone? Nobody's doing anything sensible!"

"Sit down, Dusty," Maggie said. "Quit acting like a jackass."

Dusty's mouth dropped open. He sank into his chair and stared at her.

Her dark eyes gentled. In a softer voice, she said, "Dusty, I know you only want the best for me and for David. I know you love us and that all your actions are prompted by concern for our happiness, but—"

"Hell, yes, I'm concerned. Why wouldn't I be?" Dusty interrupted. "You were concerned about David, too. You didn't think it was a good idea for him to leave the ranch. But now you seem to have changed your mind."

"Well," Maggie said, "maybe it's because something has happened in my life that has made me understand David's feelings a bit better." She smiled and reached across the table to touch Luke's hand.

Something stabbed at Dusty as Luke's weathered hand closed over his mother's, and he saw the two of them smile at each other.

"Dusty, son," Luke said, "we wanted you to be the first one to know. Your mother and me, well, we're getting married, too." His lean face broke into a wide grin, and Maggie smiled happily. Both pairs of eyes settled on Dusty as they waited for his reaction.

Dusty swallowed. He felt as if his world were tumbling down around him. First Victoria had defied him. Then David hadn't listened to him. Now Maggie would no longer depend on him. He felt adrift in an alien sea.

"Aren't you going to say something?" Maggie prompted, a glowing smile on her face. "Aren't you going to wish us happiness?"

Suddenly Dusty felt selfish. Here he was, thinking only of himself, when his mother and Luke, a man he'd always admired and respected, were so obviously in love and happy. These were two wonderful people, two people who'd worked hard all their lives, who'd always put others' needs first. These two people deserved to have whatever happiness they could find together, and he had no right to dampen the occasion with his own self-pity.

He grinned and stuck out his hand. "I hope this doesn't mean I have to call you Pop."

A wide grin split Luke's face, and he chuckled. Dusty stood and walked around the table. He pulled his mother up and wrapped her in a big hug. "I'm happy for you, Maggie," he said softly. "You deserve this. You couldn't have picked a better guy."

Then he released her and moved to Luke. Clasping the older man by the shoulder, he said, "Take good care of her."

"Always," Luke vowed, voice gruff. "Always."

The look in Luke's eyes haunted Dusty for days. After thinking about the series of events that had transpired the past week, the following Saturday Dusty picked up the phone and called information.

Taking a deep breath, he punched in the numbers he'd been given. After four rings, David's familiar deep voice said, "Hello."

Dusty's heart beat faster. "Hello, little brother."

He could almost see the smile on David's face. He certainly heard it in his voice as he said, "Dusty. I've been hoping you'd call."

An hour later he saw the smile in person. Dusty had only had one twinge of uneasiness as he'd mounted the steps to David's apartment. He hoped Sissy wouldn't be there. He wanted to see David alone this first time.

She wasn't there, but David said he had promised to call her over after they had had a chance to talk.

"It's been a long time," David said quietly, his eyes welcoming.

"Too long," Dusty said with a catch in his throat. He wanted to say more, wanted to tell David he'd missed him, wanted to say he was sorry, but the look in David's eyes told Dusty David knew exactly how he felt. No words were needed between them. Dusty felt as if a great weight had been lifted from his shoulders. His heart felt fuller than it had in months.

He grinned. "You look great. Love must agree with you."

"It does. You should try it," David said. His eyes shone with happiness and excitement as he filled Dusty in on everything that had happened in the past four months.

Finally, after they'd talked for a long time, Dusty said, "I'm sorry I acted like such a jerk."

"Hey, it's forgotten. I knew you thought I was making a terrible mistake and that you were worried. I knew you'd come around eventually when you saw that I really could take care of myself."

Eventually David called Sissy, and within minutes she was racing up the stairs. She burst into the large, bright room like a ray of sunshine, her smile lighting her face as she gave Dusty a hug. Dusty couldn't help the envy that tugged at him as he watched her perch on the arm of David's wheelchair and slip her arm around his shoulders. And when David lifted his face and they kissed—a sweet, lingering kiss—Dusty's heart twisted, and an aching loneliness gripped him.

Faces shining, they were obviously deliriously happy with each other. How could he not be happy for them? He *was* happy for them. Maybe his fears were unnecessary. Maybe it would last. And if it didn't, if they were making a mistake, it was their mistake to make, not his.

As the truth of this thought hit him, really hit him, he suddenly understood that Victoria had known that. She hadn't been interfering in Dusty's life by enabling David to break free, she had just been wise enough to give David the chance to make his own choices. And she hadn't done it to defy Dusty; she hadn't betrayed him at all. She had simply done it as a natural, generous gesture—a gesture she would make toward any friend.

Oh, Victoria, he thought. What have I done?

As he was leaving, Dusty's eyes felt suspiciously misty when he wished Sissy and David happiness and told David he'd be honored to act as his best man when they were married.

Driving home, he couldn't get the pictures of Luke and Maggie and David and Sissy out of his mind. Both couples seemed to have found something special. The ache that had started when he'd watched David and Sissy kissing had settled into a dull pain in his chest.

Too bad we can't go back and start over, he thought. Well, he couldn't, and he might as well get used to the fact. He and Victoria had had a chance together, but it hadn't worked out.

"It's for the best, anyway," he said aloud as he pulled into his driveway. "I'm obviously not cut out for marriage."

As he switched on lights in the house and greeted an ecstatic Rocky, he looked around. He had a lot going for him, more than most people, a lot more than most people: his career, his beautiful house, an adoring dog, a great mother and soon a great stepfather, and a patched-up relationship with his brother. And that was enough. In fact, that was more than enough.

There was no room in his life for anything else. Getting tied up with a woman like Victoria would probably have been a disaster. She'd have been a noose around his neck, tying him down to responsibilities and commitments he didn't need or want. He wouldn't have been free to make decisions that were best for him; he'd have had to consider her, too. Her and her daughter, he amended. Actually, he should be glad it had all turned out the way it had. He'd really had a narrow escape.

You're really lucky, he told himself as he climbed into his king-size bed. Yeah, he repeated as Rocky snuggled down next to him. He put his arm around the puppy and Rocky licked his face.

Dusty remembered the look of tenderness in David's eyes after he and Sissy had kissed each other.

Really lucky.

Chapter Sixteen

"Why are you so nervous, Mom? You're not the one getting married," Julie said as she adjusted the flowers pinned into Victoria's hair. She stood back, surveying her handiwork. "There. You look great."

Victoria studied herself in the ornate mirror. She and Julie had come to Sissy's house early to dress for the wedding, and they were just finishing. The image that greeted her from the old-fashioned beveled glass mirror told her she did look nice. The peach tones of the taffeta dress made her skin creamier and her eyes bluer. The small bouquet of peach and yellow roses, and the baby's breath pinned into her hair, were the perfect complements to the dress.

Julie was dressed identically for her role as one of Sissy's junior bridesmaids. Sissy's only other attendant was her niece, Kim, who was almost exactly Julie's age.

"I always get nervous at weddings," Victoria said in answer to Julie's question. She turned away from her daughter's knowing eyes and walked slowly to the big bay window that overlooked the circular drive at the front of Sissy's house. It was a perfect day for a wedding. Bright and sunny, with a little nip in the air—the kind of day that Houston didn't have often enough to suit Victoria.

Sissy and David were being married in the gazebo. Sissy had had a special ramp installed so that David would have easy access, and she planned to sit during the ceremony so that he wouldn't feel self-conscious.

Victoria stared out at the lines of cars entering the grounds. She took a shaky breath. The clock above the mantelplace in the guest room said three-thirty. Soon the wedding coordinator would be knocking at their door to tell them it was time to go downstairs.

Victoria's heart skittered as she allowed herself to think about seeing Dusty again, something she'd tried repeatedly to put out of her mind. Her stomach felt like a thousand moth's wings were beating inside it. She prayed she wouldn't make a fool of herself when she finally did see him.

"Mom, it'll be okay," Julie said softly, coming up behind her. "Just be cool."

Victoria blinked back sudden tears. She and Julie had made their peace weeks ago, and now for the first time Victoria realized that Julie understood what her mother had been going through. Maybe Victoria's pain over the past months had had a good result in that it had brought her closer to her daughter.

She squeezed Julie's hand and gave her what she hoped was a normal smile.

Julie grinned, her pixie face aglow. "That's it," she said. "Chill out."

The term brought a real smile to Victoria's lips, and she opened her arms and gave Julie a warm hug of thanks. Just then there was a soft knock and the door opened. The dark auburn head of Ann Shelley, the wedding coordinator, appeared in the opening. "It's time," she said.

Victoria took a deep breath and smoothed her dress. As she and Julie emerged from the bedroom, they were joined in the hallway by Kim O'Neill, Sissy's niece, who looked just as lovely as Julie in her peach colored dress.

Soon the hallway was filled with people, but Sissy still hadn't emerged from her bedroom.

Then her bedroom door, at the far end of the hall, opened, and she came out, radiant and smiling in her ecru satin and lace dress and small veiled hat. She gave Victoria a tremulous smile as she passed her in the hall, stopping at the top of the stairs for the others to precede her.

Victoria's heart was in her throat as she slowly made her way down the stairs, through the large double parlor and out the terrace doors. The golden sunshine, the rainbow array of colors in the flower beds lining the path to the gazebo, the heady scent of Sissy's fall roses, the crisp air, the murmur of the crowd as they caught their first glimpse of Sissy: all receded into the background as Victoria climbed the steps to the gazebo and found herself looking straight into a pair of brilliant green eyes.

Shaken to her soul at her first sight of Dusty, she faltered and would have fallen except that he quickly reached out and steadied her. The touch of his hand seared her arm.

Heart racing, she looked up, and for one crystal moment, it was as if the two of them were alone in the world. Nothing existed except his eyes, his bronzed face, his square jaw and firm mouth, his slightly crooked nose and his thick, burnished hair. Victoria drank her fill of him as she committed each feature to the store of memories she'd been building since the first time she'd laid eyes on him.

For Dusty, the glittering moment seemed suspended in time. He had told himself he would have no problem seeing Victoria again, but now he felt as if someone had kicked him in the stomach. She stood there in the shimmering sunshine, the latticework of the gazebo casting diamond patterns on her face, her eyes dark and glistening, her soft mouth slightly open, her slender curves emphasized by the tight-fitting bodice and soft swirling skirt of her beautiful dress. The flowers pinned in her hair made her look like some delicate goddess who had risen from the gardens to tease the mere mortals surrounding her.

When she stumbled, he instinctively reached out to help her, and the feel of her silken, sun-warmed skin sent a jolt of painful pleasure shooting straight to his heart.

And in that moment he knew.

He still loved her. He would always love her.

Stunned and shaken, he couldn't move.

For a long moment her melting eyes held his. Then the crowd's murmuring increased, and Sissy glided into view. Dusty stood back, allowing David to see his bride, and when he looked up again, Victoria was facing away from him, her eyes on the minister, who slowly began the service.

David, beaming with pride, looked at Sissy and reached for her hand. Hands clasped, they turned toward the minister.

Look at me, Dusty silently commanded Victoria. He had to see her eyes, had to see the expression on her face. He had to know if she still loved him—because he was sure she once had. But her head remained firmly turned straight ahead.

God, she was beautiful. A shaft of sunlight captured her perfect profile, and its stark, clean beauty pierced Dusty. The graceful long line of her neck, the soft swell of her breasts in the delicate peach dress, the vulnerable look of her full bottom lip: all held him immobilized. He would have given anything to be able to reach out and touch her, to kiss her, to hold her close.

He couldn't tear his eyes away from her. All through the service, he watched her, willing her to look his way. But she never did.

Victoria couldn't think of anything except the fact that Dusty stood less than six feet away from her. Her body throbbed with the knowledge. More than anything in the world, she wanted to look at him again, feast her eyes on him, but she didn't dare. She knew she'd give her feelings away, and she couldn't bear the thought that he probably didn't care, that he had probably forgotten everything that had passed between them. And she'd rather die than let him see how much she still cared.

Closing her eyes, she listened to Sissy and David repeat their vows. The beautiful words stripped away the last of her defenses. How, how would she make it through the afternoon?

At last the ceremony was over, and to the accompaniment of cheers and rice throwing by the large crowd of well-wishers, David, with Sissy walking by his side, wheeled himself down the path to the house, both of them laughing all the way. Victoria's heart ached as she saw the same heart-stopping smile Dusty had once given her bestowed on Sissy by her new husband. She fought the tears that threatened to spill over, although there were other women crying. Women always cried at weddings, Victoria told herself as she dabbed at the corners of her eyes. Yes, her inner voice scolded, but not because they're wallowing in self-pity.

Once inside the house, Victoria lost track of Dusty as she greeted Sissy's parents, Richard and Elaine O'Neill, and Sissy's brother Jack, who was Kim's father. As they turned to talk to other guests, Victoria felt a hand on her arm.

"Hello, Victoria," said Maggie Mitchell. Her dark eyes were warm and friendly, and she looked lovely in a dark green dress.

Standing behind her was Luke Capshaw, blue eyes twinkling as he said, "Still as pretty as ever, I see."

"It's good to see you," Victoria said as she shook each of their hands.

"This is going to be good practice for us," Maggie said. Then she smiled shyly and reached for Luke's hand. "Luke and I are going to be married next week."

"That's wonderful," Victoria said, meaning it, but wondering if everyone in the world was destined to find happiness except her. As the two of them walked away, Luke's arm around Maggie's waist, Victoria's throat tightened, and she wished the day was over.

For the next hour Victoria endured the toasts to the happy couple and the chore of standing in the receiving line. She kept her eyes turned the opposite direction from Dusty. She couldn't handle looking at him or talking to him. Not yet.

Her emotions were too close to the surface, the beauty of the wedding ceremony and the happiness evident on the faces of the bride and bridegroom only emphasizing the void in her life and her aching loneliness without him.

A thankful sigh escaped her as the receiving line broke up and the band began playing in the ballroom. She quietly slipped out the terrace doors with the intention of hiding somewhere until the party was over. Then she felt a gentle touch on her arm.

Turning around slowly, she found herself face to face with Dusty's crooked smile. "Hello, Victoria," he said softly. "How are you?"

Pain squeezed her heart as her eyes lifted to meet his solemn gaze. His smile faded as their eyes locked. "Hello, Dusty," she said. "I'm fine. And you?"

"Great. I'm doing great."

Victoria felt as if the air were being crushed out of her. She could hardly breathe; she certainly couldn't think of anything to say. The noise of the crowd seemed to be coming from another dimension.

His glittering eyes searched hers. "You . . . you look very beautiful today," he said. The sun glinted off his hair, turning it to molten gold. His skin glowed; everything about him looked full of health, almost bigger than life. As she watched, a muscle twitched in his jaw.

Why, he's nervous, she thought. Confused, she looked down. Why should *he* be nervous? Her own insides were quaking, but he had no reason to be nervous. Hurriedly, before she lost her nerve, she said, "It was good to see you again, Dusty. I've got to go inside. Sissy might need my help." She turned toward the open terrace doors.

"Victoria, wait," he said, grabbing her arm.

When she stopped, he walked in front of her. His hand still held her arm, and his other hand nudged her chin up so that she was forced to look at him. What she saw in his eyes only confused her more.

"Please," he said softly. "Come inside and dance with me. There's something I have to tell you."

As if she had no will of her own, she allowed him to lead her into the house. Her body melted at the touch of his hand against her waist, and she couldn't prevent a shudder from racing down her spine.

When his arms went around her and attempted to pull her close, at first she held herself rigid. But she was no match for him. As she surrendered to his embrace, she could feel his heart thudding against hers. He laid his cheek against her hair and said, "I was wrong, Victoria. I'm sorry for what I said."

She couldn't speak. She knew she should be angry with him; he'd caused her so much pain.

"Will you forgive me?" he whispered against her ear.

His warm breath sent a spiral of shivery pleasure through her. The tangy scent of his after-shave and the sensual smell of musky male invaded her senses. As their bodies melded together, Victoria could feel his hard muscles moving against her, and her body pulsed with an emptiness that cried out to be filled. She'd missed him so much. "Yes," she whispered. "Yes, I forgive you."

Fool, her head said. I don't care, her heart said. Whatever his motives, Dusty was holding her close, and that was all that mattered right now. Tomorrow would probably bring new heartache, new memories to try to erase from her brain, but right now, Victoria didn't care. All she cared about was Dusty and how he made her feel.

The song ended, and Victoria, who started to turn away, found herself firmly clasped around the waist as Dusty held her near. Emotions in turmoil, she didn't know what to do. She wanted to stay close to him; she wanted to run away. She was mortally terrified. She'd probably make a complete fool of herself if she stayed with him. Even the touch of his hand at her waist was sending a trail of wildfire through her body.

The band played a fanfare, then a drumroll. Sissy, a joyous smile lighting her face, took the mike. "Now, this is completely unrehearsed," she said as the crowd quieted down, "and he may refuse, but I hope he won't." She searched the crowd with her eyes. "Dusty, where are you?"

Dusty raised his hand and waved.

Sissy waved back. "My brand new brother-in-law, Dusty Mitchell, has a number-one hit record album, and I was hopin' as a special favor to me, he'd sing for us. To celebrate our happy day."

Dusty smiled and squeezed Victoria's waist. "Don't leave," he ordered. "I'll be right back." The crowd parted as he strode to the front of the room. Victoria's skin tingled from his touch.

After conferring with the band, Dusty adjusted the mike. "The song I'm about to sing is very special to me," he said. "I wrote it the day I flew to Nashville to record my album, and now it's a hit single." An undercurrent of anticipation rippled through the crowd as the band began to play. The melody was haunting and lovely, and Victoria was soon caught up in its sweet poignancy. Then her breath caught as Dusty's low, husky voice filled the ballroom.

"I never believed in fairy tales, or wishes that came true..." His eyes fastened on Victoria, their green-gold depths fathoms deep. "But when I saw you standing there, it was as if I knew..."

Victoria's heart beat in her throat; the music and Dusty's voice held her entranced.

"You were the girl I'd always love... no matter how I tried... you were the girl who'd fill my heart... it couldn't be denied..."

Dusty smiled at her, and Victoria's heart leaped in answer.

The music swelled, and Dusty, his eyes never leaving her face, sang, "My Cinderella girl... so full of mystery. My Cinderella girl... you're the only one for me...."

Victoria stood absolutely still as the words drifted over her like gently falling snow, diamond-bright and beautiful.

"My Cinderella girl... although we are apart... My Cinderella girl... you're the center of my heart...."

Bewitched, Victoria listened as Dusty sang the second and third verses, and her heart swelled each time he sang the chorus. The words echoed in her own heart long after the last soft note died away. Eyes misty at the realization that he'd written the song about her, she didn't know how she'd ever resist him.

Victoria floated through the remaining hours of the reception in a bemused state of part happiness, part pain. The happiness was caused by the look in Dusty's eyes when he thought she wasn't watching; the pain was caused by the thought that this joy couldn't last. This would be just one more episode in her life that she would have to try to forget.

At the end of the evening, after Sissy and David had left for their wedding trip to Hawaii, one of the remaining guests said to Dusty, "I understand you're soon to start a nationwide tour."

"Yes," Dusty said with a grin. "I'm leaving in three weeks. The tour will last most of the winter."

His answer hit her like a dousing with cold water. He was leaving in three weeks. Three weeks. And he'd be gone for months. If she'd entertained the slimmest hope that they might be able to work out something, that hope faded and died. The situation was hopeless. Dusty's life would soon take on a hectic course as he and his entourage traipsed all over the country. She, on the other hand, would be right here in Houston teaching, leading her dull, structured life. How could she and Dusty ever be compatible? She was just torturing herself by allowing him into her life.

But, oh, she wanted him. Every pore of her body was telling her to grab what happiness she could grab, and damn the consequences. Live for today, she thought. It had never been her creed.

As the last guest departed through the wide double oak doors of Sissy's home, Elaine O'Neill gave a contented sigh. Then she looked around and said, "Where did that husband of mine go off to?"

"I think he and Luke wandered in the direction of the garage," Dusty said. "He mentioned something about wanting Luke to see Sissy's truck."

"Oh, shoot," Elaine said. "The musicians are packed up and ready to go, but Richard needs to pay them. Dusty, would you mind finding him for me?"

"No problem. I'll be right back."

In the split second after he disappeared, Victoria made up her mind. "Elaine," she said hurriedly. "Tell Julie I'll pick her up about noon tomorrow. I'm going home." Julie and Kim were spending the night at Sissy's home along with Kim's parents. The girls had already gone off upstairs, giggling all the way.

"Home? But... what about Dusty?" Elaine said, surprised.

"Tell him I had to leave." Without waiting for an answer, Victoria grabbed her purse and raced outside, fumbling for her car keys as she went. She unlocked her car, slid inside and inserted her key into the ignition, praying she'd escape before Dusty had time to find out she was gone. She knew if he found her, she'd be lost.

Her prayers were answered. The car started, and within minutes she was on her way home. She purposely kept her mind blank. She wouldn't think about him. She wouldn't think about anything.

But later, soaking in a hot lilac-scented tub, head resting against the tub pillow, she allowed herself to think. And soon tears were streaming unchecked down her face.

She cried for a long time. Finally, sighing, she stood and let the water out of the tub. Drying her body and hair with a thick towel, she wrapped herself in a soft terry-cloth robe and padded to the den. Turning off all the lights except one dim lamp, she sank onto the couch.

Within minutes, she was asleep.

The sound of the door chimes woke her. Startled, her eyes popped open. Who was ringing the doorbell? What time was it? Groggy, she stood and tightened the belt of her robe. As she passed the grandfather clock in the hall, it began to strike the hour. Midnight.

"Who... who is it?" she called through the door.

"Victoria, open the door."

Dusty. Heart thumping, she just stood there. She couldn't see him. Not now. Not tonight.

He pounded on the door. "Damn it, Victoria. I said, open the door!"

Oh, God. He wasn't going to go away. Taking a deep breath, she smoothed her hair, then released the dead bolt. She opened the door.

His tall body stood silhouetted in the open doorway, one arm propped against the door frame, the moonlight playing against him. He was no longer wearing his tuxedo. Instead, his strong legs were encased in jeans and boots, and he was wearing an open jacket. "Well, darlin', aren't you going to invite me in?" he drawled.

She shrugged. "Come on in." She stood back, letting him pass, and as he did, she caught the sharp scent of his aftershave. She closed the door and followed him into the den.

He turned. Eyes gleaming, he said, "Why did you run away?"

She stared at him. She opened her mouth, then closed it.

"I'm not leaving until I get some answers," he said, his voice tight and hard.

All right. She'd give him some answers. "I...I was afraid," she admitted. Although she wanted to look away, she didn't. The time for cowardice was past.

"Afraid? Of me?" His voice was incredulous, his eyes full of disbelief.

"No. Not you. Never you." *Oh, Dusty.*

"What, then?"

Shrugging, she hesitated, then said, "I can't go through all that again. I just can't."

He frowned. "I don't understand what you're trying to say."

She lifted her hands in a placating gesture. "Don't you? I should think it would be obvious. I...I thought we had something before, but...but then you left...and I...I've never been so miserable in my life. I just don't see that we can ever work things out. So why start back up again?" She wanted to add, *I'll only get hurt, because I love you too much. And you don't love me enough, if you love me at all.*

"Oh, Victoria," he said gruffly. He reached for her.

She backed up. "No, Dusty. Please don't touch me."

His hand dropped. "We need to talk about this."

"There's nothing more to say."

"There's everything to say."

Her gaze flew to his face. What she saw was a look so tender, so soft, so loving, it made her heart stop. Was it possible? Hope, at first tentative, then more forceful, surged through her.

"Come on," he said, "let's sit down." He took off his jacket, revealing a soft blue sweater underneath. Tossing his jacket aside, he sat next to her, his arm loosely propped on the couch behind her. "There's nothing to be afraid of. Don't you know that?"

Victoria bowed her head. The last vestiges of her pride evaporated. "I can't stand being hurt again," she whispered.

"Oh, darlin'." His arm slid around her, and with his other hand, he cupped her face and raised it. His eyes smoldered as they searched her face. "Don't you know that I love you? I love you with all my heart. And I'll never hurt you again."

Then his mouth descended, capturing hers in a shattering kiss. A kaleidoscope of feelings burst within Victoria, like giant stars cascading through the night. She clung to him as the kiss went on and on and on, her arms tightening as her emotions whirled in chaotic splendor. Heart soaring, she kissed him back, pouring every bit of pent-up longing and months of missing him desperately into her passionate response. Groaning, Dusty said, "I missed you. Every day, I missed you." Then he raised his head and looked deep into her eyes. With the pad of his thumb, he brushed a stray strand of hair from her forehead. "And I love you. I love you so much it scares me."

"Oh, Dusty, I love you, too. I always have," she cried as his head dropped to her neck and his mouth trailed hot kisses against her skin. His hands slipped under her robe, and at the touch of his warm palms against her bare skin, she trembled. Shuddering against the assault of his seeking lips and demanding hands, Victoria's senses reeled. All her nerve endings craved his touch; a pulsing ache throbbed deep within her.

When Dusty felt Victoria surrender in his arms, the desire to make her his, to put his mark on her so that she would never turn away from him again, filled him. He crushed her to him, and her arms tightened around him. Her mouth opened fully under his. He kissed her greedily, her mouth sweet as hot honey.

Heart beating wildly, Dusty kissed her again and again, unable to get enough of her. His body pulsated with need; he wanted her. He wanted to brand her, to cleave her to him forever. As she moaned against him, he lifted his head and looked at her. How could he have stayed away? How could he have forgotten how beautiful she was? Perfectly made and molded with him in mind. He touched the tender skin of her breasts, savoring the feel of them against his palms. Soft. Warm. Scented. He could feel her body trembling against him. With her hair tumbled around her face, her eyes clouded with passion and her lips swollen from his kisses, she looked more desirable than she'd ever looked before. Gone was the porcelain perfection she presented to the world; this was a living, breathing, passionate woman with skin that was heated and moist and ready for him.

"I want you," he growled, giving her one last, lingering kiss, "but first we've got something to settle." He drew her robe around her and smiled.

Then he reached for his jacket, fumbled in the pocket and held something out for her to see.

The soft lamplight caused the rhinestones imbedded in the heel of the plastic shoe to wink and sparkle.

Looking not in the least embarrassed, Dusty stood, then dropped down on one knee. Lifting her left foot, he slipped the shoe on. "Just as I thought. It fits." He smiled and took her hand. "Cinderella, will you marry me?"

A delirious joy exploded inside her at his words. "Oh, Dusty," she said, "I want that more than anything in the world, but how can we?"

"How can we? What do you mean?" Amazement tinged his words.

She licked her lips. Shaking her head in frustration, she said, "It'll never work. I couldn't stand being away from you for months and months while you tour, and I can't travel with you. Even if I felt I could give up my teaching career, there's Julie. I can't leave her."

He stood, pulling her up with him. He enfolded her in his arms, and it felt so good to be next to him. Stroking her hair as he talked, he said, "Victoria. Sweetheart. I never expected you to quit your job or leave Julie home alone. But if we love each other, we can work something out."

"How?" she wailed. "How?"

"I'm not sure, but there's got to be a way. What if I try to tour only in the summertime when Julie's out of school? Could you take the summer session off?" He continued to stroke her hair and drop kisses on her forehead. One arm held her firmly against him.

Could she? Hope inched back, creeping into her like silent fog. "Well . . . maybe I could do that," she said slowly.

"And maybe you could fly out to be with me on weekends during this first tour, because I can't cancel this one."

"Oh, I know that. I wouldn't expect you to." Her arms tightened around him. She didn't want to let him go. An idea struck her. "You know, maybe I could even take a leave of absence so we could have more time together."

"See?" he said. "It might not be perfect, but we can find a way if we want to. If we love each other enough to compromise."

"I don't know—"

"I don't want to hear that from you," he said. "We've wasted enough time talking." His mouth lowered and caught hers in a demanding kiss, insistent and seeking. One hand was splayed across her back, and she could feel its heat through her robe. The other dropped down, cupping her bottom and pulling her close so that she could feel the surge of his desire for her. Her body responded with a painful pulsing deep within.

Dragging his mouth from hers, he muttered, "Say you'll marry me."

"Dusty—"

"Okay, I'll just keep kissing you until you're senseless. And I won't stop until you agree to marry me." And he kissed her again, a deep, drugging kiss that had her reeling while his hands roamed her body, lighting fires wherever they went.

"Give up," he growled as they came up for air. "You can't win."

"Persuade me some more," she said.

A wicked gleam in his eye, he said, "With pleasure, darlin', with pleasure." He untied the robe and let it drop to the floor, then disposed of his clothes in record time. Victoria's heart stopped as she drank him in, the beautiful long length of him, golden and glorious in the lamplight. She reached out, touching him, reveling in his immediate response.

Eyes never leaving hers, he reached for her, lifting her in his arms and striding to her bedroom.

After laying her in the middle of her bed, he sat beside her. Victoria shivered with longing as his eyes devoured her. He smiled. "I love to look at you," he said.

Victoria swallowed. There was a time she would have been embarrassed by his blatant admiration of her body. Now all she wanted was his touch, his kisses. His love. "I love to look at you, too."

Slowly he stretched out beside her and began to caress her. As his mouth descended, capturing the hardened nub of one breast and nipping it gently, Victoria moaned.

"Do you like that?" he said.

Instead of answering, she ran her hands down the hard muscles of his back, then around and down the front of him until she found what she was seeking. As her palm closed around the hard length of him, his mouth took hers once more. As his tongue delved deeply, she tightened her grasp and could feel the leashed power surging within him, hot and turbulent.

Dragging his mouth from hers, Dusty groaned as she held him, caressing him boldly, and his hand stroked her body, igniting each inch of flesh like fire ignited a dry forest. In seconds his fingers nestled deep, searching and finding her warmth and readiness, circling gently as she cried out from the sheer sweet agony of his touch.

"Please," she begged. "I want you inside me."

"Yes, ma'am." His fingers and mouth stilled. "I aim to please." In the moonlight, she could see the smile on his face, the look of love that was still so new, so wonderful. He raised himself up, and with one quick thrust, entered her.

Victoria closed her eyes, drawing him in, savoring his strength and heat, savoring the fullness and completeness of their union. And as he began to move inside her, she matched his moves, and it seemed so right—like a perfectly choreographed dance or a beautifully orchestrated minuet, each movement exact. And when they reached the end together, building to a perfect crescendo, Victoria thought she would dissolve from sheer joy.

Later, lying sated and feeling thoroughly and completely loved, Victoria snuggled up against Dusty. She wound her fingers through the crisp, curly hair on his chest, then let her forefinger trail down his chest and up one muscular arm. They were lying side by side in the middle of her bed.

He opened one eye. Then he opened the other. "Woman," he said, "just what are you doing?"

"Tickling you," she said.

"You'll be sorry," he warned. He started to reach for her, then suddenly sat up. Snapping his fingers, he jumped up. "I'll be right back," he said as he disappeared from the room.

Within seconds, he was back. As he stood in the doorway looking at her, one hand behind his back, Victoria thought he looked magnificent. His naked body gleamed in the dim light, and he looked healthy and strong and wonderful, more like an athlete than a musician.

She stretched, smiling as she saw a look of desire flare in Dusty's eyes. He slowly sauntered over and sat on the edge of the bed. "I have something for you, but you're not going to get it until you promise to marry me." His eyes were hooded, his voice a low rumble filled with sweet promise.

"Oh, all right," she said, pretending disgust. "You'll never give me any peace otherwise, so I guess I'll marry you."

Grinning wickedly, he withdrew his hand from behind his back and held out a small blue velvet box. He snapped the lid open. Nestled inside was the loveliest ring Victoria had ever seen. A huge round diamond surrounded by tiny sapphires, it was breathtaking.

Heart singing, her eyes met his.

Removing the ring from the box, he slipped it on her left hand. "I love you, Cinderella," he said. "We belong together."

"Forever," she said.

And as their lips met and clung, Victoria knew she'd finally found the security and stability she'd always craved. Here, right here, in the arms of the man she loved.

The End.

* * * * *

Silhouette Special Edition

proudly presents
the long-awaited ''prequel'' volume of

★ **LOVE AND GLORY** ★

by
LINDSAY McKENNA
Dawn of Valor

In the summer of '89, Silhouette Special Edition premiered three novels celebrating America's men and women in uniform: LOVE AND GLORY, by bestselling author Lindsay McKenna. Featured were the proud Trayherns, a military family as bold and patriotic as the American flag—three siblings valiantly battling the threat of dishonor, determined to triumph . . . in love and glory.

Now, discover the roots of the Trayhern brand of courage, as parents Chase and Rachel relive their earliest heartstopping experiences of survival and indomitable love, in

Dawn of Valor, Silhouette Special Edition #649.

This February, experience the thrill of LOVE AND GLORY—from the very beginning!

DV-1

Silhouette Books®

**Star-crossed lovers?
Or a match made in heaven?**

Why are some heroes strong and silent . . . and others charming and cheerful? The answer is WRITTEN IN THE STARS! Coming each month in 1991, Silhouette Romance presents you with a special love story written by one of your favorite authors—highlighting the hero's astrological sign! From January's sensible Capricorn to December's disarming Sagittarius, you'll meet a dozen dazzling heroes.

Sexy, serious Justin Starbuck wasn't about to be tempted by his aunt's lovely hired companion, but Philadelphia Jones thought his love life needed her helping hand! What happens when this cool, conservative Capricorn meets his match in a sweet, spirited blonde like Philadelphia?

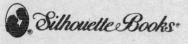

SILHOUETTE·INTIMATE·MOMENTS®

FEBRUARY FROLICS!

This February, we've got a special treat in store for you: four terrific books written by four brand-new authors! From sunny California to North Dakota's frozen plains, they'll whisk you away to a world of romance and adventure.

Look for

L.A. HEAT (IM #369) by Rebecca Daniels
AN OFFICER AND A GENTLEMAN (IM #370) by Rachel Lee
HUNTER'S WAY (IM #371) by Justine Davis
DANGEROUS BARGAIN (IM #372) by Kathryn Stewart

They're all part of February Frolics, coming to you from Silhouette Intimate Moments—where life is exciting and dreams do come true.

FF-1